# TWO + TWO

## A Novel

## MARTIN BORIS

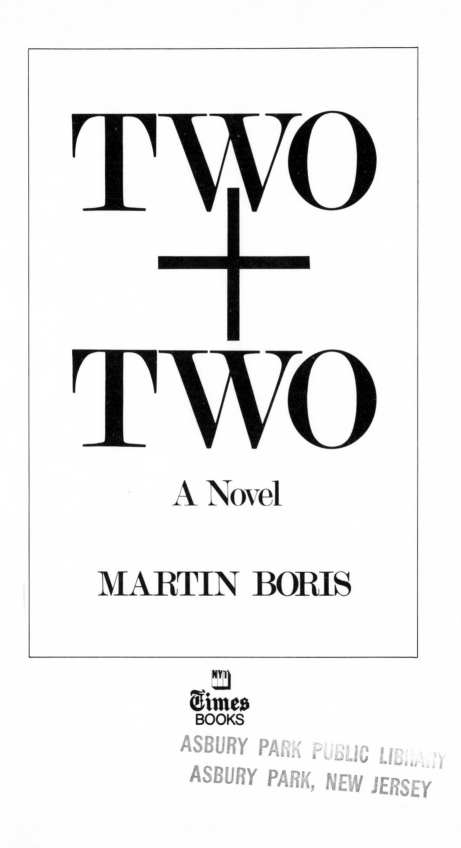

Times
BOOKS

Published by TIMES BOOKS, a division
of Quadrangle/The New York Times Book Co., Inc.
Three Park Avenue, New York, N. Y. 10016

Published simultaneously in Canada by
Fitzhenry & Whiteside, Ltd., Toronto

Library of Congress Cataloging in Publication Data

Boris, Martin.
Two + two.

I.   Title.
PZ4.B7334Tw   1979     [PS3552.07534]     813'.5'4     78-19607
                ISBN  0-8129-0783-3

Manufactured in the United States of America

To Louis Blumberg, Betty Klapper, and Abe Broizman
teachers unbeknown to themselves
and
Richard F. Shepard

# TWO
# ✝
# TWO

1

He was going to ask her to undress. Her mind was going to freeze, her tongue swell to twice its size. In the end she would dutifully and mechanically peel off her clothes and submit. Even if he had a nurse present to buffer patient and physician from each other, she would redden like a schoolgirl when schoolgirls blushed. She hoped he wasn't too horny, that he had had sex the night before and that he hadn't left the breakfast table after an argument. Small scraps of panic in a doctor's waiting room.

She wondered why in the hell she had listened to Victor. Just because he cut the doctor's lawn didn't mean she had to take her business to him. Dumb Victor. She knew what was in the back of his mind. He thought a vaginal infection was something to be ashamed of. So he sent her to Dr. Bernstein instead of old Feldman. Feldman had been the family doctor for twenty years, but Victor thought he had to sneak her off like a pregnant girl friend looking for an abortion. She was rapidly coming to a boil. I know what's bothering him, she thought. It's his name. He's afraid of a vaginal stain on his family crest. Family crest? Crossed rakes over a pile of horse manure. He's afraid old Feldman will take a tour of my insides and say "tsk tsk" and wonder who gave me this god-awful itch and smelly discharge. Victor would dry up and blow away if the world out there thought his Tessa got caught messing around.

She sat in Dr. Bernstein's crowded waiting room, aching with uneasiness and apprehension. At least a rape victim received no

3

warning. Anxiety time was cut to the bone. A smile flitted across her face like a firefly on a dark night. Gallows humor.

It was an ugly waiting room, the walls filled with pictures of New England winters, covered bridges, children on sleds, teams of horses in the snow pulling well-insulated pairs of lovers.

She hated winter. From December to March she was a prisoner, suffering in solitary confinement. Victor and the boys were no better than jailers then. Muddy boots and bad colds. If there were an early spring she got time off for good behavior, but that rarely happened in New York anymore.

The waiting room was more dreary than anything else. Dr. Ginsberg, Stephen's orthodontist, had Danish modern and Modiglianis. She liked the sad, sad women of Modigliani, those soulful madonnas. They had, for her, a deep beauty only a life of quiet suffering could etch in a face. They reminded her of her own condition, but she would never admit that to anyone.

She looked around at the other patients. On her left, slovenly dressed in torn sneakers and a yellow and white maternity dress, sat a girl with buttercup yellow hair. Huge rollers, strategically placed, tugged at the ends. She looked wired for a scientific experiment, but pretty in spite of it. Two children, a boy and a girl, with the same look of peasant distrust on their faces played around Tessa's crossed legs. Their mother appeared oblivious as her children invaded Tessa's momentarily troubled world.

The least the sloppy bitch could do is not look like an innocent bystander, she thought. Those two animals have the run of the place. If they were mine they'd be a head shorter and sore in the ass for at least a week.

She noticed with disgust the small stream that flowed unabatedly from the boy's nose and was absorbed by the sleeve of his thin blue sweater. The running nose was a more serious offense in Tessa's statute book than unruly behavior in public. The boy stepped on her foot. Tessa winced.

"Your children?" she asked, wearing her best intimidating face.

"Yes. Do you think I rented them?"

"Well, if you want to be a good mother then kindly keep them away from me," Tessa requested. "I'm here for something very contagious. Leprosy, I think. You know, where the fingers and the nose and the ears fall off."

4

The eyes of the young mother widened. In one rapid swinging motion she picked up her children and walked to the opposite end of the waiting room. Once resettled she glared angrily at Tessa. Her place was quickly taken by an old man in blue paisley pants who seemed unconcerned with the dangers of contracting a rare disease.

Tessa observed the packed room with the same curiosity she displayed when she took the subway to see her sister in Queens. There were many older people there just waiting. They did that best. They were used to it, having undergone extensive training. For them it had become a life of waiting: for doctors in crowded quarters, in drug stores, at the checkout counters in the supermarkets when they ran specials, at the movies on Senior Citizen days, at their centers where the unattached ones huddled for warmth against a cold, uninterested world, and, finally, most pitifully they waited for meals to be served by sullen children who impatiently counted the moments of their last few days in the sun.

She thought that many of them probably did not feel resentful. The waiting gave a shape to their dry, empty lives, gave them something to do between getting up and going to bed.

She watched the flow of traffic. Medical musical chairs. A young boy entered. He had black hair, black eyes, defiant and mistrustful. He looked ready for a fight. Tessa turned her head away.

He saw the "No Smoking" sign on the small formica information table that bountifully held pamphlets about cancer, nutrition, and polio shots. It triggered an immediate reaction. A hand dug into each pocket and came up with a Marlboro in the left and a cigarette lighter in the right. He sent an exhalation of smoke slowly around the room.

Mrs. Randall, the receptionist, a large woman, all in white, called to him in a booming voice.

"Please douse that cigarette."

"Hey, lady, I'm old enough to smoke," he shot back as if he had been preparing all his life for her. He smiled. His remark pleased him.

"If you're old enough to smoke then you're old enough to read. But just in case your education has been overlooked, the sign says 'No smoking, please.' That's a house rule. It applies to everyone . . . even God if He makes an appointment."

He looked at her murderously but obliged by grinding his Marlboro into the gray carpeting. In semi-triumph he plumped down three seats to Tessa's right and grinned at the large mountain of starched white. Tessa leaned over the laps of the two old men who sat unmoved and unconcerned and beckoned the young man to meet her half way.

He leaned over. When their heads met she whispered, "Do you do that in your own house? You must come from pigs."

He reeled back as if he had been scalded. After a few seconds he slowly squatted over the cigarette and dug its remains out of the carpet, then dumped them ceremoniously into the wastebasket under the formica table. He glared at his tormentors and reseated himself as far as possible from them. Deflated, he sat slumped over, head in his hands. Somehow he reminded Tessa of her husband. Two bullies.

She resumed waiting. She would never become used to it. Even if she grew as old and as mummified as the old men and women who sat now like exhibits in a museum. She pitied these chronically ill people whose only crime was growing old enough to allow their biologic sins to catch them. One woman, as small and as thin as a new maple hadn't moved in an hour. She sat there, dry and defeated, the shadows of death lengthening on her waxy face. To Tessa, Mrs. Randall appeared cold and disinterested as she controlled traffic and made sure papers were in order. She took cash, checks, Medicaid, Medicare, and Blue Cross with equal ingratitude. Tessa felt slightly diminished by such efficiency.

"New patient," she explained to Mrs. Randall as she gave the pertinent data of her medical life. "No, no Blue Cross or Health Insurance. My husband is self-employed."

"You can get individual coverage, dear," Randall suggested.

"I'll look into it, thank you," Tessa answered, surprised at the woman's warmth.

She walked the twenty-foot corridor to the doctor's office. "He'd better go slow and careful with me," she warned no one in particular as she carefully constructed her case of lechery against this unknown, unseen doctor.

\* \* \*

6

Cal Bernstein tried to rub weariness out of his eyes. Instead he spread it all over his face. Before nine in the morning a case of cardiac arrest and another of food poisoning had splintered his carefully prepared schedule into toothpicks.

First Schwartz, the jeweler, had tried the deadly combination of littleneck clams and two A.M. It had nearly proved fatal. Cal helped pack him into the ambulance and stayed with him until he heard him ask one of the nurses in the hospital about the rates. A sure sign of life.

Cal had returned just in time to answer a cry for help from Mrs. Dellaratta. Her husband was gasping for breath. Cal held his hand and heard his confession in the same ambulance that hauled Schwartz away. Sunlight had just begun to wash the west parking lot as they wheeled Mr. Dellaratta, confessed and breathing better, into intensive care. Cal's office hours would be running very late tonight. For sure Joan would have to eat without him again.

Dr. Bernstein was a tall scholarly looking man, of medium build. Fortyish, he wore horn rimmed glasses. He smiled warmly at Tessa as she sat down in a leather chair facing him.

"You're Victor's wife," he said, making it sound as though the two men were old friends. "I'm Calvin Bernstein. I'm sorry you had to wait so long. There were some emergencies at the hospital. I generally run a tighter ship than this. At least my first mate, outside, does."

"I've seen the lady in white operate," Tessa smiled. "We could use her at my house."

It was a first for Tessa. The first time a doctor had ever apologized to her. For anything.

He was almost good looking, she thought. He hadn't missed it by much, if he missed it at all. A little more hair, perhaps his nose a bit straighter. Behind the shield of his glasses he had clear coffee-brown eyes that looked into you as he spoke. At you and into you. She felt he was examining her right now, weighing things. His smile could be disarming. An alarm sounded. Warm smiles were reasons for doubling the guard.

"Doctor Bernstein," she said, "I must tell you now, before we get started, I won't take off my clothes. Okay? We can talk. You can ask questions; I'll answer questions. I don't want to seem

7

rude or uncooperative, but those are the conditions of this examination. Okay?"

Cal nibbled at his lower lip and narrowed his eyes. She was absolutely delightful, this numbskull. She had brightened up what began as another bone crusher of a day.

"Mrs. Bruno, you do have children? I remember Victor once mentioned he had two boys."

"Yes, I have two boys. What's that got to do with it?"

"Well, did your obstetrician also play twenty questions with you when you went into labor?"

"No, but he had something to take out. It was his job to take the baby out. What you have to do is not . . . physical, it just requires interpretation of the data I give you." She felt the ground loosening underfoot.

"Then take it one step further," he said. "Read about it and treat it yourself, if you're that convinced."

"Okay," she quickly conceded, "you win if you can get your Captain Bligh to sort of hold my hand."

"I never examine a woman patient alone. That's company policy, here. Always has been."

She was gradually unfreezing. She hated to admit it but the man was actually likable.

"Doctor, why aren't you writing? I intend to pay for the visit. Victor runs the business, but I run the house. Medical expenses are part of that."

"'Oh, I'm going to charge you, Mrs. Bruno. Don't worry about that. And I tape everything, play it back later so that I can actually BE with my patients, look at them, talk to them, listen to them. Writing is a distraction. That I do during the evenings." He paused, looked at her, and still found her charming.

"Now. . . . Victor said you have a woman's problem. Curious thing for an American man in the seventies to say. I thought that kind of . . . prudishness was behind us. Well, maybe he just doesn't have the words. Maybe it's my unconscious snobbery at his lack of the right words. It comes out of the closet at times. But I did poke around a bit more and he just wouldn't come right out and say what was wrong with you. Or what he thought was wrong with you."

She looked at him, and made rapid mental sketches of the

small room at the same time. The studio couch was brown and rich looking. It was older than the office. He probably had taken it with him from wherever he came. The wide space allotted in front of the couch indicated that it opened up into a bed. Either Mrs. Bernstein was a difficult lady or the doctor loved his work.

Bookshelves held the standard intimidating medical texts, the titles of which could be in a foreign language for all she knew. Family pictures, also standard, were on his desk facing him. All she could see were the frames. Two children and one wife, or three children and no wife. Perhaps other variations. She was only mildly interested. His desk was narrow, the narrowest she had ever seen in a doctor's office, probably because he wanted a smaller barrier between himself and his patients. And perhaps it was true about the tape recorder and not just another fairy tale. But maybe Mrs. Bernstein felt that the smaller desk was better suited to a smaller room. Interior decoration instead of doctor-patient rapport?

"You tell me, Mrs. Bruno, what is your woman's problem?"

Is he laughing at me? she wondered. Or at Victor? He seems too light to be a doctor, yet more what a doctor should be. Asking serious things in a personal way. And he looks at me when he talks to me, like he really believes I'm a whole person, not just an infected vagina.

"I have this itch. This vaginal itch . . . and discharge, doctor," she said with more confidence than she thought was in her. "I've had it for a week and it's driving me up the wall. It's messy and ugly and uncomfortable."

Cal shook his head knowingly, sympathetically, as if he, too, had suffered from the same disorder at one time.

"Tell me, Mrs. Bruno, have you had a cold lately? Have you used antibiotics in the past month?"

"No, nothing like that."

"Did you do any public bathing or stay overnight in a friend's or a relative's house?"

"No."

"Well, Mrs. Bruno, brace yourself. This is the moment of truth, as we bullfighters say. I'm going to take a look at it and see." Before he finished his sentence he pressed a button at the base of the telephone. Within seconds, during which her insides

9

gently churned, another starched white came in through the back entrance to the office.

This one was younger, smaller than Randall. She was dark and pretty and moved with an easy grace. Tessa guessed that she had probably danced at one time. She wondered casually if they were sleeping together. Was it her imagination or were those love letters shuttling back and forth between their eyes? She chided herself. At thirty-three she was turning into another soap opera-conditioned vegetable who saw evidence of sexual activity in every glance, every word, every action.

"Miss Sigmund, will you please prepare Mrs. Bruno for a vaginal," he said in a business-like manner.

She nodded and smilingly motioned Tessa to follow her. A little too friendly, Tessa thought. Too much smile on such short notice.

Before the door closed behind them he said, "Mrs. Bruno, it's a very short, very painless, and very impersonal examination, really. So relax and I'll join you shortly."

She thought he had led her to it nice and easily.

Miss Sigmund eased her into a shapeless white sheet with two strings top and bottom like a wide hammock. It wasn't much of an improvement in the dignity department over being nude, but it was something.

A soft knock at the door. Miss Sigmund answered it.

"Me again," he said and breezed into the tiny examination room. While she was undressing he had converted the spoken word to the written. He had listened to the tape, smiled, and wrote during certain parts, momentarily toying with the idea of preserving it intact, just for the personal pleasure. When finished, he wiped off the words as if they had never existed.

He approached her with latex gloves that made his hand look like a man with five penises. She quickly sent her mind out for a long walk by forcing it to conjure up other places, other times. He touched her. Open school week and Stephen's problem with that cold bitch of a teacher who scared him so. She was opened and pried into. His hands were knowing and did not linger long. She would have to politely tell the teacher to take a few pains and gentle Stephen over the rough spots, not force his shyness into proper behavior.

It was over before she had finished reprimanding the teacher.

10

She heard the gloves come off with a snap. Then she opened her eyes. While he washed his hands she thought how peculiar it was that her shame had never arrived.

"Okay soldier," the doctor said, "get dressed and meet me back at the fort."

He was writing a prescription as she entered. A smile spread across his face as he pointed to the chair. She sat down.

"What you have is a mild infection called thrush. Nothing serious, but it's highly contagious. You could have picked it up anywhere, in a hundred ways. It looks a great deal worse than it is. That white coating on your vagina is the organism, the infecting agent. As I said before, it's not a big deal. With the proper treatment it'll clear up in a week or two, perhaps three at the most." His glasses were slipping. Down on the middle of his nose they gave him a foxy, yet paternal look, like someone's grandfather caught in a whorehouse. To focus on her he pushed them back up his bridge.

Looking at Mrs. Bruno, earnestly, while he semi-lectured her, he realized she was quite attractive, her hair short and black and billowy. Who would have thought that Victor. . . . Well, the world's a funny place, he surmised.

"It only looks serious because of the coating and the discharge. I've prescribed a vaginal tablet and a douche before the tablet. You insert the tablet high up in the vagina with the inserter that comes with it. The douche will come with directions. Very easy to use."

"One question, Doctor Bernstein," she said, more courageous now than when she entered. "Should I, should Victor and I . . . abstain until the infection is cleared up?"

Good at reading faces she searched for a snicker, a slight smile, a sign that perhaps later on, dining with friends in a very expensive restaurant or entertaining at his home he might tell funny stories about a dumb gentile who asked screwy questions about screwing though infected. But he refused to fall into that trap. His face read only as searching for the right thing to say. They locked glances for a few seconds.

"It's advisable not to, but that's really up to you. Victor and you. If the answer is yes, you should douche immediately before and after." He leaned back in his chair, locked his hands behind his head and vaguely contemplated Victor as the lover of this woman. What he saw of the man did not impress him greatly.

"Have Victor shower well to prevent his contracting the same thing."

She nodded. Simple. As though he were telling her how to make a salad, or giving her directions to Roosevelt Field.

"Not so simple," she heard herself saying aloud. "My husband doesn't like to move himself afterwards and he doesn't relish the idea of my scooting away either. He says it's like going to a prostitute if I head for the john. And besides, he needs the reassurance. It's the only time I really respect his wishes. So I'll just have to tell him to stay away. Doctor's orders. He'd like that. To be officially told to keep hands off." She was amazed at her openness.

Cal wondered why an attractive lady, not too thrilled about having her body looked at, would suddenly open her soul to him. But strangers do that with strangers. Patients do that with doctors, but he could have sworn that this stranger, this patient, would have kept Victor's sexuality under lock and key.

"You handle him any way you want to," he said, "but if either of the two of you want sex during the next two weeks it must be under those conditions. It's a simple matter of adjustment. And if it doesn't clear up in two weeks, three weeks top, come and see me again and I'll figure out something else."

"And if it goes away, then I don't come back?" she asked.

"No, what for? If it's all cleared up, and you'll know if it's all cleared up, then there is no point to it. You'll just be throwing your money away."

She paid Mrs. Randall and left wondering how successful Doctor Bernstein could be if he didn't insist on return visits.

They all squeeze you for as long as they can. This guy must be a cuckoo, a real threat to the whole profession. She pondered the Doctor all the way home in the little Pinto. Almost ran a stop sign trying to force in all the pieces, whether they fit or not. Big white house, two expensive cars. What the hell, rich Jewish doctors shouldn't be too hard to total out, she told herself as she zipped down the Boulevard, happy to be on the other side of the ordeal.

12

Marsha was hosting this month's Hadassah meeting at which Joan knew what to expect. Two hours of group self-inflation and thick gobs of gossip the weight and texture of cotton candy, followed by Quiche Lorraine and Lobster Newburg. She could tolerate the first two indecencies, but the Newburg would surely give her digestive problems.

How could she face the tyranny of the giant scale at Weight Watchers the next day? All those grinning ill-wishers gaining spiritual points at her expense. She hated the smug skinnier-than-thou look of Dolores Abramowitz when the scale arrow proudly pointed to her own indulgences. These repentant sinners revolted her with their burning conversional enthusiasm and low-fat cottage cheese. She preferred to work with people having more normal drives, like greed, ambition, and crowd-love. Reformers were never around at the finish line.

She would surely end up with Donnatal and Pepto-Bismol at four in the morning while Cal slept as though he had just returned from a twenty mile hike. Oh, to let him know, just once, that she, too, suffered battle wounds.

Marsha has a lovely house, she thought as she parked the Mercedes in the yellow pebbled driveway close to the fifty-year-old English Tudor. As usual, she was the first to arrive and purposely edged to the top of the hill so that the others would be able to park their cars behind her. Her mind worked that way, intuitively, arranging protocol at all times.

She thought the house too nice for only a dentist's wife. It was authentic English Tudor, constructed of large blocks of gray and tan fieldstone. One of the few things about Marsha that wasn't just veneer. The heavy beams running the length of the ground floor rooms were part of the original construction. Joan loved the spaciousness of the extra-wide rooms and the twelve-foot ceilings. Each massive room meant real living space to her. She thought of what she could do with the rooms. Make each one a work of art instead of a drafty echo chamber with garbage from Sears Roebuck. Interior decoration, or its lack, was one of the crimes of which she inwardly convicted Marsha.

The house was set with geographic elegance on an interesting acre of gentle undulations, within that exclusive enclave called Hewlett Harbor. Its perimeters were a shoreline border on the southern and western ends where Howie docked his boat. Century old maples and birches grew on the north, and an area of thicket, wisely left untouched by builder and occupant, to the east completed the square.

And all this for a ninny like Marsha, a girl who saw plots and enemies all around her, whose life consisted of battening down the hatches against storms that never came. She would often tearfully complain to Joan, over Martinis at the Hunt Club, that the seltzer route man had raised his prices again another fifteen cents a bottle. It was out and out thievery. And the paperboy, who was an anti-Semite, had tossed last Thursday's *Newsday* into oblivion. At least that score had been settled in favor of the Jewish people, when she made sure to deduct the missing paper from the bill and eliminate the tip.

Joan rang the bell. The lady of the house answered, knowing in advance who her first guest was. She stood in her own doorway like a weed in a bed of flowers, thin and shapeless, coiffed in an Afro that seemed too weighty for her small head. Strands of mousy brown hair escaped hurriedly in all directions from her scalp. Joan refused to acknowledge the new hairstyle. It pained her to look at it. This, added to the overbite and a flat, almost-non-cartilaginous nose gave Marsha a mulatto look. Surely Marsha's enemies, and she created a continuous supply of them, would label her "the scrub brush with the long handle."

"After it's over I just *have* to talk to you," Marsha whispered to Joan in the empty central hallway. Joan looked briefly for an eavesdropper but found none. To Marsha there was always a need for guarded words. "It's an absolute imperative," she added.

Joan was used to Marsha's "absolutes" and "imperatives." Marsha made announcements with whispered anguish as if common knowledge of her news would severely depress the stock market, cause tremors in world capitols, and initiate hordes of suicides in high places. She treated every second of her life with the same sense of rapidly approaching doom. Early in their parasitic relationship Joan knew the girl was a victim supreme. Also a very vulnerable clown.

"Later, later, baby," Joan said. "We'll talk when our business is finished."

Once inside the mini-castle Joan felt eager to begin the meeting. People were her canvas and paints. She needed little else to unleash her creative forces. Thrown into an organization, at any level, she would soon rise to the top and become its leader. She believed in action, in setting an example, in leading her troops into battle. And she emerged victorious as few generals do today, by a combination of threats, cajoling, compliments, and the display of her own fast fading back as she flew into battle. But above all she touched. Joan was a toucher, a layer-on of hands. She touched to establish a lifeline between two souls. She touched to give a sense of the basic decency of aristocracy, and, finally, she touched because it was a disarming gesture. Who could have malice in their heart once she caressed them with her fingers?

Joan excused herself and found the powder room directly behind the kitchen. While she checked her new Helena Rubenstein face, coordinated by a computer that guaranteed beauty through chemistry and solid state circuitry, the women began arriving. With a touch of stage freight, she quickly flushed the Kleenex that wore her lip prints. She walked to the garden room where they were gathering and counted noses. All present. Attendance taken, she again reassured Marsha.

"We'll talk until we get hoarse, but after the meeting," Joan said not looking at her. Nose counting was a serious business and Marsha kept getting in the way with her insecurity. If the ninny interfered again she would be cutting, even if it was her house.

The rectangular table was well set professionally by rented

15

people. The sun, filtering through the French doors, shone its shafts of light, like golden batons, on the square, stemmed water goblets. None of the guests, except Joan, saw the beauty of the setting. Instead, they calculated the costs.

She politely sampled the quiche. It was excellent. The Newburg was a little too thick for her think-thin palate and too pasty. Proud of herself she let it pass. The coffee, altered by Sweet'n'-Low and skimmed milk, tasted good to her re-educated taste buds. She sipped it slowly and waited her turn. It came.

"Ladies . . . ladies . . . Oh, ladies of the Rosemont chapter of Hadassah," she shouted unable even to hear herself. They hadn't heard her either. As if insanely driven, they went on talking at levels dangerously close to ear shattering. But, though much was said, little was heard. Had an expert taped the cacophony and later separated out the thirty component voices, he would have heard thirty hosannas to "me" that began and ended like a fugue.

Joan was furious. She rose and tapped on the crystal goblet with an intricately patterned knife. Marsha was horrified that one might be damaged by the other. No matter. The tactic proved fruitless. Joan waved her hands for attention, but soon gave that up, too. Finally she began circling the table, putting her hands over the rapid-fire mouths of each diner. By the seventh woman the audience got the message. All grew silent and apprehensive. Joan was no woman to arouse to anger. The silencer returned to her place with a warm, knowing smile on her face. She purposely slowed her walk for the added weight it would bring to her words.

"Ladies, dear ladies," she began, "now that you've fed your overprivileged faces, now that the noise pollution has abated, and now that we've all been informed as to who is currently sleeping with whom, what do you say we get down to business?

"You know, I'm sure, that we are here for a noble purpose, girls. Let's try to attain that goal so that our passage through life is a teeny bit useful."

She spoke as a teacher to her slightly backward and unruly students. It was one of her poses. She had many and chose each one from her armory with the care that a golfer exhibits selecting just the right club from his bag. It was absolutely necessary, she realized early in her presidency, to first stun, then abuse, and finally shame this particular group into the slightest form of activity. Not because they were rugged individualists; they were neither rugged nor freethinking. The basic similarity of clothes, accessories, and hairstyle all attested to their herd pattern. Knowing them well she realized that their inaction was based on their application of patrician standards. Queens, one and all, they found fund raising, the backbone of any charitable group, beneath them. To achieve anything, to move these strange birds of paradise away from their mirrors, Joan had to first slay the aristocrat within them. Were this, however, a P.T.A. meeting (she was president of that body, too), she would have used a softer, more relaxed approach. In that game she dealt with teachers, truck drivers, policemen, and white collar workers, people who still cared desperately about education as a vehicle for upward mobility.

No sound. She finally had their attention. They watched her as if she were a suicide perched on a ledge, waiting tensely for the next insult.

"Fun and games are over for the day, my fellow campfollowers. Push the rum cake away from the coffee, push yourself away from the table, and let's get down to cases," she ordered.

She perused them again. Her Hadassah ladies were the wives and widows of doctors, dentists, clothing manufacturers, and assorted businessmen: women, if not born, then certainly quite happily adjusted to the purple.

She glanced around the rectangular table in the garden room, where the fragrances of the roses assaulted her senses and almost blunted her carefully constructed front. If she hadn't had these ladies to whip into a motivated frenzy she would have loved to open the French doors and just absorb the sweet earth odors.

Superficially Joan appeared to be one of the uniformed affluents, indivisible from the rest. The first thing one noticed was her tan. She was an inveterate beach goer from early June until late September. The reward for her steadfastness was this absolutely stunning, perpetual tan. While some wore a cross and others the Star of David, Joan wore her tan. And to her friends' amazement she never suffered a sunburn. She wore white and, occasionally, blue for contrast. The idea of contrast appealed to her, as it does to all artists whose world is the public.

Even her hair was a sample of drama. Though well kept and

17

lovely it looked tie-dyed with its strands of brown, gray, and flaxen blond. If the world of humans was suddenly transformed into one huge zoo she would be a handsome sleek lioness, proud and potent, assured and unassailable. Her eyes, as she constantly weighed her audience, were clear and brown. Five thousand-year-old eyes to which nothing came as a shock or a surprise.

"Now, ladies," she said with a little girl smile, "I've worked long and hard for this chapter. Correct?" No voices raised in opposition and she continued. "Made it Numero Uno on the east coast. It took five years and a lot of sweat to save the patient. When I took over this group, this yo-yo group, you were all a bunch of picture takers and dinner-dance addicts. And nothing more." Her voice rose, but with controlled elevation like an escalator. "Now, five years later, five long years of cracking the whip we are the *best*." She looked around, a slow pan, especially at their eyes to see if some sparks of pride were flinted off. "And my fair duchesses, we are going to stay the best."

She paused. The technique was to let the words sink in. She continued at a slower, more sober pace. "Our quota for the annual drive is one hundred thousand dollars."

The audience groaned as if in mass pain. A few low buzzes followed.

"That's a nice round number, ladies. It has a solid ring to it. And I've pledged our attaining that goal. That being the reality of it, ladies," and she glanced down, as if reading notes, "I want . . . no, scratch that out, I demand one hundred percent co-operation from one hundred percent of you." Some of them puffed on their Virginia Slims and hardly exhaled as if storing courage. "Tell your husbands they can spend more time on the golf course or with their mistresses for the duration. As of this minute your souls belong to Hadassah." She yearned for a sip of water but denied herself the pleasure. It might be interpreted as a sign of weakness.

From the back, at the right angle of the table, a hand slowly rose. It was attached to an attractive, slender blond in her middle thirties, athletic and vivacious looking, with a thin coat of worry spread on her face.

"The chair recognizes Diana Krauland," Joan said. "What's bugging you, baby?"

Diana smiled sickly, and almost inaudibly said, "I'm sorry, Joan. You'll have to excuse me this drive. I'm . . . I'm committed to a tennis tournament. I just can't get out of it. I'm sorry." She sat down quickly, her burden jettisoned.

Joan, like all good skippers who run tight ships, was prepared for emergencies. Even feint-hearted mutinies from tennis players. She readjusted her glance to a withering stare and focused on the blond who thought herself safe now.

"Listen sporty lady," she began, "you can't dance at two weddings. Your first commitment is to Rosemont and to me. To me, Joan Bernstein, Personally. You signed on for the whole voyage, sweets, and I'm not going to let you come and go as you please. This is serious business. You'll have to do your share or get out. Now," she table thumped, "you decide right now. This minute. Either you're going to smack a little ball around like Chrissy Evert or you're going to stand up and be counted." She paused.

"If you decide that wearing short pants and acting like a high falutin' wasp is more important than a new hospital in Ramat Gan, then pick yourself up and skeddadle. No hard feelings," she promised, but everyone in the room knew otherwise. "We'll just put the customary notice in the local papers of your soul-rending choice (I'll privately say Kaddish for you), and it'll be like you never lived in this community as far as we're concerned."

She had her finger pointed at Diana toward the finale, causing her to turn tennis shorts white. Before she could answer Joan stepped in.

"I also have another little thorn to take out of my finger dear, as long as we're having this little heart-to-heart. Diana, dear, you stiffed me on the cake sale last month. Don't think I've forgotten that, Billie Jean. I never forget. Why didn't you show? Not ritzy enough for you in the basement of a bank?"

Diana hung her head as if sentenced to death by a judge.

"Listen, kid, if I can bake brownies, you can rustle up something, too. Less backhand and more Betty Crocker, if you please."

Diana looked horsewhipped. An overwhelming blanket of regret enveloped her for her quarter-hearted act of defiance.

"Well," she said haltingly, "maybe I'll skip this tournament and make the next."

"Does that mean you're in?" Joan asked.

19

"Yes it does," Diana meekly replied.

"Good, good," Joan shot back, "we need you. You're a classy lady and a definite asset. I'm very, very glad you'll be with us," she smiled for all to see. "Now I'm sure we'll go over the top."

Diana warmed to the compliment. Her beaten look changed to one of pride.

Just fine, Joan thought, she'll be just fine. The bitch. She thinks her ass-showing little tennis skirt will keep her out of the ovens. But . . . she'll be fine . . . now.

"Oh, Mrs. Bernstein." A matronly lady with purple-white hair like grape juice in whipped cream, her body encased in diamonds, called to her.

Joan wheeled athletically and faced the opposite side of the table ready to field the next tricky grounder.

"I thought, and correct me if I'm wrong, that Hadassah was a *voluntary* organization, which, when I went to school, meant I could do or not do as I chose. Yes? Well, Joan, I don't think it is at all dignified for a woman my age, especially a surgeon's wife (she hammered down "surgeon" as if it were a spike) to knock at some snot-nose schoolteacher's door and beg for nickels and dimes. It's just not right. I mean . . . after all."

Joan simmered and thought of floggings. She firmly grasped her goblet and put clear thumbprints on its contours. "Mrs. Doctor Pelsky," she began, "when the ovens were going full blast, a short thirty years ago, that funny little bastard with the moustache didn't say, 'we'll excuse all the senior citizens,' or, 'sorry, my dear, I didn't know you were a *surgeon's* wife.' "

The group tittered at her sarcasm. Mrs. Doctor Pelsky was on her own as far as they were concerned.

"Listen lady," she said, "let me restate basic principles. We Jews are all in the Army, at war with the rest of the world. If the day of the final solution comes again all they'll say is 'Jews to the right, everyone else to the left.' And there'll only be two lines with no exceptions. So if it's good enough for Hitler to lump us together, it's good enough for me."

She paused, looked into her opponent's eyes for seconds before the older woman wrenched free. "So, it's put-up-or-shut-up time, Mrs. Doctor Pelsky. Are you going to stick with us less-endowed

Jews or join the other side? I'm sorry to put it so bluntly dear, but that's the realpolitik of it."

The surgeon's wife was broken. It was hardly a contest.

"Well," she whined, "I guess I can do it, even with my varicose veins." She managed a trickle of a smile.

Joan quickly followed. Now was no time to throw away a victory.

"Tell your husband, the surgeon, to get you a pair of surgical panty hose and you'll do just fine."

Joan smiled. Mrs. Pelsky smiled. The crowd smiled. Everyone loves a happy ending.

"And you know something, Mrs. Pelsky, I've got a funny feeling you'll probably be high scorer this year and get the award. You're a pioneer in this town. A legend. You know *everybody.*" The victor was being generous.

The surgeon's wife sat down ceremoniously, pleased at her elevation to legend and Joan's recognition of her new status. Of course she knew it herself but it was nice hearing it from *the* Mrs. Bernstein.

The mutiny over, Joan returned to battle plans. "Now, a word of advice, girls," she said. "When you go out collecting door-to-door, please don't dress like two-hundred-dollar hookers. We are not trying to impress; we are trying to extract," she said, stressing every word. "That little snot-nose of a schoolteacher should see just one of the girls, a volunteer for Israel, in a plain cloth coat from Alexanders, not a fancy broadtail. What I'm trying to say is don't rub their noses in the fact that you can probably buy and sell them a dozen times over."

Smugness spread like poison ivy over their faces when Joan said that. They suddenly remembered who they were again.

"Also, if it's raining you still go out knocking on doors. You'll do better. People stay home when it rains. Just remember, what we do now, what we collect goes to save lives. We need that hospital. And being a Jew, any kind of a Jew, makes you automatically committed to the survival of Israel."

They all nodded in unison.

"Also don't be ashamed to put the arm on the merchants in town. In fact, cookies, it's easier with the merchants. Especially if you don't owe them any money. And please get over the feeling that you're landed gentry and they're peons with their hats in their hands. Some of them have much more money than you. But realistically, they have to kick in. It's good for business and it's tax deductible." She ruffled her hair with her fingers and felt comforted by its healthy feel.

"And finally, you golden geese, if we don't bust through the quota, oh, if we don't bust through the quota," she sang in dirge-like manner, "I'll tell you this and you can bet your bikinis on it, there'll be no picture taking with your furs and gems. And as sure as taxes no victory dinner dance, which is why you're here absorbing all this punishment in the first place." She gently tapped the table. "Meeting adjourned."

The women looked, one and all, as if they had been doused with ice water. As certain as toys break, each and everyone of them knew that the quota would be met. Anything short of that goal would invite all kinds of hell and worse, a year of Bernstein flagellation right out of *Mutiny on the Bounty*.

Joan knew her package was tied up with a bright red ribbon. The quota would probably be met and exceeded. She knew her capabilities, knew them better than anyone else. She was dead certain that with equal facility she could organize a garden party, a trip to the moon, or a descent into hell. And with all the grace, dignity, and clear-eyed bitchiness the situation demanded she could determine the clothes, plan the menus, and organize the work crews. Without a qualm she could even shoot the stragglers, if that became necessary.

And they loved her for it. They really loved her. Not so much at first. But slowly as the project took life and form, and the princesses forgot the scourging and dimly saw the goal, their love grew. And the more she flayed them, the more they loved her. She motivated and she got results. When it was over they got their night of celebration and as Joan entered the country club they would stand up as one and applaud and applaud her until she finally cried.

She dismissed the Rosemont chapter of Hadassah and immediately felt that pair of sunny garden eyes begging her. The ladies piled into their BMW's, their Jaguars and Sevilles and left. Joan watched their cars, like parts of a convoy, slowly back down the driveway and disappear behind the high hedges. She was glad it was over.

When she turned Marsha was there as Joan knew she would be. They walked away from the sounds of cleaning up, the clatter of metal on glass, of glass on porcelain. She followed her hostess into a small den. (Marsha and Howie had separate dens on opposite sides of the house; the larger one for him, the smaller one for her.)

Marsha quickly closed the door behind her and leaned against it as if to keep out rushing hordes. A studied glance at Marsha and Joan thought that her face had aged more rapidly than the rest of her. She looked older than thirty-five. Much older. Her thin face uncomfortably held large frightened eyes. More like her mother every day, thought Joan. The years of haranguing, of suspicions and fears, with enemies and thieves were taking their toll.

"Howie's having an affair," Marsha blurted out, "and I don't know how to handle it." Her face seemed to be going in all directions. Only the eyes had stability. They searched Joan for an answer.

"You're my friend, Joan, my best friend. You're wise and you're clever. Talk to me. *Puleez* talk to me. Tell me what to do. I'm going crazy. I'll wind up with a heart attack, yet."

Joan appeared to ignore her and her bout of near-hysteria. She carefully chose her favorite seat, the one that gave her the best view of the bay. She sat and watched the sun just above the trees send yellow-orange rays that neatly cut the water without disturbing a drop. She thought, it was just a matter of time before Marsha found the bogey man under her own bed. She could almost forgive Howie.

"I shouldn't wonder," she said finally acknowledging her hostess.

"Why, what's wrong with me?" Marsha asked.

"What's wrong with you? You should have asked what's right with you. It would take less time to answer."

"I thought you were my friend."

"I am your friend. If I wasn't I'd say, 'it'll be alright,' and leave. You want to know? Okay, I'll tell you. Just stop and think for a minute. What was the first thing you said to me this morning on the phone? Do you remember?"

"No, I don't remember."

"Well, what is usually the first thing you greet me with? Come on, Marsha, it's not that difficult."

"So I sometimes say, 'do you know who died?' So what's wrong with that? I imagined you'd like to know those things."

"Well, honey bunch, you imagined wrong. I don't own any stocks in death. I don't *have* to know about everyone who died that day. It's not absolutely necessary. If it's going to affect me, I'll find out about it eventually, anyway."

"Is that all?"

"No, that's not all. You fight with every store owner in town, and over nonsense. It's one thing to stand up for your rights. It's something else again to continually stick your finger in someone's eye. Which you do over and over again. You still think your husband's a struggling beginner from Boro Park. He made it over fifteen years ago. Now act it . . . a little bit. Or else you'll be poor the rest of your life."

Marsha took the criticism poorly. She glowered and searched for Joan's flaws to offer as counterweight, thinking two negatives would make a positive.

Joan pursued her. "I passed by the other day when you were getting an oil delivery. You were standing in the downpour with an umbrella, wearing a torn bathrobe and Howie's old tennis shoes, watching the meter on the truck. And the driver was sitting in the cab to keep from getting wet. But you, dopey, were standing there like Minnie Mouse trying to make sure you weren't getting screwed out of a buck or two." Joan shook her head sadly.

"Well, I don't like getting fooled," Marsha whined. She found a strand of lint on her slacks. She swallowed hard.

Joan softened. "So what makes you think Howie's fooling around?" she asked gently with folded hands.

"Well, he's restless and he goes out a lot by himself. He never did that before. And he's so short tempered, like he's looking for an excuse to fight and take off to . . . God knows where."

With a wry look Joan sat back and slowly nodded. She was adding two and two, coming up with varied results. The after-

24

noon sun finally caught her full face. She shaded her eyes but refused to change her seat.

"Well, dear, the only sensible thing to do is put it to him straight. Say, 'are you fooling around Howie?' If he is and he says yes, you can take it from there. Throw him out or charge him a fortune to stay in. Or do what comes naturally. If he is and he denies it, well, at least he knows that you know. Sometimes when a man knows he's being watched it sort of knocks him back in the groove again, like that hand game with the board with the holes in it and the little balls.

"Of course, Marsha, if he's not and he says no, then you have another problem. Like a stale marriage. You'd better do plenty of homework on that one. But for God's sake don't sit there like a dummy, biting your nails and imagining the worst."

Marsha looked relieved. This time her face glowed, leaving only the eyes worried and sad.

"I swear, Joan, you are a blessing. So organized, so smart. And you and Cal are like unbelievable opposites. Yet you're one dynamite team."

"You think so girl? Well it's no bed of roses. I'll tell you that. Cal is the only man in the world for me. There's no one like Cal, but it ain't easy. Frankly, he's the dearest man I know, and it's my job to protect him from—the world, his patients, his employees, the tradespeople . . . any Tom, Dick, or Harry with a sad story and an extended hand. It's a full-time job. He'd give away everything, including his dirty sneakers, if I'd let him."

Joan felt compelled to continue once started and Marsha felt equally compelled to listen.

"He doesn't belong in this world. He's the simplest yet the deepest, most honest person I know and that's a compliment coming from an old war dog like me. Would you believe he sometimes goes to the office in a torn, smelly sweatshirt." Marsha's nostrils quivered as if she were smelling Cal's shirt.

"Sometimes on a bicycle. It's so embarrassing. Me with the Mercedes. But you know, he needs me. That's my main mission in life. To guard that very rare treasure. I'm not trying to put him down, mind you. Believe me, if the world were perfect, he'd be its king. Maybe it's just love, but you know, sometimes he does things and says things that are so unusual that I'm moved

25

to tears. He made house calls for one year solid, a whole year, mind you, to a colored man with cancer. Didn't take a cent and when the man died Cal even paid for the funeral. And this was before we could even afford to be charitable. So you see it's not easy living with a saint in a world of sinners.

"This man knows little about survival, Marsha, and as you well know I am its grand mistress. Nobody, but nobody knows how to survive like I do."

Marsha nodded vigorously.

"Thrive would be a better word to describe it, really. I just don't hold on for dear life. I hang on when the lifeboat turns over and I set it right, jump in, organize the rowers, and sail into port. That's me. And Cal will survive because of me. You see, I'm smart enough to know that the world needs people like him. They are its grit and muscle, but the lousy world destroys those they need the most. My job is to keep my kind away from him."

The sun, at last, had given up trying to blind her and found another part of the den to turn orange and yellow. The bay grew darker, almost blue-black. A boat with a red and white sail drifted off in the distance. It looked as if a little boy with a string were pulling it.

"So I run things at home," she confessed, "because he'd only make a bloody mess of it. Cal hasn't the time or the desire or even the feel for it. If the gardener asked for two hundred a month, he'd pay the two hundred. Or three hundred, or whatever. I know what gardeners get. You do, too. And so does Howie. But Cal? A complete blank. He could live in a lean-to. Just give him medicine twenty-four hours a day, a bowl of Rice Krispies for breakfast, a steak at night, me once or twice a week, and honey, he's in heaven. Me, too, frankly about the sex part, although it's not what it used to be. I'm very deficient in that department," she smiled shyly.

She felt awkward showing Marsha eight-by-tens of her very private life, but it was in the spirit of things and it was only a little peek. With all her peculiarities, Marsha was her best friend. She made sure to turn the pages fast.

"But you sound so ruthless, Joanie. I knew you were efficient and hardworking and blunt and honest, but ruthlessness is new to me." She seemed genuinely shocked.

"What's wrong with that? So I'm ruthless." She said it with the same degree of conviction she would have employed had someone asked her her religion. "You call it ruthlessness, I call it singlemindedness. Knowing what you want . . . and getting it."

It began to grow near dusk. The sun's rays ceased their attack on Marsha's landscape and withdrew behind the horizon. The hostess reached out and flicked on the lights.

"But you're not cruel," Marsha said. "You could be very cruel, especially to me. But you're not. And I'm such a nothing." She searched Joan's face begging for a rebuttal.

Joan reached over and patted Marsha's nobby knees soothingly. "You're not a nothing, baby. You're silly and petty, sometimes, but you have many fine qualities. You're loyal and kind and generous," she added, not knowing what else to say.

"And I can't be cruel, Marsha. Cruel is small and sick and obvious. Damned wasteful, too. It's letting pettiness rule you. Mine is on a leash . . . where it belongs. I never let it get in the way of what I want. And when I see it in myself, I beat it down like a weed patch. There's never a reason to be cruel, but there are many reasons to be ruthless.

"And as long as you're looking at my wrinkles," she continued, "you might as well know that I'm afraid, sometimes. Terribly afraid." Her voice trailed off like a puff of smoke in the wind.

Marsha was tilted slightly out of orbit. Her ears were full of the sounds of idols crashing down.

"You afraid? I don't believe it. What have *you* to be afraid of?"

"Listen, kid, I'm forty plus. I'm past the pinnacle, now. Downhill is the next stop. Who wants a forty-year-old Jewish Queen, regardless of all the accessories? I'm . . . I'm just not sure of Cal for the long haul. He's missed too much in life. I know it, maybe he knows it, too. I hope not. He's a volcano ready to explode. I see him there smouldering, smouldering, sending out a few rumbles. Luckily the man's never strayed before. At least I don't think so. I hope he hasn't," she said when her ears heard her voice.

"So what do I do, you ask? I give myself another job. Me. Taking care of me is my other vocation. I work two shifts," she

27

smiled. "Between taking care of Cal and taking care of me, I say pretty busy."

Marsha giggled knowingly.

"Just keeping my weight down takes God knows how much time. And the right clothes and the tan. Do you think it's all done with a twitch of the nose? Just look at my nails. Small precise wonders, no?" They were oval-shaped unstrung pearls. "And the hairdresser. And the cosmetician. But it works, believe me, it works," she said.

"It's selfish and it's vain, I know, but it's also altruistic. If I take good care of me I'm fit and proper to care for Cal. And that's the way I keep my ship afloat. So, baby, don't think that it's smooth sailing for my doctor and me. It's a question of fighting off the wolves every goddamned day of the week. I'm just as much on call as old Doc Bernstein."

Joan left after that, but returned moments later. The Mercedes would not start. It lay there in the driveway, like a mule, ignoring her cajoling and curses.

"I'm stopping the check. Just had the alternator replaced," she said as she dialed the service department. "And it's the same damned thing, again. This time they're going to send a service man down here to fix it."

"Don't be silly, Joan. Mercedes never sends mechanics out. That's unheard of," Marsha said.

"You think so, huh? Well, ninny, don't bet your bloomers on it. I know Sam Conte, the service manager. He's my assistant at the election board."

She stood in the doorway, arms akimbo, tapping her foot like a metronome counting the minutes. Very few of them went by before a small red van, barrelled up the driveway. After a few more the wrong was righted. Only a loose wire.

She gave the mechanic a dollar and flourished her best oh-thank-you-for-coming-to-my-aid smile. The car sprung to life and she flew away waving goodbye to Marsha positioned in the middle of her rear view mirror. Her tires kicked up a dusty smoke screen behind which she vanished like a sorceress. That bit of magic was really unnecessary. Marsha had long ago grouped her with wizards, magicians, and other practitioners of the black arts.

The weighty stillness of May. Everything seemed heavier in May, especially in the marshes. The air was thick and appeared to slow the light, distorting it before it eventually reached him. Nature looked pulled out of shape, as if Picasso had given it lessons. Gulls overhead flew more slowly, decreasing their usual number of swooping arabesques. The songs of the marsh birds were belabored, too, as if they had to push their notes against an invisible tide. Even the flowers showed signs of lethargy, their perfumes contained within their petals.

Nothing stirred in the tall grass fatigued by the overwork of being alive in May. Occasionally the cattails gently waved from side to side without the aid of a breeze.

Cal sat in his usual Friday spot, on a torn beach chair that he had rescued from a premature grave. He had snatched it from the garbage spot in back of the house and hid it, bent and torn, in his car trunk. He felt comfortable on it. The webbing had adjusted to his body.

He, alone, knew of the tiny finger of land that extended into the inlet. Attached to that finger was a thick hand covered with magnificent oaks, impenetrable raspberry mantraps that clung like barbed wire, and trees whose names he did not know that sent out long thick tendrils criss-crossing with strands from other nameless trees. Whole webs of tendrils formed hostile barriers that kept Cal confined to the finger. In the winter when the jungle dropped its guard he would explore inland. With ease he would negotiate the half mile to the Cedarwood golf course, where the primitive land bowed to the majesty of well-behaved grass. Since no explorer ever left the safe haven of the eighteenth hole he considered the jungle private property.

Though a life-long resident of Brooklyn, and unused to the sight of green growing things, Cal took root in the compatible soil of Nassau's South Shore during the great migrations of the late fifties. The Bernsteins were one ripple in a series of eastward waves that comprised the exodus of the middle class from New York City. Without a Moses to lead them they fled first to adjoining Nassau County and later on to Suffolk, east of Eden. After World War II when the real estate brokers split blocks, when a new black face next door decimated a neighborhood, when the Jewish boys from Flatbush, Pelham Parkway, Bensonhurst, and Crown Heights began to make it big and the non-Jewish boys grew families, as the rents grew faster, the City dispersed its tax base in an almost football-like pattern.

The top level of the new diaspora, stock brokers, advertising executives, fledgling professionals, sons and sons-in-law of clothing manufacturers deployed short right, just over the city line into the Five Towns, or short left, to the North Shore duchies of Great Neck and Kings Point. Both communities, north and south, offered easy access to the city and the pristine purity of all-white living. Lower middle class Jews who could not afford three thousand dollars in taxes went long and to the right in middle Nassau, populating the towns of Merrick and Bellmore. The non-Jews with small incomes and large families, barrelled straight up the middle to Valley Stream, Elmont, Lynbrook, and Hicksville. Many settled in Massapequa close to Suffolk where square box houses were counterbalanced by low taxes and G.I. mortgages.

It was Joan who chose that area starting with Inwood and running due east to Hewlett, commonly called the Five Towns by some, the Gilded Ghetto by others. She was certain that the thirty-five hundred dollar tax bite created greater safety against *them* than an alligator-filled moat and a ten-foot-thick wall of solid stone. Cal, oblivious to the fine points of reghettoizing, followed her lead blindly since the center of his world, man and his illnesses, could be found everywhere and anywhere like grass, like the Jew.

He stared at the empty canvas. It stared back silently accusing

30

him of the low crime of sloth and the high crime of no talent. But he was content and felt years lighter. By some magic process he was at one with Van Gogh in the cornfields and Gauguin in Tahiti.

A gray-white gull pierced the stillness with its raucous cry of discovery. It wheeled and dipped widely in its arc, warning the marsh's residents of the intruder even though Cal's residency had begun back in January when opaque ice patches had crackled underfoot and the cold air had burned its way into his lungs.

From his vantage point, he was well hidden by the tall reeds, but he could see the drawbridge in the distance and the boats chugging by. His Fridays were fantasy days. Inventory taking days. A chance to burrow within himself, to surface, with a treasure of sorts and put it, loosely translated, on canvas. But he painted poorly and he knew it. Absent was any feeling for form and line and texture. There was no real difference between the paint on his pallet and the paint on the canvas. Both were unused. Once, as he stood in line at the hardware store to pay for batteries for his tiny throat flashlight, he had seen the display of artists' paraphernalia and had shelled out forty dollars more than the fifty cents he originally came in to spend.

Painting pictures to hang in the Louvre was of secondary, even tertiary, importance. What did count, was the chance to hear himself. A chance to find that trapped miner tapping, tapping on the wall of his tomb. Cocoon would be more accurate. One is placed in his tomb, but one builds a cocoon out of the elements of his own body. Was the miner still alive? He wondered. Everything had to stop, the phone calls, the nagging demands of domesticity. All had to be quieter than a whisper if his voice was to surface. If there was still one left. The doctor had his doubts.

His brush strokes were whisper soft, they just kissed the canvas lightly. He felt serene. Adjusting to May was like getting a second wind. There was not enough heat to drive him inland, yet it was warm enough for him to go barechested and roll up his corduroy pants.

He sighed languidly. Half the morning was invested in watching occasional squadrons of swallows practice attack maneuvers overhead. They dove as a single wedge, then broke apart, only

31

to regroup above yet another target. Cal could see that they hardly needed practice being expert at all phases of their war games. "Fantastic, fantastic," he mumbled through clenched teeth.

Weightlessness weighed heavily upon him. The gravity of his total involvement in matters of life and death suspended, he needed more time to adjust to floating free. The bay appeared to ripple without a breeze. He wished he could capture the fecundity of the marshes in May through his unwilling paintbox. But he was just too inept and would never submit to the regimen needed just to master the fundamentals. He could not hope to be an artist, but he could speed the miner to the surface in first class transportation.

By noon he had sketched the barest outline of a blue crane standing serenely, in the narrow neck of the inlet. There was beauty in abundance to that graceful slant of neck and the reverse curve of the wings. The model had infinite patience with the artist's ineptness. He stood, staring at the water for what seemed like an hour while Cal traced and retraced false starts and gross errors of proportion. It was all so easy and effortless; he was losing himself at last. Now if the crane can only hold out, he thought.

The tall grass rustled behind him. He hardly heard.

She was startled to see him, but knew who he was at once.

"Hullo. You're Doctor Bernstein. This is quite a coincidence," she said while her face indicated otherwise.

"Coincidence?"

"Sure. First the office, now here. Did someone tell you I walk a lot? Have you been following me?"

He put his brush down slowly. "No, I've been in this area for almost six months. I have squatters rights. I can even show you a painting from April with snow on the ground."

Which funneled her eyes to the canvas. She frowned. "No thanks. It's probably worse than this."

Convinced of his innocence and coaxed by it to make amends she said coyly, "I hope you practice medicine more skillfully."

"I do. The smearing isn't good. In fact it's quite lousy. I don't care since I'm my own critic. Except for you. It gives me something to do while I sit here and hide."

"I thought all doctors played golf or tennis on their day off."

32

He nodded more to dissolve her suspicions than to agree with her prejudices.

"They do, most of them. I can't stand the game myself. Boring. Boring as hell, really . . . Mrs. Bruno?"

"Yes, Victor's wife . . . remember? The lady with the vaginal itch and the chip on her shoulder," she smiled. "I thought maybe *he* blabbed to you about some of my other peculiarities. Besides being a breeding ground for funguses."

"No ma'am, just a case of no-fault collision."

Her eyes clean-swept the tiny circle of Cal's gear.

"No beeper?"

"No beeper. I've been beeped enough to last a lifetime. Not too long ago it was part of my anatomy but I had it surgically removed. The operation saved my life." He grinned weakly as if he had told himself a private joke. "I need a day all to myself."

She smiled. "I thought I was the only goofball in the whole world who ran and hid. I guess I'm not so strange, then."

"Unless we two are the last of the breed," he speculated toyingly.

"A possibility. I never thought of that," she said playing his game.

Awkward silence. Both wondered who had the ball. The crane, insulted by Tessa's intrusion, flew away, his large wings sounding like the noise of rugs being beaten.

"Listen," Cal began, unsure of his general drift, "I have more than enough lunch for one. Some nice Swiss cheese, lettuce, some fruit. Even a pair of cold beers attached to that line in the water." He pointed to two strands of fuzzy cord tied at one end to a round rock.

"How about it? Would you share them with me?"

She paused, pursed her lips and said, "That's a very tempting offer and I accept. Swiss cheese and beer happen to be high up on my gourmet delight list. All we need now is a book of verses and paradise enou'."

"I'll recite 'The Star-Spangled Banner' for you," he said as he spread his khaki blanket, almost completely covering the finger of land. "It's the only poem I can think of right now."

They subdivided the contents of the knapsack. The Swiss wedges were uniform. A feat of engineering. They looked a little wilted

33

but smelled tangy and inviting. A head of lettuce with thick green leaves, broke easily into quarters. Dixie cups of Russian dressing and mustard came out last along with the plastic utensils sealed in Saran Wrap. An assortment of oranges and apples were left in the knapsack wrapped only in their own skins. Tessa wondered about the efficiency expert who devised the packing order and the wrappings. It frightened her a bit.

Cal fished the beers, cold and wet, out of the bay, happy as any fisherman with his catch. They sat Yoga-style at opposite ends of the blanket and ate with their fingers.

"I take it your infection cleared up. You didn't come back to see me."

"It cleared up, but you'll have to take my word on it. I've no intentions of letting you play doctor, here."

He laughed and threw up his hands in mild surrender. "Sorry, I was just talking in general. I should know by now not to talk to you in general. You're a very specific person. Forgive me. And I was *not* aiming to get your clothes off. That was a hell of a job the first time, when you had to."

She grinned and dipped a cheese wedge into the Russian dressing. It was very good Swiss.

"You know, you seemed tense as hell that time, the first few minutes anyhow. You don't appear terribly shy, you don't seem to have that untouchable virgin syndrome. You're more open and candid, really, than most. Free from hangups, I think."

"Well, I'm not shy about most things. In fact, I was surprised myself when I clammed up that way. It's not like me. I'm quite open. You saw that during the last part of the visit when I blabbed the whole thing out. Like you were confessing me."

"You're not the only one."

"I am to me," she shot back, then relaxed her guard. "It's just that . . . that, I really find it difficult to put into words. Not that I'm overly modest, I just haven't been in that part of my head in quite a while."

"It's like driving a car. You never forget," he said.

"I'll tell a person, my innermost thoughts, like I did in your office, but being handled and touched while I'm not in full control of myself, that's a different thing."

"Even when a doctor's doing it," he probed.

34

"Even when a doctor's doing it. The subconscious clam-up is still there." She began to stumble. "I can't draw the line between the two points, but I think it's something like an assault on my person. Tell me it's silly, or not modern, I still can't help it. And it's not an easy thing to verbalize. I never have, till now, and probably never would have if you hadn't sprung me to lunch alfresco."

"Look at that," he said. "That's what the whole profession needs. More open air centers."

"I'm not talking to you as a doctor," she said and he saw thunder and lightning in her eyes.

He held back on a easy answer and wiped the beer cans dry. "I had hoped not," he said yanking off the tabs. Their eyes watched each other as they drank. The beer was anesthetically cold. It stung on the way down. Cal felt slightly drunk before the liquid entered his stomach. Her eyes had something to do with that. Then he remembered that the tabs were still in his hand. With a neat little flip he tossed them into the inlet and watched while they stumbled to the bottom.

"You still haven't told me what you're doing trespassing on my territory, Teresa."

"Tessa."

"Okay, Tessa, confess. Nothing illegal? You're not growing marijuana or smuggling guns, are you?"

They laughed lightly. She was better at it than he. When he laughed his eyes were not involved. They remained impassive, cold, impersonal. A complicated face with curves and pockets, jagged edges and loose ends. One eye was ever so slightly higher than the other. Like Lincoln. His profiles were slightly different. He had a straight nose that decided at the last moment to bulb slightly at the tip. She determined just then that he was handsome.

"Nothing as exotic as that," she said soberly. "How many times can you scrub a bathtub? My babies are in school. I'm just not the homebody type, so I took to walking. Beaches, backwoods, country roads. Today's my day for marshes." She looked around as if seeing it for the first time. "It's my first trip to this spot. I found it quite by accident and I swear I won't tell a soul." She grinned feeling that he was enjoying the teasing.

35

She drew down on him. "Was I really intruding? Should I go?"

"No times two. You're perfectly welcome to share it with me. Have another piece of cheese."

She accepted his offer. They ate everything except for the fruit. It was his ace in the hole. He would attempt to hold her here with apples and oranges.

"Are you committed to a timetable? Do you have to be somewhere, soon?"

She nodded no, tingled by the course they were blindly following.

"Good," he said happily, "then sit here and let's talk for the rest of the afternoon. I've got some fruit and forty-three years of history in the bag and I'd like to know more about a lady who walks the marshes and is frank and open."

A sudden breeze, the day's first, caught in her short black hair and played fondly with it. His attention was focused on her. She was attractive, he decided, round delicate face and saucer eyes. Black saucer eyes that lived a life of their own, had moods and moments. She wore a man's plaid workshirt and a pair of worn jeans that made him more conscious of her body than during his brief examination of her in the office.

A type, he thought, young shiksa, mother of small children, intelligent, slightly bored, slightly daring to be here dallying with me, accepting my offer of lunch.

"Listen, doctor. . . ."

"Oh not that terrible word, not here. My name is Cal."

"Okay, Cal," she said, "I'll sit here until five on one condition."

"That I don't try to seduce you?"

"No, I can handle situations like that, thank you. What I mean is you'll have to talk about why you're here and not, say, in a Tennis Club or at a lawn party or some other place like that. I want to see if you fit the frame I made for you. It's kind of selfish, I know, but when I'm satisfied, you can ask me whatever. I'll answer truthfully, too. Is that okay?"

"Sure, sure, that's fine, Teresa."

"Tessa," she corrected. "I'm not a Teresa."

"Tessa," he stressed. "That's fine with me. There's enough dumb talk on TV, in living rooms, at tennis matches. No harm in trying something . . . with sense to it."

36

It was so smooth, he thought, such a nice flow to the way she talks, the way we mix. I like it. I like her. It's like swimming with the current. Not like tennis, like Cedarhurst tennis. You have to be careful with Joan's friends, what you say, how you say it, who you say it to.

"Where do you want me to start?" he asked. "I don't think you want me to go back to the Dark Ages when I was born." She laughed at that and he appreciated it. He was playing with her and she enjoyed it. Skillfully he peeled one of the oranges. It was a navel orange and Cal disrobed it after one continuous rotating motion. He handed her her half.

She looked at him wide-eyed and innocent. It made her moon face more lunar and her saucer eyes the size of soup bowls. "Any place you want to start is fine with me. I'm just a guest here. An accidental guest." She accepted her orange portion without acknowledgement.

Cal followed the path of a pair of deer-brown ducks out of the watery cul-de-sac that was formed when the two strips of land almost joined together like fingers holding a pinch of salt. The aquatic couple swam side by side, their rear ends tilted upward like bobbed noses.

"You see, doctor," he began, "I've been a doctor about nineteen years. A good one, I hope." He reversed field. "No, that's being falsely modest. I *am* a good doctor. I've put my heart and soul and every waking minute into it." He shooed a fly away from his orange and peeled off a plump section. "And probably a lot of sleeping moments, too, if what my wife says is so. She claims I diagnose in my sleep and even make house calls." He smiled and quickly turned it off like a light switch. "It's been like a religious calling and up until recently I've considered it a blessing. I was a truly happy man, content, unquestioning, undemanding. I thanked my mother and father a hundred times a day for what they did for me."

Tessa listened, nodding where appropriate.

"They had a grocery store in Brownsville, that's a section of Brooklyn. . . ."

"You needn't explain, I have relatives there."

"Well, it was a momma and poppa thing where pop had a thick pencil behind his ear and wrote down the prices on brown paper bags and totalled by hand. With butter that came in tubs and pot cheese in big gold-colored tins. He'd get up at four in the morning on Sundays when couples were coming home from dates to take in the bagels and the bialys. Mom worked with him seven days a week, yet they thought they had a good life. No one ever told them that it was slavery. And if they knew they kept it to themselves. That little store on Hinsdale Street was their factory and it turned out only one product, Calvin, the Doctor."

He separated another orange section, partially lost in the world of tub butter and bulk pot cheese. It did occur to her that he was perhaps trying to exorcise the memory because of the guilt that clung like barnacles to it. Those cold eyes were seeing the world of his childhood again. She did not feel rejected, though.

"Every nickel they scraped together they sunk into me. Everything. For their only child, for their reason for living. Here I was, I often thought to myself, a big strapping galoot, and I had these two gnomes slaving for me, with smiles and looks of ecstacy on their faces."

He tore the orange rind into small bits and tossed them into the bay. They floated away with the current. Two or three sections, like white upturned palms, actually made it to the open waters beyond. For a few moments the air was heavy with orange aroma.

"It was 'doctor, doctor, doctor' from the moment I could walk until I finally had the diploma. Then it became 'my son, the doctor.' They must have ground up pages of the AMA journal and fed it to me with my strained carrots. Probably, no, for sure, they both would have shriveled up and died if I decided to become the President of the United States or another Shakespeare."

The day grew progressively warm. The sun seemed rooted to one spot directly overhead in order to listen and punish them for their abandon. Tiny drops of perspiration appeared on Tessa's upper lip forming what seemed to Cal a small tiara. She has lovely full lips, he thought and speculated on their taste. He suggested that they move inland, under the trees, to escape the solar eavesdropper.

They relocated beneath a large maternal oak with many low heavy branches like outstretched arms. Tessa instantly felt protected and hidden by the tree. It was a heady feeling.

"And I loved it," he continued. "I ate it up. We were good partners, my parents and I. They joyfully did their part and I did mine. They broke their backs lugging cases up from the basement and hauling cases back down. Both of them. When I tried to pitch in my pop said. 'What kind of a business is this? I don't try to study your books, so don't you muscle in on my racket.' And mom, her favorite words were, 'The books, the books, get back to the books. You gotta be the best to get into medical school. Anybody can schlep cartons. We don't need you for that.' They never had a kid to help them. To them that was a waste of money. All for me." There was a sad melody to his last sentence.

"They sound like marvelous people," she said.

"So for love or for shame or because those chopped-up AMA journals got into my system I threw myself into it. Got straight A's through high school, through college, and through Med school. Body, heart, soul, head, everything that belonged to all three of us was thrown into that big, fat pot." He formed a pot with his hands. "And D-Day came. I made it. And what's more I came out of school shiny and untouched by greed. Not like my fellow sufferers, like animals let out of a cage, raring to make it all back in a year, hungry to catch up on life after eight or nine years on Devil's Island. Becoming a good doctor was my obsession and it remained that way, in spite of everything."

"Mmmmm," she hummed not wishing to sever the line of narrative.

"Do you want me to go on? Do you want to start?"

"No, no Cal, you finish. If I think you're running off at the mouth, I'll tell you. Remember, I said I was direct."

"An example," he continued. "One of my first patients was a Mrs. Rizzuto, from Glenwood Road in Canarsie where I first hung out my shingle. A sweet lovely Italian lady with eyes bigger than yours. Her husband worked for Sanitation and raised the most beautiful plum tomatoes I ever saw in that black Canarsie soil." His face grew sober as a mourner's. "When she came to see me it was too late. Don't even know if I could have helped her if it were diagnosed earlier. Cancer study was so rudimentary then. It seemed that some other doctor, an established, successful man in the area pawned her off on me because he didn't want the anguish of a terminal patient. It meant seeing her die daily,

39

facing the family, and signing the death certificate. No doctor wants that . . . burden.''

He paused and with one fingernail removed parts of the orange rind that had lodged under the others. Cal was reliving the Rizzuto experience, not just narrating it. It still had the power to hurt.

"The first thing I had to do, once the diagnosis was confirmed, was get it off my chest and tell her. She had to know.'' Tessa read the pain in his eyes and around his mouth. She considered stepping in but didn't, reasoning that it probably would have been more painful for him to stop midway.

"I was sick for three days. Really sick, with physical symptoms. I had this nauseous pounding headache.''

She turned on her other side, the ground under her being firmer than marsh ground. Cal noted, somewhere, that her hips and thighs were extremely good.

"Also had diarrhea, off and on, mostly on.'' A bite-sized grin tickled his face then quickly disappeared like a comet. "Then I got hold of myself, told myself I was a doctor, well, a beginning doctor, anyway. It was my responsibility and my obligation. So I told her one night when I had no appointments. (I had very few appointments anyhow, at first.) I needed the whole evening.

"I cried first, I remember. I hadn't cried since I broke my leg in high school. And only then because I had to miss some tests and jeopardize my grades. God, I was lucky. I got it all out to her before the tears started. And then she cried. Not as much as I did, not hysterically, not emotionally, but . . . sort of naturally, like when you cut a plant and the sap flows. She had been expecting that kind of verdict.''

Tessa said, "We Italians take some things better than you might expect, watching the stereotypes in the movies.''

He nodded perfunctorily. "Then I had to go through the whole thing again the next day with her daughter, a beautiful young high-school girl, with hip-length hair and the face of a saint. Maria was the oldest of the six and she told me she had a right to know. I thought so, too. The family would become her burden. We cried then, too, but only after Maria started. I was learning. But I was terribly distraught throughout the whole experience. And Mrs. Rizzuto, this terminal patient of mine,'' and his face shone, "a very devout Catholic, ended up comforting me. She really pulled me through. Every day she came to the office to cheer me up. Brought a big bag of plum tomatoes. Every day. And the sight of that dear lady would only intensify my symptoms. To this day I'm overcome with grief whenever I see a tomato. I can't even drink a glass of tomato juice without getting a huge lump in my throat that keeps it from going down.

"I went to her funeral and afterwards remained friends with the Rizzutos. Maria's married now with her own kids and she comes out every few months for check-ups and minor things. We're very close.

"So," he said, returning the Rizzutos to the past, "what I'm trying to say, in a very roundabout manner, is that I'm a very dedicated man. Or was. Was, because recently I've begun to think that someplace along the way I lost something. Maybe something I never had, maybe something that died in infancy. I don't know, Tessa," he said with eyes that sought answers of her, "I think I lost me. I can't even call missing persons because I don't have a description. I know that I'm a diagnosing machine, an instrument of healing when I'm lucky, when the government and the paperwork don't completely neutralize me. I'm a father and a husband, lousy in both cases; a Jew and an American, also second-rate. But where the hell is that seed that Mom and Pop Bernstein tossed into the wind? Where is the *me* in me? So damned busy and so damned sure I was in becoming a doctor that someplace along the way I forgot to become a person. And that, Tessa, is the bottom line, as my wife likes to say. That's why I sit here, like Van Gogh, trying to do something I hardly understand in order to find something I'm not absolutely certain is missing. For sure I know nothing about color or texture or anything artistic, but I do have the urge to put something down, to let it flow from my head to the canvas. The impulse is there; the talent isn't."

"There's plenty of talent around, anyway," she said.

"Well, I feel better, so help me, I feel better. I come out here week after week, get tanned and filthy, but it is so good when the sun goes down and I've a solid day of nothing under my belt. It's like pouring water on a parched field and hoping that something, anything will sprout. And who knows, really, I may just be fooling myself. The field may just be a desert. Not a damned thing underneath, nothing at all." His voice sounded hollow and thin.

41

"But I sit here and smear and listen for growing things. I've always been an optimist. Somehow a lot of good will come of it. It has already. I feel very comfortable with myself. Like all my debts are paid. And look, you're here. That's a damned nice dividend."

She liked that. It was a nice way to end a spell. He was buzzing around her. She couldn't fault him for that. In fact she would have been disappointed if he spent all his time on himself and ignored her.

"Now," he said, his spirits and his voice rising, "you tell me what the source of your energy is."

She changed positions again. This time she sat with her back pressed against the tree trunk and her knees raised almost flush with her tiny breasts.

"First of all," she began, "a small cop-out. I'm not as introspective as you are. You Jews are a marvelous people. I've got a thing about Jews. You've cornered the market on self-probing. I guess it's all tied up with the pushing around you've gotten for centuries. It must have made you turn inside and learn every inch of that landscape, seeing you had none of your own. I'm afraid I'm just a beginner, but, novice that I am, I see I'm in a blind alley. So I take off, go on expeditions. I don't know what the hell for, either. Maybe if I found it I wouldn't even know it. Maybe it passed by already."

In the distance, to the southwest, a graceful, expensive looking yacht approached the drawbridge. Both ends of the bridge rose jerkily, and stood at attention. After the boat passed through both arms rejoined to form a bridge again. Tessa and Cal watched the proceedings in silence.

She continued. "I'm a restless sort. I gave up home economics, child raising, and television. I guess I'm just your garden variety bored housewife." She reconsidered and withdrew her thumbnail portrait. "Not really, though," she said. "I wouldn't want you to think I have an ordinary problem. I'm more complex than that, my situation is more involved than just homemaker blues. I don't know if Victor talks much to his customers, if he ever mentions us. I doubt it. He's a little ashamed of me and he's very confused."

"No," Cal said. "I've only spoken to him once or twice. About

42

hedges and bushes and things like that. We're both not overly communicative. And Joan handles the home front."

"Well," she said scratching her back against the rough bark, "I'm three years older than he is and probably a hell of a lot more than that emotionally. It makes for problems. Serious problems. Our marriage was an arranged thing. You're probably smiling inside and saying that it's impossible, that those things don't happen in America. At least not now. But they do, and it did happen to us. Old Manny Bruno and my father worked out the details twenty-five years ago. Maybe they should have gotten married to each other, those two old bastards," she said with a wide swath of disgust clearly showing on her face. "They certainly deserved each other. They were certainly more of a match that we are, Victor and I.

"So, what I'm trying to say, without becoming graphic, is that I have a problem." She smiled at her low estimate. "I have a large number of problems. And they're not solved by long walks in quiet places. I'm old enough to know that most problems in life have no solution. Unless you call death a solution. But they do put spaces between them, breathing room. And that makes it bearable. Most of the time. Do you see a lot of that in your patients, doctor? Cal?"

"Don't do that," he cut in quickly.

"Do what?"

"Try to put up a wall after you've said something painful, something revealing."

"Was I doing that?" she asked. "I was doing that," she answered. "I'm glad you stopped it. Why did you stop it?"

"Because I like you and because I don't like walls."

"You and Robert Frost."

They returned to the grassy finger that pointed into the bay. The sun had journeyed a great distance across the sky in their absence. He held her hand a bit too long as he hoisted her up from against the oak. She did not fight it.

The canvas and the paint box were undisturbed. The late afternoon rays were less intense and they sunned themselves.

He decided on a quantum leap. Actually the decision had been

43

made earlier when the sight and sound of her touched something very deep within him. And perhaps "decision" inaccurately described a process in which internal systems were acting for him.

"I want to see you again, Tessa. You're damned good to talk to and to be with. I've enjoyed today tremendously and I'd like to encourage a friendship."

His first attempt, in a very long while, at the seduction game. Since Maria, years ago. He was sure that he would fail miserably.

"I thought that's where it was going," she said soberly, "and I asked myself why. I'm past thirty. Not bad looking, but sure as hell not fresh and lovely."

"I like you. Isn't that enough? Do I have to give reasons? Answer in fifty words or less?"

"No. No, you don't, Cal, and to be quite frank with you, I thought about it, too. That it would be nice. Very nice," she reiterated and let it hang in the air.

"But," she continued, when she was sure of what she was going to say, "hold off on sex . . . for a few weeks. I'm not very modern. I need time. Let's just spend a day a week for a while, a month or so, together. Then we'll do whatever makes you happy. I'll be ready and eager then, maybe."

He held her chin lightly, kissed her full bare lips. For the first time he noticed she was without lipstick. She tasted of oranges and beer.

"I'm leaving now," he announced. "Can I take you home or drop you off somewhere?"

"You can take me home. We're not lovers yet. Officially. There's no need to be discreet."

4

"Cal, I feel sooo English. Hot tea on a blistering summer's day. Breakfast on the verandah. It's positively colonial."

Joan usually felt expansive on Sunday mornings. She was practically soaring as she hummed "I'll See You Again" and set the round glass patio table for breakfast. She poured the tea with an exaggerated elegance into two miniature loving cups made of porcelain, then pensively surveyed the latest crop of roses. The bushes were heavy with American Beauties. She viewed them with pleasure and pride from the small flagstone patio off the kitchen door. All was right in her world, life bountiful, everything in its place . . . almost. The week had passed productively, smoothly . . . almost. Why did he have to start up with her?

Surrounded by *The Times*, Cal, dressed in faded, torn bermudas, and still sleepy, thought she was her usual Sunday morning Joan. He listened to her sounds of well-being and knew how sweet and sticky she could be with her tea-and-crumpets. He read a letter of gracious thanks from the Swedish doctor who had studied American family practice from his office last March. The handwriting went out of focus as he thought of the strange mystery of a girl he had kissed and plotted an adventure with only days earlier. Joan flitted about buttering little rolls with oleo-margarine (how many times did he have to tell her he was capable of buttering his own bread?).

"Why didn't you tell me my mother called?"

"I forgot," he said matter of factly, without raising his head over the letter.

"And that you hung up on her?"

"I did not." He put the letter in his lap and looked at her with a subdued earnestness that said "I may be soft but don't you push too hard." "I was . . . abrupt . . . maybe, but I did successfully fight the great urge to cut her off in mid-word. I did *not* hang up on her."

He was using that exaggerated Broadway play tone that often confused and annoyed her. Though I am usually direct, I become standoffish, pompous and obfuscating when it comes to that woman, it said. Using verbal camouflage helps me bury my true feelings, it said. Joan knew the code. And it almost always deeply hurt her.

"What has that poor woman ever done to you to deserve such . . . such disrespect?" She wasn't sure how to end the sentence. It wasn't really disrespect. "Contempt" would be more accurate if it came from someone other than Cal.

"Oh, don't take me down those roads again, Joan, please. We fight for hours. We get no place. We waste God knows how much of our life over that woman. She just isn't worth it."

"Cal, she's my mother." Said defiantly.

"You're welcome to her."

"And she's your mother-in-law and your children's grand-mother."

"Two of God's greatest blunders."

Finally he let the Swedish letter drop to the floor. The Sunday spell was broken. He had blundered into the minefield of Pearl Fialakoff, Joan's Tiger tank of a mother. As with many things in their life together, she came in pairs. The mama Joan knew and the one that Cal swore he knew better.

"She says you slammed the receiver down so hard that it nearly shattered her eardrum."

"Joan, I am not rude. Even to her. I was rushed. I was on the other line with Arnie."

"Oh. . . ." She hesitated. "What did he want?" She angled her-self against the glass table and peered down with interest at him. The half glasses she wore gave Cal the distinct impression that he was back taking English Lit. in college, discussing Chaucer with his instructor.

"The usual, lunch and drinks in some expensive restaurant in the city."

"And what did you say, if I'm not being too curious?" He wondered if he would be graded on his answer.

"The usual. That I can't make it. The pressure of the practice and all that."

"But you tell him that all the time. Really Cal. . . ."

"I guess I do, but he still doesn't get the message."

"Arnie Feingold," she crooned and looked past the roses at the snowballs just beginning to blossom. "How is that wicked, wicked man?" she asked, knowing that the question had the power to unleash a storm.

"Depends on what stage of the phone call you're talking about. It's great with the money from the four shops rolling in (can you imagine, Joan, he calls his Medicaid centers shops), and the cars, and his women. He talks about his stable of hookers as if he had just found his penis. But after about ten or fifteen minutes the shine wears off." Cal sat back in the caned, cushioned chair, interlocked his fingers, and spoke with ease. Joan was glad that he was easing his way into Arnie. And beyond, she hoped. He was quite touchy about the early years and didn't like being reminded.

"He told me he's been indicted for fraud, embezzlement, and a bunch of other illegal things. He says it's nothing. He said it at least ten times. Then he finally admitted being scared as hell about going to jail."

She evinced a deep interest in the Fall Fashion section of *The Times*, where she found something just right for Laura, if only the girl would permit an opinion. She takes after her father that way. Stubborn, stupidly stubborn.

"And?"

"And he asked me to run his 'shops' for him if he has to go away for a while."

"And what did you say?"

"No . . . of course. I'm not a shopkeeper. I thought you knew that," he said acidly.

"You could at least have lunch with him once in a while. Whatever you don't like about him isn't catching, Cal."

Despite her frequent hints, Cal was legally finished with Fein-

47

gold. There were no hard feelings about the dissolution of their partnership. They had called it quits on good terms. It was definitely not the bitter taste of yesterday that caused Cal's reluctance to see him. The incessant pounding of Arnie's here and now bored and wearied him. If boredom were his dish all he had to do was attend the next meeting of Joan's Community Chest. Success stories bored him; he was more attracted by failures. At least there was variation, and probably truth, too.

While Joan, who clearly wanted the tricky conversation to prosper, left for more cream cheese, he went back over the history of their medical association. After five years together, suffering the torments of medical school and internship, the apparently small differences between Arnie and him grew geometrically during their partnership. Arnie would bring a patient back three to four times past the medically sound cut-off point solely for fee. Then, too, he would calculatingly frighten a patient with a dire diagnosis, then take the credit for a remarkable recovery. Reputation building. They dissolved their tottering marriage the week he caught Arnie falsifying treatment records for Medicaid reimbursement "just to get back what they screwed us out of."

Joan breezed out of the kitchen with a tray of cheeses and an opinion she was dying to hit him with. "In trouble. Hmm. Well I'll bet if the two of you were still partners that would not have happened. He would have kept to the straight and narrow. You were good for him and he was good for you, Cal." Joan pointed at him with the cheese knife italicizing her point. If she only knew how motions like that annoyed him.

"You know it's a lie and yet you repeat it as if it were the Pledge of Allegiance. Joan, he's a thief and a liar and the day he was born they set aside a cell with his name on the door. He screwed around with the Anatomy professor's wife to stay in school, he cheated on Natalie when we were just getting started, he even stole from me until I put a stop to it. Can't you get it into your head that our partnership was a match made in an insane asylum?"

Joan looked surprised and hurt. She refused to surrender the idea even though he thought he had it beaten to a pulp. "Still, opposites attract. You *could* have kept him honest with your

48

strength of character. He respects you. And he would have helped make all our dreams come true. When we had dreams, that is."

Cal suddenly grew weary, as if, lost in a jungle, he had come to the same spot for the tenth time. "Are we back to that again? God. All our dreams come true. Like a Walt Disney production. 'Our dreams.' Who is the 'our'? You and your mother? Of course, you and your mother. You don't have to be a genius to figure that out." He was getting sucked in against his will. She was wiping out his Sunday with these obvious provocations. Why couldn't she see that?

"You know, you just have to know, that her control of you has given us nothing but trouble all our lives together. In all our plans I never once spoke about reaching the top of the salary mountain. And you just refused to believe me, you and mama. I wouldn't be surprised if you sat with her, back in the beginning, and said, 'Sure, sure . . . let him talk. *We* know better. We'll make something out of him in spite of him, the lemish.' "

"Kindly leave my mother out of this. She has her own problems."

"All self-generated, I'm sure."

"Don't be so sure Doctor Dolittle. We're not talking about chicken pox or the clap, you know. We're talking about people, complex people, a subject you're not terribly familiar with. We're talking about my mother and her problems. But what the hell do you know about either things in your little small shell?"

"What do I know? I know for years every time you opened up your mouth her words came out. Like the Dybbuk." He felt regret as she became visibly agitated. He thought it a damned shame that their only two points of passion were in the bedroom (fast fading) and over her mother (growing like a weed). With the children there was detente, over money, his surrender, gladly. Over anything else one of them turned and walked away like a reluctant witness to a crime.

"Leave her out of it, Cal. The *whole* family was unhappy when you dissolved the partnership."

He pounced on it. "The *whole* family? Joan, you must be kidding. What *whole* family? I didn't have a *whole* family leading me by the nose. I had a seven-year-old and a four-year-old and you

49

and your mother. Your mother was the *whole* family. That Jewish steamroller. She felt, then you felt. She got cut and you bled. And there I was, pissing away my talents by just doing my job, practising medicine as I saw fit. So the big bucks didn't roll in from padded GHI and Medicare claims. The double billing techniques, the huge office complexes with more rooms than a whorehouse just never materialized. She was, you were, unhappy as hell when the return on investment wasn't as planned or as good as Arnie's." He pulled up short. He was running away with himself.

"I know she died more than a little when you dropped Arnie and married me. She had plans and you had plans. Pearlie and Doctor Feingold were as close as itch is to scratch. I don't know, I don't care, and I'll never ask why the two of you broke up but I do know that when you did, mama practically sat Shivah for a month. I've got a long memory Joan for insults and abuse and I remember her cold fish look when I came into the house. I remember the fights with her, over my spending so much time in the ghetto hospitals. Arnie wouldn't waste five minutes in those toilets. Whenever we'd go there for supper I'd feel that Fialakoff freeze. Even when I brought the money home you looked at me like you were Oliver Twist with the porridge bowl. I didn't say too much then, Joan, and maybe I should have, it might have changed things. Who knows? Well," he continued without coming up for air, "it's too bad for you and for mama that I'm not Arnie Feingold."

She listened impatiently, anxious for a break in his words. Finding none she sliced off a sliver of Jahrlsberg and gave her mouth something to do.

"That is damned unfair, all those accusations, and how you distort. All my mother really wanted was a comfortable life for me, for us. Is that so bad? Why the hell do I have to teach you basic living like you were my child instead of my husband?"

"I passed the course, lady, without your help."

"Not as far as this teacher is concerned. This teacher figures you must have some kind of learning disability."

"Because I refused to be brainwashed?"

"Because you are so damned insensitive to what a mother wants for her children. Why is it so hard for you to understand that when you don't get the most a certain amount of disappointment sets in? So she was miffed when I married you instead of Feingold. . . ."

"Miffed? She called me Dr. Schlemiel for months until I told her to stop."

"Oh, that was a joke. Her way of teasing. Don't blow it up, please. Remember, she's had a hard life even though there is money. You really can't blame the woman for feeling resentful at what she considers lost opportunities."

"Can I blame her if she infects her daughter with the same resentment? Do I need your permission? Is it okay if I hold her responsible for souring you on the kind of life we wanted, or I thought we wanted?" He made the correction before he thought she would.

"Oh that's gone, Cal," she said, eliminating it with the flick of her wrist. "I did at first, sure I did (I am still my mother's daughter), but it's gone. I've adjusted very nicely to only semi-success."

"You have, I must say, remarkable powers of recovery, Joan. You really know how to make the best of a bad situation."

"Oh, save your sarcasm for some of those deadbeats who owe you money."

But he refused to allow a wrist flick to wipe away twenty years of history. There was no place secret enough to hide something as gigantic as Joan's disappointment in him.

"Then how come every time you were frustrated with me or after your mother finished raking you over the coals you'd go and hide in some executive committee?"

"You are over-simplifying," she said tapping her spoon on the table.

"And then pretty soon you didn't need a reason to run."

"Wrong, wrong, wrong . . . and even if you are right, a little bit, what was I *supposed* to be doing while you were out there saving the world by wiping noses? I'm not the coffee klatch type and I can't *stand* ladies' book clubs. I'm just not a homebody. Of course I had to get out and into something . . . or I'd die. You don't rest easy because Mr. Katz's pressure won't come down and I have the same problem because my UJA contributions won't go up. So that's how it is and that's how I am. My mother may not like it, but I've overcome that, too. Yes I have. Screw her. And screw you, too, buster, if it pinches."

51

"So it's surfacing. That's been one of your problems for a long time. There's always been the two of you fighting for control. I see it in the tension in your face when she's here, the way your eyes narrow and you pick at your nails when you're on the phone with her."

"Oh shut up, Cal. I hate you when you gloat. You don't even know how to gloat. And you can't make me angry. We're past that stage. (She wasn't, but he didn't have to know that.) I don't need your ten-cent psycho job. It's not your specialty. Stick to making house calls." Then the realization stopped her dead that it was Sunday, it was sunny and hot and the beach would be delicious. She brightened. "Cal, I simply won't let you make me angry. Truce. It's much too hot for this kind of heated discussion." She smiled at him. "It's been a lovely week . . . really and we must be good to each other, today. Please."

Cal settled for an easy peace. He finished his tea and as a concession played The Boston Pops instead of Mozart. He thought again of Tessa. He needed the serenity of a household in quietus to conduct his affair with the lady of the marshes. Operating on two fronts is an impossible manoeuver.

Victor heard the key turn in the lock with an exasperated jiggle that was solely hers and was on his feet before she opened the door.

"Where were you?" he demanded.

"Out."

"Out where?"

"Out . . . where I'm always out on Fridays. With Cary Grant in the Casbah." She examined the mail on the hall table.

"It's not funny, Tessa. How come when I need you you're never around?"

"Shit. I'm always around. That's my trouble. I'm *too* visible. One day I'm not here to wipe noses and I catch hell for it. Even Roosevelt wasn't indispensable."

"Goddamn, Tessa, don't talk in riddles. Don't lay your fancy college education on me, all over me."

She hung the car keys under her name on the little rack in the hall with hooks in the shape of fingers and walked the six steps up into the kitchen. He blocked the way.

"Victor, I don't know the password so let me up anyhow." She said it wearily. That usually deflated him.

"Bitch . . . bitch mouth. I needed you and you weren't there."

"I can't always be there, Victor. I'm not a rake . . . or your car. See, I've got feet and those feet have a mind of their own and when it's Friday those feet know it and they get restless. So forgive me and my wandering feet, Victor, and tell me what's bothering you."

Victor got lost in her words. Tessa knew that all she had to do was bombard him with language and he would forget his anger, real or imaginary, just or unjust, potent or weak.

"It's Gralnick."

"What's a Gralnick?" A fungus infection? . . . a tree blight? . . . a tool?"

She was joshing now with him, on purpose. Little boys have to be tickled out of temper tantrums and Victor was many parts little boy. She knew perfectly well that Gralnick was *the* Mr. Gralnick, the famous clothing manufacturer who lived in Woodsburgh with his two Rolls Royces, a large, strange looking skinny dog, and a wife of roughly the same description. After ten years she still had not uttered one word to Victor, not one solitary word even though he had seen her at least two hundred times.

"Gralnick is the dude on Raspberry Lane."

"Oh, that Gralnick," she finally owned up. "What about it? Did you screw up his hedges, too?"

"No, no, Tessa. I'm serious. Don't fool around. I'm talking about money."

"Oh, money . . . well, that *is* serious, Victor. I'm sorry I funned around," she said escaping to a higher level of comedy she knew was above him, therefore safe, therefore private, therefore harmless.

"Whaddaya think the stinkin', rotten, lousy son of a bitch Jew bastard did?"

She shrugged.

"He didn't pay me today. I did the lawn and asked for my money and he stiffed me. He ain't paid me in four months. I did the spring clean-up, I seeded and fertilized, and all I get for it is the same crap I've been getting for four months now. 'See me next month, I'm on my way out to play tennis, or go sailing.' Last

53

month the fuck asks if I accept Master Charge. What the hell does he think I am . . . a department store?"

"Victor, Victor . . . calm down. What's the point in getting all steamed up?" She moved in close to him where she did her best work and tugged at his belt. "Just sit down a minute. I'll get you a beer and we'll talk about it like people."

"If anyone did that to poppa he'd throw garbage on their lawn. Then charge them to clean it up. And collect on the spot, too," he said ruefully and waited for her rebuttal.

It came quickly and it was soothing. "Poppa and his ways are gone, Victor. A thing of the past. We're living in a different time. We use more finesse, we're more business-like. Manny is horse and buggy; we're S.S.T." She took five seconds for the tranquilizer to work. "You know what might be a good idea?" she asked, planting seeds.

"What?"

Then the boys came in, sweaty and wild-eyed from play. Their black hair hung limp and shiny around their foreheads.

"You gladiators shower and change into fresh underwear. Your daddy and I are discussing high finance. Big numbers. Come back in about half an hour and I'll feed you some lion meat." They left almost as if they didn't hear a word she said.

"I once saw in a movie," she said, "when somebody was trying to collect some money from some low-life he pretended he was the guy's accountant. He made it sound very big business. And it worked. Or was it his lawyer? Whatever. P.S., he got his money the next day."

Victor's face was generating hope, doubt, and confusion. "I don't know. I can't sound like a lawyer or an accountant. I'm a *paisan*. That's how it will come out."

"You want me to do it, Victor? I'll be your accountant's secretary. Okay?"

His face was left with one surviving emotion. He was overjoyed.

"Tessie, Tessie, baby, that would be great! Do you think you could pull it off?"

"Sure, Victor, sure. After supper you get out his folder and I'll call him."

"Maybe he's religious and don't pick up the phone on Friday night. Some of them do and some don't and you can't tell by looking at them which is which."

"We'll see, Victor. After the kids are fed and I've got them in front of the TV or reading a book I'll become a secretary. But listen, Victor, I want you sitting right next to me. I want you right there when I sell him the secretary line, or if I have to switch over to some other method. I don't want you to tell me later that you knew nothing about it."

"What other method?"

"I don't know. I think as I work."

"Okay, Tessa. You're the . . . I mean that's okay with me."

"Boys," she called.

A squeak of sneakers on the steps. The boys found their places at the table. Tessa served them a beef stew that had been prepared the night before when the world was slightly different, before a doctor had shared his lunch, his biography, and a mild kiss with her.

"What have you bandits been doing this afternoon?" their father asked.

"We were playing with the new boy Raymond, daddy," Stephen, the spokesman for the two answered.

"Who's Raymond? Where does he live?" their father suspiciously asked.

"You know, daddy. He moved in when Bobby Ingrassia moved out."

Victor dropped his fork as if it were red hot.

"The niggers? You were playing with niggers? What the hell's the matter with you kids?" Victor's eyes drilled holes in both his children.

"Kids," Tessa cut in, "what kind of boy is this Raymond?"

Happy to submit to a different interrogator, Victor junior spoke up. "Oh, he's a nice boy, mommie. He talks so different . . . like sing-song but he's not rough or mean and his daddy says we can come over anytime and play with all of Raymond's toys as long as we put them back."

"And his mother gave us Good Humors she's a nurse," Stephen said using the run-on sentences that children his age are famous for.

55

"Where's the harm, Victor?" Tessa whispered when her husband reached over toward her for more peas.

"They're niggers, Tessa. That's the harm," he whispered back.

"They've got to be more than that to be harmful. At least to children. Stay out of their play life, Victor. They need all kinds of friends."

"Tessa, they're. . . ."

"Don't use that word again, Victor. It doesn't tell a thing about them. If the boys don't like this Raymond kid, if he's loud or a roughneck they'll back off. Don't do to them what your father did to you."

"I never played with n------ them."

"I mean try to control their lives."

"It's not the same thing, Tessa."

"It is. The only difference is in the incident. The important thing is that both fathers are trying to shove their kids into a mold. Their own private molds. It's the same thing."

Victor sidestepped the issue of Raymond's color and poured himself a beer. It was only a delaying action, he knew. Tessa never left anything in midair. If there was to be peace in the house, and he wanted that essential more than almost anything, the problem of his boys' friend must be nailed down.

"Boys, it's okay. I give you my permission to play with Raymond. But, if he ever plays nasty and starts hitting, you get in your licks and you get back home . . . pronto. You hear?"

"Okay daddy," they said, not really sure that the matter of playing with the black boy whose mother served Good Humors was ever in doubt. Instinctively they knew, as all children know, who sat on the throne in their household. Mother had the last word on almost everything despite the noise daddy made.

"You heard what your father said," Tessa added. "Come home fast if you see there's trouble."

Victor roughhoused with his boys while she cleaned up the mess. Why, why, why did she think she might nurse him into manhood? Schoolgirl dreams. Her marriage to him and her father's death, occurred just prior to her own recovery from a teenage obsession with self-hate. The marriage was supposed to be a golden opportunity to save the man who had rescued her. Victor would travel the same road and survive a dehumanizing father. She would see to that. As she waited for him to get better, he got worse. In truth she hadn't the knowledge needed to save him. But her recognition of that came too late to do either of them any good. Actually he didn't get worse. He remained the same, but the stakes got higher. He was both son and husband. She realized then that he would never free himself of his father's grip. By attempting to snip the ties that bound him she just became the frying pan to Manny's fire. She pulled and Manny pulled and Victor floundered.

Tessa lost patience with him. Then she considered a divorce, a lover, a career. She abandoned each in turn. Then Cal came along. She wasn't sure where he would lead. Her knowledge of Jews and their extra-curricular mating practices was minuscule. Books filled the house on why people hurt people, family problems characterized by a strong father and a weak mother. She had read Ibsen until the new feminists came along. She accepted them —then rejected their shrillness, their femachismo. What she saw of her life did not make her free. It just made her more knowledgeable about her cage.

Before the boys were born it occurred to her that perhaps she was making profit on Victor's weakness. Using him. Sex was never a strong urge of hers. Was she being noble by caring for Victor's whipped soul because his body, because any man's body held no promise of rapture for her? Was Victor, in essence, a smoke screen for her own battered libido?

By the time the boys were independent she came to realize two overriding facts. She *was* a sexually functioning woman, thank God, and she was bound forever by ties of gratitude, and by two children who needed both parents to become functioning adults themselves. It was this sense of entrapment that drove her to long walks, that had induced her to give more encouragement to a stranger than she ever gave to her husband. And receive more stimulation from it.

"Remember, Victor," she said when the dishes were away and the boys were neutralized, one by *The Partridge Family* on the tube and the other by *Treasure Island* on the page, "I'm handling it as I see fit. Don't have a hemorrhage if I lie a bit."

Victor nodded vigorously with his head and his large black, marble-sized eyes.

57

"Mr. Abraham Gralnick, please." She paused and inhaled while someone went to get the manufacturer of woman's clothing. "Mr. Gralnick? This is Mr. Vincent Lorenzo's private secretary speaking." Pause. "Mr. Lorenzo's firm does the accountancy and legal work for Victor Bruno Landscaping and Gardening as well as other interests." Pause. "Yes, that's right, the gardener. We noticed an open account going back to last November for five hundred dollars." Pause. "Yes, we do work rather late at night. We're an unusual firm. Our people are mainly of Italian extraction. We don't follow the usual business procedures. You see, we are *family* oriented." She paused, inhaled deeply while the words seeped into Mr. Gralnick. Tessa looked very cool and very secretarial. Her cigarette dangled at a sophisticated angle that was customary for cool secretaries. She winked at Victor. "There is no point in assuming an indignant air, sir. *We* are the injured party. You owe us the money. And quite frankly, Mr. Gralnick, we want payment."

Victor flew off the chair next to Tessa. He blanched at first, over her lies, then grew as indignant as he thought Mr. Gralnick might be at the other end. She put her finger to her lips then pointed at the chair. Like a tamed tiger he came back and perched.

"I really don't think that would be wise, Mr. Gralnick. In the first place, all gardeners are part of families and one family would never undercut another by stealing another's client. That's just not done. I'm sure that you've heard how we ethnics operate and how we stick together. And if you should start up with a stranger, well, Mr. Gralnick, you are in business and you know what incompetence is like. Why, some idiot might even accidentally poison your dog through negligence. We've seen that happen over and over again. Chemicals left around." Victor flew out of the chair and began to pace the floor.

"Oh my God," he softly swore. "She's bringing in the Mafia. God, God, if poppa ever knew he'd kill us both."

Tessa squinted angrily at Victor. He quickly returned to his seat. She nodded sagely into the receiver. "I am not making threats, Mr. Gralnick. We are a legitimate firm. I thought since you've been customers of theirs for years you deserve the courtesy of a phone call before this oversight went out of sight." Then a long pause. "No, I'm sure that there will be no trouble. None whatsoever." Pause. "No, there's no point in disturbing the Brunos at this hour. I do believe they're at a concert with Mr. Lorenzo and friends. But I'll leave a message with them to pick up the money in the morning." Pause. "Yes, yes this wipes the slate clean. No hard feelings. Nothing further will be said . . . or done." Pause. "And thank you, Mr. Gralnick." Pause. "Do we want new clients? Why do you ask?" Pause. "Well, that's terribly nice of you, Mr. Gralnick, but Mr. Lorenzo has more clients than he can properly service now. So . . . good night, sir."

Victor ran his hands through his thick hair, picked his nose, scratched the sides of his neck, hoisted up his trousers, and sputtered and bubbled like an angry tea kettle. Small guttural sounds escaped his mouth. All this to express his dissatisfaction at the tack his wife had taken to bring Mr. Gralnick around. It was . . . dishonest . . . sneaky . . . underhanded and he said as much to Tessa who turned and gazed at him with a Cheshire smile from ear to ear.

"So I lied," she said. "You told me you wanted the money. I saw he wasn't going to hop in the Rolls and run it down to you. So what's wrong? I did a little arm twisting."

"I don't like to twist arms."

"You like to have your arm twisted?"

"No."

"Well, he was doing that to you by not paying. That snow job he gave you in tennis shorts was arm twisting. He wasn't honorable so I wasn't honorable." She saw that he still wasn't satisfied. "Listen, Victor, I did it because you asked me to. For myself I don't give a damn whether he pays or not."

"Suppose he tells my old man? You know how *he* feels about the Mafia. He'd be mad as hell."

"Victor, stop measuring everything by the way Manny might feel. Measure by the way Victor feels. Did it really hurt you when I said a few dishonest words? Did it?"

"Well, no . . . but it was sneaky."

"Big deal. The five hundred dollars of yours, of yours, Victor, that he's holding is like stealing. We recovered stolen money that belonged to us."

59

"I guess you're right, Tessa. It's just that . . . that I think I do a good job and I should get paid for it. Don't I do a good job, Tessa?"

"Yes, you do a good job. And you know it."

"As good as my old man did?" He came closer and stroked her ear, a sure sign that they would not just go to sleep tonight.

"Better," she said. "Better. Manny just gave what he was supposed to. You give more. Ask Mrs. Bernstein. Didn't you redo her hedge because she said it wasn't one hundred percent?"

"You gave me hell for that, Tessa, remember?"

"Well you loused up the kids' Sunday. That doesn't mean I approve of it, but it does show that you care. Not like the phone company or Lilco. It shows a one to one caring. That's hard to find today, Victor."

"You know I work hard, Tessa, because I want you and the kids to have a decent life. You know that, don't you?"

"I know, Victor, of course I know. And you don't have to keep saying it. Honestly." It depressed her that she could not match him gift for gift, his toil for her love.

"Gee, Tessa, things are getting better between us, aren't they?"

"You really think so?" she said, refusing to perjure herself.

"Yeah. I remember when we first got started . . . all the problems. They're gone, Tessie, they're gone. We ain't exactly identical twins, but we're getting there."

Oh, God, does he really believe that? she asked herself. Then she felt horrible, realizing that he did, and worse, that out of kindness and gratitude, she had fostered the notion. Long into the night she lay awake hating nothing worse than kindness and gratitude.

5

For a month of Fridays they invaded remote beaches on the North Shore of Nassau and Suffolk Counties, oases the sparse population found inaccessible and unsuitable. Not enough sand, too many rocks. But wonderful to explore because the shoreline was an unbroken series of small arcs, each one setting the stage for the next.

Then reversing direction they went toward the buzzing city, in the eye of the storm, to tramp the quiet marshes of Jamaica Bay that yawned like an open mouth west of Kennedy Airport. Soft bogs that were hidden away like bastard children of sea and shore.

And strolled tiny pocket forests in the middle of the Island that offered emotional asylum even though bordered by the Long Island Expressway or Northern and Southern Parkways. Even though the sounds of traffic roared dully in the distance like thunder.

They talked incessantly, believing the lean limited present could be stretched like a body stocking to cover years of flabby past tense. It almost worked. But, as in any cram course, they forgot the details of each other's lives, only dimly remembering the highlights. Births and deaths of loved ones, children's names and characters, injuries suffered and imagined, thoughts saved for a rainy day or a sympathetic ear, all seesawed with impressions of the land they walked. It was as if a zoom lense had been placed on their lives and internal geography came into focus as external geography fuzzed to the background. And the reverse.

These Fridays were quickly touched with silver and gold. They became treasured memories in their own time, even before they had the chance to become distorted. Having no combined history, Cal and Tessa created one, building emotional ties horizontally for what they lacked vertically. And it was all so natural, so simple, so effortless. Sex, as yet, had not intervened. He kept his word, as she expected him to. Their laughter was not forced, their conversation flowed with few obstacles. It was a rare and lovely honeymoon.

Tessa had five sisters, all living, married and regularly pregnant, much to her disgust. Cal had two children, whom he spent an undue amount of time outfoxing. Each of them agreed that they individually and as a unit had a healthy, subdued view of money; he because he had enough and she because she required little.

The weeks of discovery flew away like flushed birds. They held hands and kissed in Wildwood State Park deep in Suffolk County standing on a ten-foot boulder in Long Island Sound. He caressed her shoulders, her bare brown shoulders, while ankle deep in the brown backwater of Floyd Bennett Field at the western end of Jamaica Bay, in full view of a family of mud-brown ducks. At the Cedar Beach Golf Course east of Jones Beach they raced along the watery skirts of the Atlantic, a race he was pleased to lose because she kissed him as consolation, and he kissed her back as congratulations. Two winners and no losers.

This Friday morning there was a chill in the air, rare for June. Cal felt October ambitious. The chill acted as catalyst to their growing sense of each other, an impetus to push on until everything became shared knowledge. Today Cal would put on display the most valuable pearl in his collection of hidden Long Island wonders. Today he would share with her that undiscovered, inaccessible cove at Bayville, where Nassau's north coast suddenly turned in on itself like a crooked finger. He had mystically honed in on that spot one rainy Sunday in September when his soul felt as uncomfortable as the humidity. It had been a transition period in his life when something unknown was seeking to establish contact.

More than a year had passed since he first discovered the place and claimed it as his own, but he clearly remembered that narrow tree-canopied lane miles from the main road. Something in him had almost physically demanded that he stop that first time. Too much a man of science and a watery agnostic to believe in voices, he had tried to go on. Something inside him had forced the car to a halt. He remembered laughing a little over it, about how silly the whole damned piece of theatrics had been. But the feeling had been strong. He had sat and sweated even though the air conditioner was on.

He parked on the shoulder parallel to the narrow lane and eased out of the car. The clouds had begun to speed up, as if in reply to his challenge. Early fall leaves crunched beneath his walking boots.

The crackling acted as a messenger to the entire forest community. Nothing moved. The birds listened. He struck out through the thorned underbrush, not knowing where he had to go. When he found the place, he knew he had been looking for it.

He had stood facing a solid, tangled wall of thorns and vines. He could go no further. The sound of the surf grew louder, more insistent. With a branch, he pushed aside the tangled wall. It moved like a curtain. Behind that curtain was a small bluff, like a box seat at the opera. It overlooked the entire Sound as far as the eye could see. A small loop of a beach, perhaps eighty feet in semi-circumference lay below. He had been surprised to find himself so close to the shoreline. The thorns and the vines had warped his sense of distance. Though he was out of breath from fighting the underbrush, he ran the rest of the way downhill to the beach. Part of the pristine beauty was due to the delicious fact that the beach was well hidden from all sides except the Sound. And even on that side a row of jutting black rocks stood guard like a company of riflemen. Cal was thrilled. He had arrived at the center of the beach just as the first rain fell. Turning his face to the sky he welcomed the attack, he was overjoyed, his soul was shining. Like a circling dog he settled finally for a spot and stretched out, surrendering himself to the rain. Then for a brief instant, he sensed he had died and was born again. He remained prone until he felt foolish. When he felt totally ridiculous he got up and left, but he retained the aura of rebirth for weeks afterward.

The mystical nature of that baptism slowly washed over his mind as he once more parked on the soft shoulders of the narrow road.

"What a delicious place to be raped and murdered," she said as she gathered both handles of her plastic picnic bag and kicked out of the Buick like a paratrooper.

"Evidently, young lady, you've never been raped or murdered or you'd walk a little softer," he said.

He opened his trunk, pushed aside some of his son's sports equipment, and dredged up his khaki blanket. Tessa joined him at the forest's edge, a dungareed pioneer in tassled moccasins and owl-sized Polaroid sunglasses.

"You'll have to kiss me because we're on a dangerous mission. We may never come back. Also because you look so fresh and alive and lovely. Simply lovely."

They kissed without touching.

He kissed her, too, because he was very much alive today, because he was on parole, and mostly because he would finally have her before the day ended.

Recalling the way, he walked in first and she followed behind like a Chinese wife, passing along a rudimentary path through the bramble until they came to a lush wall of vines. It was enough to discourage the casual stroller.

"Dead end, Cal," she assessed. "What do we do now, brave leader?"

"The living end really," he returned. "The wall is to chase away the sissies. But we're experienced trailblazers. Come, Tessa, give me your hand."

They locked fingers and Cal led her skillfully around the green barrier, angling and twisting as he went, poking and thrusting with a branch as he did before, but this time with some skill.

Tessa was clearly impressed. Her face shone.

"Oh, Cal, it's lovely. I want half of it. Give me half of it," she insisted. "I can't believe it. It's so tiny and isolate. Shangri-la with a beach. No, it's a mirage, I swear, a goddamn mirage." She was gushing like a waterfall after a heavy rain. He looked at her and grinned knowingly.

Then she seized his hand and yanked him. "C'mon," she cried, "let's not just look at it. Let's feel it and taste it and soak it up. C'mon," she gently commanded.

At the water's edge she dropped the picnic basket, kicked off her moccasins and negotiated the small concave strip of beach as Cal had done, a year earlier. She returned, finally to Cal's arms, nearly knocking him down. He held her firmly, his sweet prisoner, bursting with the pride and pleasure of a donor.

"I give it all to you, baby. A present. Just give me visitor's rights."

"No, just half," she whispered. Touched by his generosity she brushed his cheek then let her hand fall away as if it were loosely tied to her shoulder and not really under her command.

"I'll settle for half. Keep something for yourself, Cal. You never know when you might need a place to run to."

"But I want to . . . give you things I love, things that move me," he said with a blend of solemnity and subdued gaiety. "It's yours, every grain of sand, every drop of water, even the lousy flies. The only way you really own something is to give it to someone you love." Then he quickly added, "It's free, on the house." His voice grew stronger.

"Oh," she said and the world stopped for her for a brief second. She hadn't been prepared for love so soon. Not an unexpected guest, it had arrived before the table was set.

She circled him slowly as he uninhibitedly shouted over and over again his offer. When she found an opening she leaped at him playfully, threw her arms around his neck and kissed him with unexpected hunger that surprised even her. It was the right time to uncork the feeling that had been blossoming within her for weeks.

"When, Tessa?" he asked almost painfully when they grew tired of kissing in the warm sun.

"Today, Cal, today. I swear. I'm ready and I want it, too," she said hoarsely. "But not here. It's too raw, too crude. I want a bed. I want somewhere where it's soft and comfortable, where I can lie still for a while afterward. I'm excited, but I'm not a teenager. Some comfort to go with my feelings, please."

"We'll go back to my office, later. I have a studio couch I used to relax on during a long day, when I had lots of long days. It'll do fine."

65

"I thought that was for you and Miss Sigmund," she half-teased him.

He grinned. "I just ask for a good day's work from my staff. Besides, I'm not a skirtchaser. I never went out of my way to look for other women. You were a gift from the gods. And I'd never turn down that kind of a present."

She kissed him again, less passionately this time. A transitional kiss. One to bridge the distance between the beach and the office couch. He understood and spread the blanket on the warm sand paying more attention to it than it really warranted.

"Hold out at least until after lunch."

"I'll try," he said.

She was a wanderer and soon became uneasy as a mere object of the sun's beneficence.

"Enough of sunbathing. Too much is bad for the skin," she said and put her soft cotton shirt back on. "Let's walk a little."

Together they explored the shoreline. She wanted to see how difficult it was to approach their beach from east and west. The water fell gently against the rocks as the pair made their way from one end of the arc to the other. They held hands and in their bare feet leaped from rock to rock avoiding sharp edges and the sure splinters of driftwood.

"There is absolutely nobody here," she said.

"There was this terrible disaster. We are the only two left in the world. Good afternoon, Mrs. Eve."

"I'll bet no one in the world knows about this paradise," she said.

"I'm going to swear you to secrecy. It would be a crying shame to let them in on it."

"Right," she agreed. "They would probably put up a Carvel or something."

"Probably."

He watched the back of her heel as she hesitated before going on to the next rock. Layered, yellowish, puckered skin. Her feet were as fresh and unmarred as a young child's. "Probably never wore high heels," he thought. Lovingly he watched her efforts to find beach treasures, things the sea reluctantly surrendered. She

66

squatted, examined, and threw back what she could not use. A well-mannered lady. At that moment he knew he loved her. It had to be false, this suddenness of love. No one loves in a blinding flash of discovery. Love is usually at the end of a slow-burning fuse. It starts small, unnoticed. Then it hits you. You must have been blind or stupid not to have noticed it. It becomes the towering fact of your life.

Yet, with Tessa it came too easy. Lies come easy. Truth was supposed to come hard. The truth about his life, about his standoffish relationship with Joan, about the kids and the practice, about everything on this earth. He knew that his entire existence had to be examined and dissected every so often. He had to earn his birth certificate constantly. If it was too easy, if it was said fast, it was a lie.

But all of a sudden I love her, he thought. And it is true. He should know better, man of science and all that crap. Love and the glands. Why did looking at her unmangled virgin feet create such nonsense? It had to be false. But it didn't explain why he suddenly loved her.

It had grown too warm in the sun. They retreated to the box seat bluff under some evergreens where they had command of the entire hidden pocket. Tessa sheltered her eyes and tried to read the markings on a blue sailboat that skimmed by.

Ordinarily he would never stare, but his eyes feasted on her. It pained him to do so. A sharp ache in his chest, like angina, gripped him. He wasn't acting or feeling himself. She had put on a large floppy hat, with yellow polka dots and a long yellow ribbon, then gazed at him provocatively. She looked blowzy yet sophisticated like a princess on hard times. Just the right blend of ennui and earthiness.

With the right clothes, the right makeup, she'd be stunning, he thought. Too stunning for me. He pulled himself up short when he realized what he was doing. Strange . . . strange and stupid, to reject my world then end up trying to fit Tessa into it. He shook his head and ran his fingers up her arm.

"What are you smiling about, you deep, devious man?" she asked.

"At you, at the day, at this tremendous sense of freedom I feel. God, Tessa, it's marvelous."

Then, impulsively he reached up, snatched Tessa's hat and put it on his head.

"Yeeeoweee. I'm Sunbonnet Sue and I'm ready for all you hard-up miners," he shouted while prone, his legs flaying about like an overturned lobster.

She laughed and laughed and still laughing sat on him in order to retrieve her hat. He would not surrender it without a fight.

He reached up and, seizing the back of her head where her hair began to curl away from her neck, pulled her down on him. She flattened without resistance. They kissed hungrily. He reached up under her loose shirt and found her unfettered breast. She did not discourage him. After a few seconds, during which she heaved and tossed on him gently, she kissed his ear and whispered, "Later baby, don't take me now. It's only eleven o'clock. I never made love at eleven o'clock. It's bad luck." Cal reluctantly let go. They lay on their backs and held hands.

"Why did I let so much time escape?"

"What are you talking about?" she asked.

"I've been in Sing Sing for years and didn't know it. And didn't care. Or knew it and cared but was unwilling to help myself. Now, all of a sudden, I've been pardoned. And I could kick my ass up the Hudson."

"Baloney, you could have gotten out anytime. You had the key."

"Not so. I've fallen in love with you and that's the key. Now everything is shooting by very quickly."

He turned over on his elbow and looked at her.

"These past few weeks, the walks and the lunches just punched a hole in the dam big enough to drive a truck through. Out pours this whole flood of things about me and my zombie life that probably would have died of suffocation if it weren't for you."

"Or someone like me."

"I won't even consider that even though you may be right, smart-ass. I know what you're saying smart-ass. You're saying, 'grow up . . . it takes two, both you and me to be in love with you.' So what? *You* did it . . . along with me."

"That's about right, Cal. You know, I could have passed in and out of your life a dozen times. But if you weren't ready for it, there'd be no walks, no conversation, no love, no nothing. Don't put all that weight on my shoulders. I carry enough."

"Well," he said, "forgetting about the time factor, I'd like to think that there's something special about you, or about us together, that it took only you to help me find me. Now don't push against that too hard. It's a very negative approach. I'm happy this way."

"Sometimes the negative way is the most honest one."

"That kind of honesty is overrated. Sometimes we need little lies or gray areas to get by. I was heading for something when I began painting. It was a step in the right direction. But I might have gone that route forever if it wasn't for you. Now, I'll lose it if I try to put it into words," he confessed, slightly annoyed at himself for being so poor at self-exhibition.

He grasped a handful of sand and let it slip through his fingers mindlessly.

"I'm trying to change things. It's difficult to do, but I must. It's an absolute necessity. Can you understand that, Tessa?" He looked at her intensely. "I've reached the end of a long trip and now I'm starting on another one. I'm at the highest degree of sophistication I can get to. Simplicity. Fancy meals, fancy cars, all the complexities of spending a good income don't interest me anymore. Joan would say that it never did, but that was because I was never in her consumption league. That binge lasted twenty years and at times I thought it was good, even great. Then I became restless. No one saw it, I think. Then the painting. That was fine . . . until you. Now, I'm churning again and for something different, something better, something truer for me. Do I sound . . . irrational? A year ago when I was drawn to this spot, I was looking for something. I'm convinced it was a loving relationship. I must have that, Tessa. I don't want a business partner. I've had that in the office. It didn't work. I have that at home, now. It works, but it isn't enough. Can you understand me, after just a month Tessa . . . ?"

"No."

". . . that I'm not just looking for someone else in the sack, a different pair of hips, a different someone all the time for an hour or so of clinical sex?"

"That I understand."

69

"Well, I'm just not built for politics, or affairs, or intrigue. Like Joan. I want . . . I need someone to be simple with, to be deep with. It's really quite simple, though I would guess that not too many people understand the feeling."

"I understand it," she said, "mainly, I guess, because I need that, too."

"Tessa, by some kind of instinct I knew that I found it, as soon as you told me my painting was lousy."

She made two quick decisions. The first, to suppress a grin about the painting, the second, to prepare an early lunch.

"Isolation is great for knowing myself. I've had that for some time now. It's good . . . but you know that. You've practiced it so I don't have to convince you. I know me. Now I'm coming back for seconds. I want to know you, too."

"And so you shall," she promised. She had few qualms about the offer. He would have no obstacles to overcome with her.

They ate off paper plates. Tessa introduced him to her egg salad, one of her famous successes and one of his forbidden foods. He ate heartily without silently counting cholesterol.

"Know something, Tessa? I got a bigger kick out of seeing your face when I wore your hat than I did when I got the new Buick. How did I live so long without touching you?"

Tessa was moved, almost shaken. She cast her eyes down and stroked his fingers.

"Cal, wherever we go, whatever happens with us, I think I'll always remember what you just said."

She threw her shoulders back and smelled the moist ocean breeze. She smiled. Her mind was bubbling. It is no trick at all to have someone fall in love with you. You send out signals, you show interest, you make yourself attractive. That's penny-ante stuff. But to have someone feel he wants to be open and free, to have someone choose that path with you, is strong medicine. She felt flattered and that seemed to pull invisible cords within her, making her body taut and firm.

"But we better eat up," she said, "or maybe I'll cry."

"Not that," he said, "anything but tears. We have some good times ahead of us."

They finished off the smorgasbord from two very different kitchens. Joan's tuna salad and margarined Rye Krisp, Tessa's

70

egg salad, fried chicken, and boiled potatoes in jackets. They ate quickly and sparingly as if they were late for an appointment. The birds were given more of their lunch than they had.

"What about Victor?" he asked as they drove back to his office.

"Well, what about him?" she replied, almost defiantly. "I certainly don't love him, if that's what you want to know."

She loses her temper fast, he mused, then dismissed the thought as unimportant.

"No, I know that already. You made that clear. What I mean is what kind of a life do you have?" He felt shameless in asking since he was about to share the man's wife, regardless.

She sat back allowing the cool air to bathe her face, and tucked her long legs beneath her. Getting comfortable to begin an uncomfortable narrative.

"Well, hon, to know Victor you have to start with old Manny Bruno, his father." She stared at the dome light in the ceiling. "That man is a corker. Out of a movie. He and my father were emigrant buddies for years. What they call *goomba*, compatriots."

It was the first time she ever used an Italianism. Cal was mildly surprised. Never really thought of her as an Italian. Not that it cut into her loveliness, it just tilted her a bit.

"I mentioned it before. They fixed the marriage. Shook on it, or had some vino over it, or something. Victor and I were as good as married before I got my first period."

Cal nodded as she spoke, very pleased that the Meadowbrook Parkway heading south was virtually free of traffic. They would be in his office very shortly. But not quick enough.

"Just so happened that I was born three years before Victor." She searched for the ashtray, her hand cupping the Marlboro. "Didn't mean a goddamned thing to either of them. So, I grew up without options, relieved of the whole courtship process."

The exits flew by, Cal ticked them off one by one in his head. He glanced nervously at the digital clock on the panel. Every minute that passed was stolen from him, from them.

"The week before we got married old Manny asked to see me in his office behind the greenhouse, where he wrote out the monthly bills. No, not really," she clarified, "he didn't *ask* to see me, he demanded it. Like he was royalty. Funny," she said, slow-ing her pace, "he was a Socialist, too, outside the home. Hated Mussolini and said so, I'm told, even when it was dangerous. But at home . . . a fascist. Well," she said dismissing her small diversion with a wave of the hand, "I remember he kept me waiting for what seemed to be a hundred years (I was so green and scared then) while he made out a few bills with an old-fashioned ink pen, the kind we used to use in public school that you dipped in the sunken inkwell."

Cal nodded, affirming the memory, smoothing the path of her narrative.

"Little beady eyed bastard he was. When he finally figured that I had sweated enough, he looked up over his glasses like a judge, and asked, "Are you a virgin, Teresa?" He pronounced my name in the Italian way, like he was talking to a Teresa with a gold tooth, wearing black all over. I felt like I committed a crime."

"Well, I told him straight out, 'None of your damned business.' His face fell to the floor and his glasses slipped off. I could see the empty spaces, like open graves, where teeth should have been. Then he slapped his glasses back on his face and became livid. I actually saw his face go from white to beet red in a flash. Imagine anything on this earth, or in it, not being Emmanuel Bruno's business. Well, *he* couldn't. He sat there and cursed me like hell. All that *mala femina* crap. What really bothered the old snake wasn't that I might not be pure enough for his sonny boy, but that I had the brass balls to shut him out of my life, just like that."

She looked at Cal who confirmed her judgment with his eyes. He could see the scene. It became as real to him as if his own virginity was called to the bar. They entered Southern State Parkway about two, and the sight of it, practically empty, acted as a whip. He accelerated rapidly.

"After all," she continued, "he asked the same intruding questions of all his potential daughter-in-laws. And got the same answer. Oh yes, poppa, from all of them. Bullshit," she snorted, "they were all deflowered before they hit sixteen. I know that for a fact. And by other guys, too. Also hard fact. But, being devious, political, and not too cheeky, they made their accommodations with old Poppa Manny, as long as it was on his terms.

72

I was the rebel, the anti-Christ in short shorts and no bra and he tried to chop me up for fertilizer every time he saw me."

"You were doomed from the start, poor kid," he said. He looked at her to show his reflected anguish. He looked at his speedometer, too. He was doing over seventy. "Passion was pushing the pedal, officer," he planned to tell the traffic cop, poetically, if he were stopped.

"He got me alone, right before the wedding. I'll never forget it. It was the day we made reservations for Puerto Rico. Victor went to Friendly's to get ice cream. Manny told me, 'Now I'm giving you a nice boy; be good to him.' 'Of course I'll be good to him,' I answered, all white-hot and flustered, 'but I'd rather you gave me a man, instead.' He burned me with those pig eyes of his and said, 'Better for you I didn't. If I did the two of you would kill each other and I'd never have grandchildren.' That, my love, was and still is, old Manny. That is the kind of man that raised my husband and with that background you'll understand about Victor."

"I guess I can put together the rest of it," he said. "Victor went from the frying pan into the fire and back again."

"That's about it. Victor did whatever poppa wanted and got hell from me for it. And the other way around. But I took care of him." She stretched to full length. "You know, I went to college to become a teacher of the handicapped. I quit in my junior year because I had a cripple in my own backyard. I had Victor. His poppa insisted Victor get going on the grandchildren. So I quit and got married and hung around the house waiting for the stork. I earned my degree in the field."

The parking lot of the medical building was deserted. All the professionals declared a moratorium on sickness and death on Fridays. Cal parked in the back, out of sight from passing traffic. They sat in the car, sealed off and cooled while she tied up the loose ends of her history.

"I'll never forget that Christmas party when Victor stood up, proud and shining, to tell our combined families, about a hundred men, women, and children, that I was going to have a baby. It was at Poppa Manny's place, that Florentine ranch of his. Poppa stood up and offered a toast to Emmanuel Victor Bruno

73

the second. The bastard was thinking in terms of lineage and royalty and all that nonsense. I pulled at Victor's pants until he finally told the old windbag that we decided on Stephen, if it was a boy, after my dead father. Well, Manny walked straight up and slow, no . . . he didn't walk, he marched . . . over to Victor, who stood about a head taller, and slapped my teddy bear of a husband right across the face. Not once, but three times. Like in a Three Musketeers picture. Poor Victor, my heart broke for him, he just stood there and cried. And in front of both tribes. He cried like a baby. I had to drive us home that night, it had so disabled him. He couldn't sleep with me for weeks afterward. And in front of my mother and all her children."

She stiffened and smiled as if she were coming out of a trance. "So that's it. That's Victor and that's Manny. My husband is still his prisoner."

The keys fell out of Cal's hand. She giggled girlishly as he made a mess of opening the office door. First the knob wouldn't turn. Then the door caught on a thick brown envelope that the postman had dropped through the mail slot.

"A case of honeymoonitis?" she chided.

"Nonsense. I'm simply very happy. It happens. I'll have to grow into it."

He turned the couch down and it became a fine place to make love. Tessa was undressed before he could turn around to help her. He sucked his breath in and wondered if he should fondle her first or undress, too. He did both.

When they were comfortable she scooped his face with both her hands and kissed him furiously. The sun escaped through the half-closed blinds and put stripes across her body creating an undulating effect that raised his fires even higher. He was overwhelmed completely. His hands were everywhere. She worked slower, more methodically, as if she were the older and wiser of the pair.

"Listen, love," she said between strokes, "no fancy Five Town screwing. Make it standard and make it long."

He desperately attempted to honor both her commands. It was damned hard to follow orders. Damned hard. He closed his eyes

74

to avoid the sight of her fine striped body vibrating to a rhythm only she heard. It was bringing him too rapidly to a boil.

Tender. She was very tender in all her actions, saying not a word during the half hour of high excitement. Cal was enormously pleased. Joan talked incessantly, day and night. She even badgered him during their lovemaking. There was no way he could shut her up. He tried insults, entering and leaving her body, but to no avail. She was ever demanding, demanding, demanding. New techniques, repeated requests to extend and heighten her orgasm. Always more, always different.

Tessa, almost in complete silence, except for the soft moans, took and gave pleasure as if it were the most natural exchange possible. Cal dove for pearls within himself and surfaced with the best he had to please her. He held back nothing. It was as if he had been saving it for years.

"Don't go yet," she begged when it was over.

"I'm not going anyplace, love," he whispered between kissing her flesh. He whispered not out of fear of detection or embarrassment, but because love flowed easier on a whisper. "I'm just going to lie here with you and talk and hear your heartbeat."

"Cardiology?" she smiled.

"Communication," he replied.

He lay with her, spent and panting softly. His heart pounded against the walls of his chest like a lion testing the strength of his cage. For a brief instant he felt guilty and ashamed. What if Joan should suddenly appear, after shadowing him for weeks? What had he done getting involved with another woman? But the feeling passed quickly. A shooting star on an August night. By the time it was noted, it was gone. He had something left, though, his residue of pleasure in its purest state, this deep contentment. It destroyed the shooting star.

They had hours left. Neither made a move to leave the couch.

"Can I tell you more about Victor and myself?" she shyly asked.

"I was hoping you would, but I thought maybe I had pried enough. I don't know yet what you consider private property, where the borders are. But I want to know whatever you want to tell me." His fingers, like small streams, flowed from her thigh to her knee and then upstream again. He buried his face in her hair surrendering to an impulse as old as their first meeting. She seemed almost oblivious now to his attentions.

"Victor is a baby, a very difficult baby. He's uncomfortable with women, with me. When we talk seriously, as seriously as he can get, he paws the ground like a dog. He's more comfortable with his friends, that clique of creeps he grew up with. Sports nuts. He'd rather watch football on Sunday and Monday than make love to me." Then sadly, "He'd rather do almost anything than make love to me."

"Damn fool," he interjected.

"On weekends . . . forget it. Those bums of his stink up the house with cigarette smoke and burn holes in the furniture. But I grin and bear it. I'm hospitable. I grit my teeth, but I'm hospitable."

Cal worked her shoulders, transfixed by their soft gentle slope. He dwelled on them while she lay on her belly and looked at him looking at her.

"I curse in the kitchen, but I come out with the six-packs and the potato chips and I'm all smiles. And these six greasers he huddles with clam up like a secret society when I come and start up again when I leave. I feel like a damned den mother with those mangy animals in the house.

"Love," she said disgustedly. "He thinks love is something that happens once every two weeks, when he's all gassed up from a night out with the boys and comes home at three and rips my P.J.'s off. Twice a month I get raped by a drunken teen-aged teddy bear."

Cal wondered if he should be angry at or grateful to Victor for his amatory pattern. Before he could decide she added, "The only thing his father gave him, besides the business, was a razor strop. The one old Manny used on his boys when they showed any signs of independence. Victor used it once on Stephen. Thought he was honoring his father when he put stripes on the kid's little behind. But I cut the damn thing to ribbons and threw it in the garbage. Victor just shook his teddy bear head and looked as if someone kicked him in the testicles."

"So why do you stay with him?" he asked and felt foolish for asking. "You'll only continue a life of misery."

76

"Listen, Cal, understand this," she said as she propped herself up on her elbow exposing a fine outline of breast, belly, and thigh. "Victor is a baby. Victor needs me. I'll probably never leave him. He'd wither and die if I left. The family thing is too deep, even though I'm modern and supposedly intelligent. Right now, in the back of my mind I'm wondering if they'll remember that it's Friday and they're supposed to go to Margie's next door until I get home. My other two babies. And in a way, I guess, I care for him, too. Like a mother loves her crippled son."

"But Tessa, that's slavery." Cal had been contemplating sex again, her outline encouraging him, but he forgot about it, for the moment. "It's against everything modern and humane. It's against everything women have been working for and achieving," he said, feeling foolish for carrying banners.

"Is it?" she asked. "Is it slavery if I choose to be a slave?"

"It's still slavery, with or without your consent."

"So be it," she concluded. Then tenderly stroking him just below his ear she added, "Cal, listen to me. Without your hands making so much noise."

He locked his fingers and held them captive.

"I love you," she said. "I tell you this freely and honestly. I want you again and again. I want to see you forever. It's been damned good, this day, this whole beautiful month. Talking like this, making love like this, is food and air for me. And I was starving. I want it to go on and on. But for me and for you, too, this is a second meal. Your survival doesn't depend on me, and vice versa."

Cal started to say something. Tessa cut him short by sealing his lips with her fingers.

"Victor's does. You need me for a second world. Okay a better world. But you *could* live without a second world. It would probably be rough knowing how tired you've grown of the first. But listen, love, it's a matter of priorities with me. I must tend to the most severely wounded, and Victor is nearly a basket case. It would be out and out murder if I ever left him."

Her words tamed him into silence. He lay there, looking at his solid wall of books, a spent and toothless lion.

"So it's like this, Cal. You can have me anytime you want. For days, for weeks, given a little notice, even during my period, if

77

your nice body so dictates. But eventually I go home to Victor. House rules. There'll be enough of everything for both of us."

Then she invited him in as if to prove her point. The second encounter was longer and more tantalizingly pleasurable than the first. He took his time.

An hour left to their day. It was almost dusk and the rays of the sun, an anxious voyeur before, were gone. The room was almost dark. What light remained seemed to lovingly hug Tessa's every feature.

"Oh, one thing. It may embarrass you if I say it, but I'll say it anyhow. Please, please, please . . . no gifts or presents. Our time together is present enough. Pay for lunch, or the motel, or wherever we arrange to go, but nothing past that. Agreed?"

"Agreed."

She kisses him smartly to seal the bargain. There was no sex left in it.

"Did I tell you that I love you?" Cal asked.

"Yes, today. But what about Joan? Do you love her, too?"

"Yes, I think so, in a few ways. I've given it some thought."

"Then you love us both?" she asked and answered in one.

"Yes."

"Do you love the butcher, the baker, and the candlestick maker, too?" she asked, trying to be wicked, or simple.

"Don't be facetious, Tessa. I was being as honest as possible. Our own situations are parallel. You can see that."

"There is a similarity," she agreed. "And I wasn't trying to be cutting or funny. I just wanted to know where the boundaries were. I just want to see if you were serious."

"About loving Joan?"

"About loving me. I guess it wasn't funny the way I phrased the question. I just wanted to know about me."

"Very serious."

"I'm glad," she said and sunned him with a broad smile. She had not smiled since they left the beach. It felt warm and invigorating.

"One thing, Tessa. I'm going to tell Joan about us. Do you mind?"

"No. That's up to you."

"I know it is but you should know whatever there is to know."

"Do you expect trouble?"

"No, not really. I can handle Joan. She won't hassle you. Still, I don't want anything hidden from you. No surprises."

Tessa seemed amused. And pleased.

"Don't worry. I don't get upset. Want to see my medals for bravery?"

"Only after I've seen what I want to see."

"You sweet lecher," she said and popped out of bed. "Now take me home before I'm completely scandalized." She dressed as quickly as she undressed.

"Drop me off in Genovese's parking lot. My Ford's there. Now that we're serious adulterers we have to be careful."

She kissed him again. "That's also our goodbye kiss for today. Do we have an appointment for next Friday?"

"Unbreakable," he answered.

"Fantastic," she replied zipping up her fly.

He thought of ways to tell Joan. Started down a hundred different roads and got lost. Never once did he consider not telling her. He could lie and let it grow into a monster; he could tell the truth as he knew it, or really, as he felt it. Both alternatives were, for days and weeks, unacceptable. Joan would get hurt either way. That was the simple truth of it.

The children were out for the evening. Joan and Cal were alone. It would have to be tonight. Not because he felt terribly guilty, but because it bothered him that he knew something that affected their lives that she didn't know. Well, maybe he did feel a little guilt. He had met Tessa back in May, slept with her and talked of love in June and now at the end of July, had made more trips to her body for sustenance. He reasoned that his love for Tessa had now set and hardened like a cement walk and he could rightfully think of it as accepted fact. The diagnosis had changed from strong feeling to absolute certainty. It was time.

The house rested with the children away. The Nazi had stormed out after a shouting match with his mother. She buzzed him waspishly for leaving a trail of sweaty clothes from the shower to his room. He grumbled about his being picked on (his conditioned response to any form of criticism), and flew away like an angry, noisy bird, slamming doors behind him. Probably he was now playing cards and swapping sexual lies with his cronies.

The Bitch, sullen and moody, at the start of her menses, sought asylum with another sullen and moody princess at a neighboring castle. Cal was acclimated to these rapid changes of weather, the intermittent showers from his daughter, the thunder and lightning from his son, Peter.

"Where did she go?" Cal asked almost disinterestedly.

"To see Bambi, I think."

"Is that picture still around? God, I remember as a kid. . . ."

"Bambi Levinson. Her father's the one who was indicted last year for fraud. The film distributor. Remember?" she said, her annoyance just on the verge of surfacing.

"No, not really. How can parents name a kid 'Bambi'? Don't they know what a burden they put on the poor girl? Minnie or Sadie would have been better. God, Bambi."

They sat in the kitchen alcove quietly eating half grapefruits. The dining area stuck out like a top hat from the straight brick line at the back of the house. Joan had designed it that way. Sunlight always streamed in from one of the three sides. She needed sunlight with her meals the way a coffee addict needs his brew. During breakfast the rays entered from the left, covering the gray formica table with a pearly coat. It was a tepid cup of sun, but it sufficed. At lunch it shone over her shoulder from the center windows and helped her read the mail. And she served dinner just as the dying rays angled in through the western window on the right.

"Muriel Levinson is a nut," she said. "What do you expect from nuts who smoke pot in their living room and sit around like statues practicing Yoga or T.M. or E.S.P. or whatever they practice? I once walked in for a donation and there they were, the six of them, the Levinsons, the Watchers, and a couple I never saw before, sitting on the kitchen floor staring into space."

"So what did you do?"

"What did I do? I waited until they came out of their trance and made him write a hundred dollar check. The lousy thing bounced and the next month they indicted him."

"And what kind of a kid is Bambi?" he asked trying to run communication lines between them in the hope that before the night ended he could bring himself to use them.

"What kind of a kid?" she repeated, "a kid like Laura, spoiled, indecisive, rich in material things, impoverished of spirit, initiative, and all those things that make a person alive. They have as much pressure on them as wild geese, yet they're unhappy.

81

Most of them have shrinks. In short a bitch, like our Bitch, like all her friends, like the whole generation."

She cleared the table.

"We said that we would be patient, that eventually they'd all come around. Remember, Joan, about short term and long term, about late bloomers and different drummers?"

"I remember, Cal, but you remember, too, that some hothouse plants, raised scientifically, hygienically, with the wasted love and care of a doting father and mother never bloom or flower or bear fruit. They just rot away."

She loved those two last lines. She would use them again to stiffen soft backbones at the next P.T.A. meeting.

"The subject is children, not roses. You just can't take the comparisons too far. It's not fair," he said.

Joan felt that she was put in check again. An infrequent occurrence, their being alone together. As the years accumulated, they built alternative worlds to the one they shared. Did the walls behind which they hid from each other just grow, like Topsy? He often had these thoughts during lunch while she shunned the certain indigestion it would bring. He pondered facts; she adapted, but only when unable to change them.

It was tacitly agreed that they enter each other's emotional life only when asked in. Lately, the invitations were rarer than kindness. She had not told Marsha the whole truth. She was several stations beyond afraid. But a system of checks and balances saved Joan from touching bottom. Fears about a husband in transition grew numb when she stood at the dais or meted out assignments to subordinates. From that rose-colored vantage point she concluded that the arrangement wasn't too bad. After all, relations between them were often cordial, even friendly. There were no emotional valleys in bed, but neither were there peaks. Perhaps being over forty is like living in Minnesota before they grew wheat, a flat no-man's-land where nothing ever happened. She could accept that if it were a normal growth pattern.

Luckily each had many outside obligations. Actually medicine was Cal's major activity. She did not count the painting. It was only a quirk and would pass when he realized that it was one patient that would never get well.

Lately, they had begun to feel increasingly uneasy in each

82

other's presence. There was simply nothing to say. Except to talk about a girl named Bambi. It had begun to look as if it had all been said years ago and filed away. The talk about the Levinsons was nonsense, she thought. Who cares about the Levinsons? Who cares if they sit and stare into empty space with their empty friends or walk on their empty heads? But, she thought, if Cal wants to talk meaninglessly, it was fine with her.

Before Tessa, Cal had accepted the emotional vacuum that spaced him light years away from Joan's life. No real reason remained to become closer friends or deadly enemies. This evolution occurred, unseen and unheralded. The marriage that had begun as a deep necessity had arrived, after twenty years, at the safe harbor of convenience. Joan would have preferred it otherwise. Her love remained a survivor of that boredom, which few hearts can survive. She compared their life together to a roaring fire reduced to white ashes wherein a small but steady fire glowed. But she preferred not to be pressed about it for fear that too much exposure might extinguish those sparks.

They ate a cold salad for supper. Joan hated to cook during beach months. It was so easy to leave the sand at four, shower, and prepare something that required ten minutes of cutting and chopping. Crisp green lettuce leaves, hard pink tomatoes sliced horizontally in thick sections, thin strips of white meat turkey and whole deveined shrimp. That was the ideal supper. The whole thing took fifteen minutes to prepare. It was low in calories, especially with the substitute Russian dressing, and it was nutritious.

He sat hunched over a large wooden salad bowl, his mind elsewhere, as usual. She chatted more than usual, until he began to steal a shrimp from her.

"Hey mister, watch it. I saw you."

"One more or less won't matter," he said and downed it, making her argument academic.

She frowned, something she hated to do. It deepened lines on her face. "I can practically see the cholesterol lining your arteries. They're getting narrower and narrower." She shook her head ruefully. "You may be a good doctor, Dr. Bernstein, but you're one lousy patient."

No matter what he thought earlier, it had been wrong to post-

83

pone the inevitable. This weight around his neck was growing heavier by the minute. The lettuce sounded crisp as she chewed it. Then he realized that he was doing the chewing. Where had he been the past half hour?

She sat opposite him reading *Newsday* and eating a celery stalk with little beaver-like bites.

"Listen, Joan, to hell with my arteries. I have something to discuss with you. Something important."

"Don't you think your arteries are a serious matter?" She held the celery stalk extended as if it were a cigarette. It gave her a bored, silly, sophisticated look that just did not go with the celery. "After all, men your age are so susceptible to heart attacks. Dear husband," she said, cupping his hands with hers, "I am trying to preserve you."

He withdrew his hands as if hers had thorns. "And you brush it off as if I were trying to sell you a magazine subscription."

Cal bristled yet he felt guilty about withdrawing his hands so quickly. He tilted the brown brass chair and stared at her. She was acting again and it annoyed him. He thought she should save that for her ladies.

"Not the long suffering wife tonight, Joan, please. The kids are away and we can talk quietly." He put down his fork and pushed away from the table. It won't be easy, he thought, looking at her long and intently. She won't let it be.

"Leave the dishes. Come into the den. You can do that later," he ordered.

She felt uneasy. He could do that to her with a stare, with half a sentence. It just knocked her off her pins.

From the standpoint of tactics the den was not the best of battlegrounds for him. It was the only room she decorated herself without the aid of Mrs. Twenty Percent. The walls and ceiling were a robin's egg blue. Because of the fluted paneling that enclosed and surrounded the room, the paint showed darker at the top of the ridges and lighter in the valleys. Dark, then light, then dark again. Joan loved the drama of the interplay. The wicker couch and chairs had royal blue seats and backs. Carpeting was thick and light blue, the color of the snowballs outside the kitchen window. Even the rolltop desk, in the corner, near the Andersen

84

windows had been stripped bare of its mahogany pigment and redone in a blue close to the color of the Atlantic at Jones Beach about seven in the morning. She had gotten it that way by taking Bob Golden, the hardware store owner, out to a breakfast of clam chowder and french fries. She had placed him on the school board, so he dutifully blended and reblended until they were agreed that her desk and the waters off Jones Beach had the same decorator.

Cal sat in the rocking chair and gently set it in motion. Only last year she had rescued that antique from a scrap heap, one Sunday in Sullivan County, and refurbished it in a kind of rose-blue tone. It felt massively Victorian, like money made before the turn of the century.

He looked at her, her face glowing and almost felt tongue tied.

"Well," she said.

"I've been seeing another woman for the past few months. I'm in love with her."

"Okay," she said with a clipped finality, as if someone had told her that her library budget had been vetoed.

"Do you want to talk about it?" she asked.

"Of course I want to talk about it. Did you expect me to say it and get up and walk away as if I told you it was raining?" He found his tongue. The words were coming easier.

"Certainly not, Cal. What I meant, really, was that it's your move. You brought it up, you continue. That's what I meant. Certainly it must be discussed. Go ahead, please."

Her eyes never left his face. She made sure of that. This was no time for weakness.

He continued. "I didn't go out and look for it, Joan. I swear I didn't. It just happened. I've never been involved with another woman before. But I'm in love with her. I'm sure of that as I'm sure of anything." He felt suddenly liberated. His shoulders drew back reacting to the release.

She pressed on. "And you say this . . . thing has been going on for months?"

He was on trial, he realized. Guilt established, the inquisitor was now in the process of determining the depths of his corruption.

"Since May."

85

"Uh huh," she said weighing, weighing, weighing, their eyes locked on each other's.

"You've been sleeping with her since May?" she asked gingerly.

"Since the middle of June. What's that got to do with it Joan?" he asked. "Once or ten times, I've said I love her. The numbers change nothing."

She blinked and turned away for a moment breaking their hold on each other. "You're a son of a bitch, Cal. A rotten, good for nothing, whoring bastard. You know that, Cal? You're no different than any other ass-chasing son of a bitch, two timing adulterer."

He felt caught off guard by the outburst. All he could muster was, "You're right, Joan, you're right. I'm terribly sorry about hurting you." He bent over toward her. She backed away. "Joan, I didn't go out of my way to hurt you. Can't you believe that? Do you think. . . ."

In clipped precise tones she said, "I don't know what to think. All I ask myself is 'how could you do such a thing to me at this time in our lives, in this community?' After all the sweat and struggle to get us here you come to me with this this . . . craziness. You bastard, you goddamn bastard. You just destroyed our lives. You know that Cal? You just destroyed our lives. And furthermore why the hell are you telling me this? For once in your life can't you just be like everyone else and hide it? Men do, you know."

"I can't, Joan. I thought by now you'd know that. I know you longer than anyone else on earth. Except Arnie." He stared at her and thought she was more upset by his honesty than his transgression. "And lashing out like that doesn't solve a thing."

She looked at him, as if just awakened, and said nothing, her mouth an empty cave. Finally, she confessed, "I know, I know, but I had to say it. It's how I felt. It was too enormous to swallow or reason away. I'm just not that bloodless. I was terribly hurt and I had to strike out at you."

She paused and her strength almost reached pre-shock condition. "Now, let's have the rest of it. I'll behave, I promise."

"There's not a hell of a lot else to tell. I met her by accident, painting one Friday. We talked. I was . . . captivated. I pursued her. We found we care for each other. That's about it." He tried to be truthful and yet at the same time expose as few emotional outposts as possible.

"Oh is it?" she shot back. He dug in for another assault. "I suppose she's young and fresh, with a flat stomach, a little ass, no wrinkles and she worships the hell out of you. And you love it. It flatters your well-hidden ego. Makes you feel young and alive and all that horseshit. That's the way it is, isn't it, Cal?"

He recognized her search and destroy tactics. Find the weak spot, bring up the heavy stuff and wipe him out.

"That's kind of crude," he said.

"But true, right?" she followed quickly.

"Not true," he patiently answered. "She's in her thirties and married. She has plenty of her own problems and she sees me as I am. She's not the groupie type." He glanced out the window, realizing with surprise that they were surrounded by dusk. Dusk through a blue filter.

"Then can't you see that the little bitch is probably after your money, or your imagined money? Sure, she sees that you're an established doctor and you live in a big white house, plenty of all the goodies. She's poor with nothing but bills and brats. And she wants a piece of the action. Can't you see that, Cal? Well, lover boy, you tell your courtesan that everything is in my name (she lied and they both knew it was a silly lie). I'll make sure you never see a penny of it. I'll make such demands on you that you'll both end up working for me and the lawyers. And you'll beg to come back after she takes off."

Cal switched the lights on and returned to his chair shaking his head sadly. He was stung by her caustic vindictiveness. It was years since he had had to face such a withering attack. Hell, she has every right to, he thought.

"And I'm sure, absolutely sure, she's a shiksa to boot," Joan declared knowingly.

"Yes, she's not Jewish, but that's also an accident. I didn't go shopping with a list in my hand. I didn't say, 'Let me see, I could use a lover. She should be a Christian, five foot six, about a hundred and twenty-five pounds. . . .'" He discontinued that line of sarcasm as a fruitless attempt to match hers.

"But you sure as shootin' got one, so what the hell's the difference if you went looking for her or she found you or you found each other? The results are the same. I'm low man on the totem pole." She clenched her teeth. "I don't relish the idea or fact of being low man on the totem pole. For your sake and for mine, Cal, I'll destroy her. I'll find out who she is and I'll wipe the floor with her. I'll do it. You know I can do it."

Cal seized her hands and held them until his knuckles turned white. She thought he was about to strike her. "You'll do nothing of the sort. You try to hurt her, Joan, in any way, and I'll leave. I'll just pack up and take off with her and you'll never see me again. Is that what you want? Think carefully before you do anything that foolish. Now, we were talking," he said and slowly released her hands and backed away. "'Keep it that way. Don't threaten me, don't bully me and we'll talk."

She stood up. "My throat is terribly dry. I have a pitcher of iced tea. Do you want some?"

He nodded.

"Good. Sit here I'll bring it in."

She returned immediately with a pitcher and glasses. They needed the break, she reasoned. Things were getting out of hand. Once seated she began again. "Of course I didn't mean any of that, Cal. Please forget it. You were very honest and very embarrassed telling me about it, about her." Her face had regained its composure. It was as if the tea were a rapidly acting tranquilizer.

"You're ashamed of what you're doing. I can see it in your face. What is the matter with you, Cal? Tell me, let me help you."

He was no boxing buff, never played chess well, but he recognized the maneuver. Something to do with feinting with one hand while readying the other; giving up a knight to get the queen.

"I'm not embarrassed. I'm not ashamed, so help me, Joan. I'm just uncomfortable. I'm uneasy about hurting you, I'm uneasy about having to submit to cross-examination and trial by abuse. I know I deserve it, but pretty soon you'll have gone too far and we'll have nothing to talk about. Is that what you want, Joan?"

"No, Calvin, I want to talk. I think I'm over the shock, now. I *do* want to talk. But please understand, I never thought this would happen to me. I hoped we'd slip quietly through middle age and grow old without any fuss. This is a terrible shock to me.

I'm not myself. I knew you were beginning to grow restless. Dissatisfied. An expected thing since you grew up missing so much. I figured you might want to move out west, or buy a boat. Go back to school and teach. But another woman? Never."

She relaxed, leaning back against the pillows of the couch clutching her drink.

"You know, Cal, sometimes I'd torture myself with the thought that you might wander. But somehow, oh, how can I explain it, it was like a bad dream that you knew was only a dream and you'd awaken soon. So I never took the nightmare seriously. Now that it's happened I can't wake myself up and I don't like it at all." She whispered her last sentence as if somehow she had run out of word fuel.

"I don't like it either. I mean about its effect on you. I'm not geared for hurting people. Some people do it well. My first impulse is to take the pain myself."

"Then give it up, Cal. Maybe we can work it out later, when you've gotten back to your senses," she said, finding what she thought was a hole.

He frowned. "I thought I was very clear about Tessa. I'm in love with her. Fact. Fact. It's no casual one-night stand. I will *not* give her up. That has to be the starting point. I won't give her up."

She bit her lip, stared into the frosty tall glass of iced tea, her glance almost dazed, her eyes refusing to accept the signal to moisten.

"Oh, Cal, what's wrong with us?" she asked. When did you stop loving me?" Without waiting for an answer she continued. "Really we've had a lovely marriage, all things considered. Fine children, in spite of the fact that they are very difficult at times, though not as difficult as some. It's a good life, Cal, the house, the practice, the life in town. What's missing? What did we lose? Where did I go wrong?"

Her voice had a beggar's quality to it and he felt uneasy with beggars. She was too good to beg. If she were trying to get to him through the back door of fake pity, if it was another ploy, it would only make him more distrustful, more prepared for the next assault. If she were truly a mendicant it would not work either. His course was fixed. As far as he could plot it, of course.

He took a deep breath and held it as long as he could. "First of all, Joan, love . . . our love . . . everybody's love has a history, an evolution. The kind we had at the beginning, the noise, the aggravation, the tumult of becoming a doctor, raising a family, working for goals, with all the fighting and the truce in bed, afterwards . . . that's gone. I admit that. Certain things die naturally or change into other things. You know it, too. And, as a matter of fact, you wouldn't want the same kind of explosive relationship we had at the beginning. It was too edgy, too much friction with your mother. I could take her then, I was afraid of her. I couldn't take her now."

She was ready for him. "Well, I certainly don't want this middle-aged madness either, and from you, of all men, Cal. So straight, so honorable. I would never have guessed."

He thought of her then, as some old prospector, searching the canyons of Wyoming, for a gold strike, tapping against him, looking for hidden caches of shame.

"I thought I knew you so well," she said and broke off a corner of a cinnamon Graham cracker. "'No, I really do know you, and you are making a big mistake, thinking you can solve your problems on top of another woman. It doesn't work that way. And sure as you're sitting here we need each other. You know, Dr. Bernstein, and I'm sure you know because you spend a lot of time putting things together, we supplement and complement each other. We're two symbiots, you and I. Two old veterans who listen to each other's stories on the back porch of an old soldier's home. Don't forget that. I know that because I know you."

Cal twisted uneasily in the rocker at her distortion, at the hint of an intimacy with a long lease. Her technique was flawless and his discomfort was a half-and-half mixture of the feelings that her assessment was grotesque and that it was accurate, too. Once they were very close. Once was some time ago.

Quietly seated, sipping his tea slowly, he gave her her chance to wear pain like a crown. But he would have to get on with it. There was more to say. Much more.

"Now, let me tell you how I really feel," he said, "or try to tell you. It won't be easy. Most of my feelings I've kept sealed in Mason jars. But the time comes . . . and I guess this is the time."

He finished his tea and placed the glass on the bar to his right.

"There is no warmth in our marriage."

"But I love you, Cal, I really love you." '

"I know that."

"Then you don't love me."

"I never said that."

"Then what is it? Maybe I missed something."

"You didn't. All I said was there's no warmth."

"I'm not a cold person. Are you ever displeased in the bedroom?"

"No."

"Then what?"

"I guess it's more me than anything. My needs are changing."

"But I'm giving all I can."

"You're cold, Joan." He said it more easily than he thought possible.

"Would you want me to fawn all over you and tell you how wonderful you are?" Her voice cracked slightly. A hairline fracture that Cal noticed. "I won't do that, Cal."

"I don't want that."

"Then what?"

"Some tenderness, some warmth."

"I really don't have much to give. You get it all."

"I know that."

"Then what?"

"It's not enough."

"You foolish man," she chided. "Do you think you're going to get it from a young shiksa who doesn't know you like I do after twenty years?"

"She's past thirty. That's not young for this kind of thing. That's Marsha's age."

"You've become an expert on affairs?"

"You don't have to. It's common knowledge, today. Like who presidents sleep with and what the C.I.A. is up to."

"And you want to be in step."

"You know better than that, lady."

"I don't know better. I don't think I know you anymore. You frighten me. You've wiped me out tonight. Totally, with this thing."

"It's done."

"It's not done," she said the hairline crack widening. "'I just won't allow you to walk all over me and say 'it's done' like they stole your bicycle or you lost a patient. It's not done. It's not done."

"Then it's not done, Joan. Have your say. Keep at it."

"Are you going to keep her?"

"My bicycle? I'm not going to give her up. That's the third time I've said it."

"I mean are you going to set her up in an apartment or anything? We're not that rich, you know. I'm not going to deprive my kids of an education so that you can toot your horn in some love nest."

"No, no, no. She wants nothing from me. Except time."

"Time. Time," she said. "Twenty years is a lot of time. Add to it the five years before, when Arnie introduced us, and you have a quarter of a century. But I'm still willing to learn. Tell me about our life together that you don't like. I can still change, if I have to."

"You really believe that, Joan?"

"Listen, mister, I'm fighting for my life. Don't cut me down like that. Give *me* some of that time you're so anxious to spread around."

"Joan, listen. We just never grew together, like we should have."

She seized on that, as an addict his fix. "Are we supposed to become one entity, a Joan-Cal, or Cal-Joan? Sorry, my husband, that's not what my life's all about. You've got your thing, your stethescope, your scalpel, your little prescription pad. I've got mine, too. Was I supposed to be the little woman at home while you were swinging between worlds?"

"You're trying to bury me with words. I recognize the act. God, Joan, I know I hurt you . . ."

"You sure did."

". . . but we're not going to have it out if you intend to wallpaper me. This isn't a P.T.A. meeting."

She paused, realizing she had made a tactical error. "Sorry, I'll tone it down. Talk to me Cal, I'll listen. I'll really listen, this time."

"She doesn't fully understand me. I'll concede that. You're absolutely right. But you see, she accepts. She accepts and loves. You don't accept. If there's something you don't like, you change it, or try like hell to change it. I don't know," he said frustrated with his inability to nail it down. "There's a warmth in her you don't have, you never had. It's a live-and-let-live warmth. She says 'I love you and I accept you,' period. You don't. With you it's tolerating without appreciating. Like a stern mother with a backward child. Like with me. With you it's 'oh that silly husband of mine. Yes that's him. He did it. But, what can you do with him, the big dumb dope. The lovable dope.' It's the supreme put-down, Joan, to be laughingly tolerated. I feel (and he searched the floors and ceiling in vain) less than the man I know I am, with you. I don't like it, because I'm not that schlemiel at all, not the standard Jewish eunuch. Lately I feel the need to be self-protective with you for fear of being sawed off at the end of the limb. And you know damned well, when you operate, you can really saw someone off at the ankles, at the knees, at the testicles."

"Then I'm a real Jewish bitch. Is that what you mean?"

"I didn't mean that one hundred percent derogatorily, although you are, and you do, and we both know it. At least face that. Besides, there's nothing to be ashamed of. You do it quite skillfully, and usually very nicely, and for a good cause. I used to go to meetings, remember?"

"Now who's sniping at whom?" she asked.

"We're flying off at tangents. Let me spread it out," he said. "With her I'm open, naked, utterly without guile. (She snickered and he regretted his choice of words.) It's a clean feeling. She doesn't store up my words in a data bank and hit me with them later, when it's advantageous to do so."

"Like I do."

"Like you do."

"Joan, with her I'm not afraid of being mousetrapped, or had, or out on a limb. She's not possessive, materialistic, jealous, vindictive, class-conscious, domineering. . . ."

"Like I am."

"Yes, sometimes. She's the damn freest person I know. She's made me interested in people again. As people, not as patients. Not as sick, disturbed bodies but as someone to reach out and

93

hold." He began to feel foolish saying these things to her. He blocked out how foolish she probably thought he sounded and decided that he would finish.

"You don't know what it means, you just don't know what it means to me not to be told that I'm wearing the wrong shirt for my pants. Or that I'm ordering the wrong dish at the restaurant."

"Big deal," she said.

"To me it is. It counts a great deal. I may become a person yet. Joan, I know it may sound silly. Many things people our age do to alter forty years of mistakes do seem silly. But they're necessary, even life-saving. That's how I feel. If nothing else, you must respect that."

His voice, at first weak and tinny because of the hostile audience grew sure and firm. "Hell, I certainly don't want to hurt you and those two monsters we live with (a dash of smile) but it's fact now, I won't back away from it."

"You keep saying that little disclaimer, about not wanting to hurt us, but that's dishonest. You're dishonest," she said nonchalantly, not as anger, but as simple fact.

"You're not telling the whole truth, sweetheart," she said and didn't really mean "sweetheart." "I know too much about you, Cal. You've been searching for years for something. A chance, maybe, to explore one little stream. I gave you plenty of room in that direction, sweetheart, but it can't be one hundred percent. You live in a house with people."

He shrugged. Why did she keep after him with guilt like it was a suit he had made to order and refused to claim?

"I take it from our heart to heart that you don't plan to end your relationship soon?"

"Joan, how many times do I have to say it? Should I have it tattooed across my forehead? Should I have a sweatshirt made saying, 'I won't give her up'? What shall I do?"

"What do you plan to do, then," she asked.

"Well, I don't want a divorce. This may come as a shock to you after all the shooting on both sides, but I think, no, I know for certain, I still love you."

"You just said you loved her."

"I know what I said."

Shocked. "And you love me?"

94

"Yes."

Horrified. "You love us both?"

"Yes."

Amused. "Oh, you're crazy, Cal, you're absolutely crazy."

*He* wasn't amused. "You know damn well I'm as sane as you are. I just happen to love two different women. Different women for different reasons. I thought about it for a very long time. There are parts of my life with you, there are parts of you that I love very much. I want to hold on to that."

"Cal, I don't come in parts like a chicken."

They stared at each other. She gave in first. "You're serious. You're really serious. You want to eat your cake and have it, too."

"Please stop throwing little pieces of folk wisdom at me like they were snowballs. That's not going to stop me, really."

Shocked, horrified, amused, she said, "You want us both, both of us. You want me when you want me and her when you want her, too." She threw her hands up to the ceiling asking for divine intervention or at least guidance.

"You're repeating yourself unnecessarily, Joan."

"Well, understand, you Mormon, I never expected *that*. I'll have to give it some thought. A lot of thought," she added ponderously. For the first time since the sun set she was totally in the dark. Then Joan asked, "Who is she, this miserable bitch," and smiling about it to defuse his anger she tacked on, "just being funny, Cal. Don't get defensive. After all, I think, Dr. B., I have the right to know, don't you? Don't worry, the shock is over. I'm not going to run out and shoot her, or anything. We don't do those things today. You know very well that I'm a proper Jewish Queen," she smirked.

He thought about it. Certainly it would be foolish to withhold what she could easily find out for herself.

"Okay, Joan," he said. "I'm not ashamed of her or the affair. The only reason I haven't gotten into that is I didn't want her badgered or harassed. She lives in town and you do have a bit of influence. You can hassle. She doesn't need the hassle."

"I said I wouldn't, Cal. I just want to know for reasons of pride. C'mon, Cal, who is she? Do I know her?"

"No, you don't know her. Or maybe you do. She's Victor's wife."

"Who's Victor?"

"Victor Bruno, the gardener."

"The gardener's wife?" She was back to shock again.

"Oh, I don't believe it. You are too much, Cal. I swear you are too much. You finally decide to take a mistress and it's some low Italian. You really have no class. I'm hurt. I'm absolutely mortified. How could you do this to me?"

"Joan, you don't know her." He was burning slowly. "How could you be so definite?"

"You know, I think I'm getting upset again." She forced out a twisted laugh. "At first I was only hurt and angry, but now I'm downright mortified. You bunny hop from me and to some dumb Italian's wife. Where's that lofty patrician air of yours? You dislike breaking bread with some of my friends because you say their husbands are lowlifes, yet there you are fooling around with some pasta eating mamma mia. Oh, I just hope you haven't signed your real name to any motel register. I'd die of shame."

The phone rang separating the warring parties. It was for Cal. He answered, paused, then advised the caller to discontinue his medication. He would call the pharmacy and prescribe a more suitable drug. That done he re-entered the room.

"I know what you're trying to do, my fine indignant friend," he said, plumping down in the rocker again. "But it won't work. So help me, it won't work. You're not going to cheapen me. Or her. Tessa is a fine, intelligent woman and all your snobbery and phony indignation won't change that fact. Not one iota."

He poured himself the last of the tea knowing that she watched everything, the way a cat watches a nest of baby birds. He closed ranks. Nothing had changed and he was at the point of refusing to accept any more punishment. He thought of packing and finding a room.

Joan, speed reader of signals reversed gears. "Let me make another pitcher of tea and we'll talk some more. Is that alright, Cal?" Can we talk some more about it?" She was being cutesy, he felt. The lady enjoyed her shifting moods. It shattered and confused the enemy. But Joan never really thought of Cal as the enemy, just the surrogate enemy. It was that Italian's wife she was gunning for.

"If it's to take more abuse then forget it. It's been a rough day.

96

On both sides," he said wearily. "I've plenty of records to update."

"No, no," she cooed. "Please, I was hurt. You don't blame me, do you? I struck out at you to hurt back. Understand, please. We'll talk sensibly about you and her and me. See if there's something meaningful, salvageable in all this. Something left to hold on to. . . ."

What Joan meant by "meaningful" was the ammunition necessary to win the war she had by no means conceded. There would be a fight. There would have to be a fight, she thought. That was something she knew right away. You just don't turn the keys of your life over to a gardener's wife.

If she only were not so afraid of Cal. His very openness melted her rockets and heavy hardware. His very ability to walk on water and say "no" softly, blunted whatever she could send his way. Damn him! If he were only a normal stupid, devious man. But then she would have fewer functions if he were. Round and round in a circle she went and it was beginning to unnerve her. If all the scheming was for Cal, and she thought it was, very often, then why was she preparing an indirect assault against him through that Bruno slut? Of course, to save him from himself, for himself, for her, for the world. Confusing. She would have to return to it later.

She moved closer to him while basking in the exuding warmth of her day at the beach. She still felt very attractive. How could this dear, child-like fool settle for so much less? Men must really have keepers. That was the crux of it.

If Mrs. Bruno was like Mr. Bruno it would be no contest. She would send the tramp for first aid after a few cutting remarks. Back to the compost heap with her and Cal would return to the fold hurting but whole. Until the next one, perhaps. A small cloud on the horizon. But, first things first.

"We won't talk about silly things, about what she looks like. If you feel for her, I take it she's all there. Or what she does for you that I can't or don't. Self-punishment is not my game. Besides you spelled out my deficiencies already."

"You just asked, you know that, of course. I have the text of your first principles. Let's get down to basics," he said curtly. "I won't leave unless you make me leave. I'm comfortable here, with

97

you, with the Bitch and with the Nazi. I told you I loved you. It wasn't a handout. I meant it."

"I suppose she's told her husband, too," Joan asked matter-of-factly.

"I really don't know, but I imagine so. She's very honest."

"Honest? How honest can she be? She's sleeping with someone else's husband."

"Back off, Joan, don't draw me into that, again," he warned. "You said talk and I took you at your word. This isn't talk. It's badgering."

"She's got children, I suppose? Lots of children?"

"She's got two boys. Why?"

"Because I'm trying to picture her in my mind. If I know her better, I know you better. That side of you, you say, is a stranger to me. Maybe then I can discover why you went off the deep end."

"That's ass-ways, Joan. You know me as well as you ever can."

"Obviously not well enough, Cal. But I'm not going to try and throw myself at your feet and ask for another chance. I don't live that way."

And they talked for hours, ending in the same spot. She gave up badgering and invective as tools seeing the boomerang effect it had. Something of Tessa was learned by her prying. A college-educated girl, almost, with two children and an ox of a husband, yet a solid basic girl with passion for Cal and pity for the ox. And probably she never told her husband that she was carrying on with Dr. Bernstein.

Her next move was clear. She would work on the lady in question and end it all that way. Cal need never know. Her spirit quickened at the thought of a new project and she was buoyed by the knowledge that it was a very important one. She was eager to begin.

"Cal, I'm tired," she said, full of life and adrenaline. "There's nothing more to do now. Maybe time will straighten this out. I'll try to think positively. I swear I will. Give me time."

He hoped she meant her overly rational words. It was too late in their combined histories for shenanigans. Somehow their words tonight, even the ones with booby traps and thorns, gave him a greater sense of freedom than he had ever known before. He sat until three the next morning filled with admiration, awe, disgust, and ten forms of wonderment at those adulterers who keep their affairs from their wives, while he backtracked the last three month's *New York State Journal of Medicine*.

Near the center of Cedarhurst, at the apex of the triangle formed by its two main streets stood a Burger King. This omnipotent sovereign, innkeeper to free men, had the cheek to invade the Kingdom of the Five Towns. A kingdom of artsy-craftsy boutiques that sold solid gold pillboxes for three hundred dollars, of shoe stores whose cheapest pair cost a Ulysses S. Grant and of dining establishments where a small repast for two required a knight's ransom.

Fearlessly this King of the Burgers had built his bastion and raised his pennant within eyeshot of many shops flying the regal colors of Gucci, Calvin Klein, Estee Lauder. Inside were tons of chopped beef interlaced with chemicals developed by the alchemists, gallons of catsup prepared in jugs like reserve plasma, infinite rounds of anemic looking french fries, to bedazzle both serf and nobleman so that each might have it their way. It was a terrible eyesore to the natives.

As in many a fairy tale, this black-hearted villain had bewitched many of the subjects of the Kingdom of the Five Towns, as Joan discovered waiting impatiently in its large, crowded parking lot. Teen-aged boys and girls, dressed in the nouveau-poor uniform of their generation, faded jeans and workshirt, entered and left the area, with regularity.

Disgusting, she thought. They all look the same, like little dirty dolls. She looked at her watch, the Mercedes clock dead from the day she bought the car, and squirmed uncomfortably. It was hell for her to arrive early and be made to wait in an area so degrading for a confrontation with someone below her standards. And her timing might be off. That delicate psychological advantage she was used to might melt in the early August noon. This was not the best place to handle it. She smiled. No matter, she would handle it well.

A little detective work and she knew that Mrs. Bruno and her two boys would be here this day, this hour. The fact was one of many she had gathered during the week. She even knew that Tessa's boys were B students in school with excellent records in behavior and attendance.

"One o'clock," she muttered and checked the dryness of her armpits. That tramp always comes here around one every Tuesday. Certainly tells a lot about her, the inconsistency of the woman. Oh, that foolish man, she thought.

Workmen with tank tops sat on the creosote poles around the parking lot and ate, drank, and talked. Cars dashed in and out. People floated past her view like kites. When the hell is she going to feed those kids?

Her thought was just completed when a dark green Ford of questionable age entered from the "exit only" driveway of the lot. The driver parked in the section clearly reserved for the manager, the car's right wheels covering the yellow borderline between the next spot. As if on cue three of the doors flew open. Stephen and Victor junior jumped out. Their mother emerged more slowly watching the boys.

Joan, slammed her door, stiffened her spine and approached Tessa. She managed a noncommittal smile.

"You're Tessa Bruno," she asked almost timidly at the tail end of the smile.

"Yes I am," she replied.

"Well, Mrs. Bruno," Joan said, "we have something in common."

"I can't imagine what," Tessa answered.

"Calvin Bernstein," his wife quickly shot back.

Tessa's face lit up like a Jack o' Lantern on a dark night. The situation assessed she decided to wing it at her own pace.

"Say," she said, "he's my doctor, too." Tessa held her look of innocence as if she were posing for pictures.

101

Joan made absolutely certain that their eyes met when she replied "He's not my doctor, he's my husband."

"Oh," Tessa replied. "Say, listen, will you excuse me a minute?"

Without waiting for a reply she fished a five-dollar bill, the only bill, from her shirt pocket, a man's white dress shirt with the sleeves rolled up and with tails that flapped when the breeze caught it, and handed it to the older of the two boys standing quietly in her shadow.

"Stephen you feed yourself and your brother. Go ahead, you know what to get. Start without me. Go on, what are you waiting for? I'll be in in a few minutes." The boys finally moved off: "No junk now. Just the cheeseburgers and the coke. And put the change in your pocket, Stephen. Don't leave it on the tray like last time," she shouted after them.

Joan, too, watched them go, slim, dark, quiet boys, with the same deep lovely eyes, black curly hair, and olive skin. They looked so easy to raise.

"Your car or mine, Mrs. Bernstein?" Tessa asked when she saw the boys through the glass doors, each with a tray in his dark little hands.

"Mine, if you don't mind. I'm wearing white. And cleaning bills are so damned high."

"Okay with me," Tessa replied with a soft shrug of the shoulders. A deceptive softness, as she had no intention of allowing the fancy lady to sneak that one past her, "but I may soil your upholstery."

Joan looked at her for a few seconds without blinking, and headed for her car, Tessa alongside her. They both took time after seated for first impressions. Joan was pleasantly disgusted. This female's dressed hideously. Those dungarees . . . early Salvation Army. I'm sure she's got pasta stains on them and probably her panties are two days old, she thought. But it was the shirt that stuck in her mind. The middle button was open or missing. Mrs. Bruno's breast, unsupported by bra and floating free was quite visible from Joan's seat opposite her.

Shaped like a long, low fishhook, Joan scoffed to herself. She was deliriously piling up points. Low, then slightly tilted upwards at the base. They should be higher and firmer for a woman in

102

her thirties. Probably from years of no bra, or from too much handling. She was happier with the latter alternative.

Tessa still had the boys under surveillance. Finally, when she saw that they were seated by the window, when they pressed their noses to the glass and made funny faces at her, she was ready. She turned to Joan, breast-gazing, and said calmly, "I'll listen to whatever you have to say. I'll listen politely if you talk politely. Just two things. Don't get hysterical and don't talk down to me. Okay?"

Joan arched her back up against the soft real leather of the seats. "I've never been hysterical in my life. I'm certainly not going to start now. And I won't talk down to you. In spite of what you may think, Mrs. Bruno, I'm not that way at all. Don't be fooled by appearances."

Like you are, Tessa thought but didn't say. She would rather all Mrs. Bernstein's cards were on the table before she played her own hand.

Joan paused and surveyed the enemy again. The woman was sort of attractive, not striking, not the drop dead flashy young thing that a forty-five year old man goes A.W.O.L for, but attractive in a non-Jewish sort of a way. Despite the absence of makeup, despite the handicap of clothes that could get you locked up for vagrancy. Tall. About as tall as the Bitch. Probably, no surely, the girl has little class, no finesse. Just a low class, flash in the pan, Italian housewife. Slovenly, undisciplined. She was disappointed in her husband. What a damned fool Cal is, she thought adding up the columns. Her spirits began mountain climbing. All she has is about ten years on me, if that, and a one-night-stand prettiness. Not too much to overcome. She felt worlds better. From the driver's seat she would be magnanimous, even chummy.

"Frankly, Mrs. Bruno," she began, "you really don't *look* much like a husband stealer." Joan wondered if she appeared academic enough, anemic enough, while trying to silently waste her enemy. "You look more like a nice average housewife." In case the shiksa didn't know it, she was trying to bury her with non-hysteria. She could play the game Tessa Bruno's way and beat her brains in, too.

Tessa nodded as if Joan had uncovered a rare and precious

truth. "And you don't look at all like the type of woman who lets anything go, Mrs. Bernstein," she returned. "So I guess we're both not really what we seem to be. Or maybe we're both not very perceptive. But you'll have to forgive me. I haven't had much experience with people like yourself, so I can hardly judge."

It caught her unprepared. Joan felt as if her face had been slapped. Surprisingly the thrust exhilarated rather than insulted her. Was it beginner's luck, this tit for tat? She really should have felt insulted by this snot who didn't even wear eyeshadow. Joan took her eyes from Tessa and looked at her slacks. The crease was still there, despite the humidity. Smoothing them bought her some time. Perhaps she was sitting too close to the girl to really be effective.

Tessa waved again to the boys whose eyes were barely visible over the tall plastic containers of Coke. So far so good. No blood, no tears, not an insult that had a bite to it, yet.

Tasting frustration, too proud to spit it out and too smart to swallow it, Joan said, "Let's not go astray, Mrs. Bruno. I'm here for just one thing, one important thing. I want you to stop seeing my husband. He's my husband, Mrs. Bruno, he's my husband. I want you to break it off for everyone's benefit."

"No," Tessa answered with the same tone of voice used earlier when a door-to-door salesman had attempted to sell her Fuller brush products.

Seconds of silence that seemed to stretch to the moon.

"What do you mean no? you just can't say no, period. You might say, 'no I love him,' or 'no, we need each other,' or some such patented nonsense. I'm sorry, I just can't accept a flat no."

"Mrs. Bernstein, it's that simple. I'm not having open house on my soul today. The message is the same if I just say no, or no with explanation."

"Wait, wait," Joan said, "don't get huffy. This was not supposed to be a one question meeting. I mean, this is a very complex thing. We're not exchanging license numbers after a dented fender. You *are* sleeping with my husband. I have the right, I think I have the right to bleed a little. No? Don't you think I'm part of the scene, here. Or just scenery? I'm the third part of this . . . triangle or quadrangle."

"Mrs. Bernstein," Tessa said, feeling more at ease now, "I'm damn aware of you and your . . . situation and me and my situation. Regardless of what you might think I don't go around hopping in and out of beds, destroying marriages left and right. I'm no husband thief."

"I didn't say you did, Mrs. Bruno."

"You didn't have to, Mrs. Bernstein, it's written all over you in capital letters."

"Like hell it is," Joan said, then reconsidered.

"Well, you must understand that, if it's so, it's a natural response," she said. "After all, I've been rejected, for a younger woman. It's very difficult."

"That's not entirely true, Mrs. Bernstein, and you know it. It's not the classic situation. It's more complicated than that. If you want to discuss it on that level, fine. If not, I can go home and see the same simplicities on television. *Edge of Night* or *All My Children* has plenty of garbage like that."

For the first time since she entered the Mercedes she felt at home. She was over the hurdle with the haughty, cold woman. To her surprise Joan was less and more than what she, at first, seemed to be.

"Now you know damned well, that neither Cal nor I, intend to ask for a divorce. For different reasons, sure, but we don't want to change a thing. But if you want to feel classically injured go right ahead. It'll cloud matters, Mrs. Bernstein, but only for you."

"You want to share him with me, Mrs. Bruno? Is that what you want?" Joan asked.

"Just the part of him you're not using, Mrs. Bernstein. You're a smart woman. You must know that a good part of the man is just sitting there, wasting away. Really, what Cal and I have doesn't touch you in the least," Tessa said. She felt as if she were back student-teaching the handicapped, going over what must be clear as crystal to anyone who just listened.

"And your husband. Does he know? Does he approve?"

"Victor knows. I told him."

"And how does he like sharing?"

Tessa looked at her, then grinned. "Not that I'm required to tell you, but he cursed me for a few hours, called me every name he could think of. He's got two sets, English and Italian. Even took a few swings at me. . . . Then he begged me to call it off, too. But I told him basically what I told you. No dice." She paused. "It ends when Cal and I decide to end it. So Victor accepts it now because there is no alternative. You do the same, Mrs. Bernstein. You'll save yourself a lot of wasted energy."

"What kind of man is Victor, to back off so easily?" Joan asked.

"That's none of your business," Tessa snapped. "A very sick man, a very helpless man who needs me. And I'll take care of him. There's never been any doubt of that. Now at least, we have a more equitable relationship."

"Equitable relationship." Joan would have to piece that together. Tessa kept popping out of the pigeon hole Joan stuck her in. Joan was puzzled. She knew Victor only as a gardener, a giant bear of a boy, with smouldering eyes. That big bully look should have been enough to send the shiksa back to her pots and pans. Not this shiksa, though. She was spunky. She could have been used for one of Joan's committees.

"That's all very nice," Joan said as she slowly caressed the tan arm rest. "But you must realize, Mrs. Bruno, that I am very influential in this area. Quite conceivably, now listen to me carefully, I'm not saying that I would, mind you, but I *could,* make life very difficult for you and your husband. He has a business here. A good business. And a reputation, also good. He's very well liked. All my friends say so. Can you imagine, think now, can you just imagine what it would do to his business if somehow the word got around to these Five Town queens that their gardener's wife has been fooling around with one of the kings? Can you picture it? Why they would pull up their drawbridges and freeze out poor Victor so fast you could catch a cold in the draft. So that, Mrs. Bruno, is something to consider. A vague possibility, sure, but not one to completely dismiss." She stood back and waited for the body to fall.

"Do you often do that?" Tessa asked her calmly.

"Do what?"

"Accomplish one thing by threatening *not* to do another? I guess it's a pretty good trick when it works. I guess one of the beauties of having power is getting things done, quite a lot of things done, just by mentioning that you have this power."

"I didn't threaten you, Mrs. Bruno. I simply stated what might happen, not what will happen. It's not the same thing. I don't have to pussyfoot."

"I got your poison pen message and it's the wrong way, I swear, Mrs. Bernstein, trying to zap me like that. I'm apolitical on all levels and I really don't know or care how deep you are into this community. I just smile at the neighbors and mind my own business. Maybe it's not the ideal way, but it takes me to sundown. But consider this: If word did get around, somehow, that the lowly gardener's wife and the influential lady's husband were fooling around, that wouldn't put any stars in the influential lady's crown, either. Now would it? It might even hurt Cal's practice, too. Seems to me we have a sword with two sharp edges. You should have figured it out yourself, that's kindergarten stuff for you. I'm just a dumb shiksa and even I figured that one out."

It was funny, Joan thought, here is Tessa, the three little pigs in her brick house and there she was, the big bad wolf and she was all tuckered out. But she had to plunge on, she just wouldn't walk away with nothing. There had to be a way. Nobody is invulnerable.

"Forget my threats Mrs. Bruno. please. I made a mistake.

"Now," she announced, her slate wiped clean of blunders, her hands folded in her lap, "let's talk like sensible people, you and I, instead of his silly dueling." Joan was running out of ideas. It had to work. She studied the younger woman with renewed interest. Her hair, rich, black and uncoiffed, curled nicely at the nape. Joan wondered where she had learned her smarts. Then she gave up wondering because there was work to do.

"Tell me honestly, what does Cal do for you?" she asked. "No, I don't mean sexually or anything like that. I'm not interested in dirt. I mean what does he do for you financially? We can talk about that. Maybe, I can match or beat your present arrangement. I'm not a poor woman, and we. . . ."

"Do you mind if I smoke here?" Tessa asked taking a Marlboro from her shirt pocket.

"Go ahead, go ahead," Joan replied, annoyed that Tessa thought so little of the offer as to cut the string on her balloon and let it float away.

Tessa lit up, inhaled gently and exhaled in slow motion. Joan

107

was not optimistic. Tessa smiled a knowing smile then laughed in small spasms. Stephen and Victor smiled back thinking she meant it for them.

"You're a million miles away, Mrs. Bernstein," she began. She searched for an ashtray. Joan came to her aid. "I love Cal. I love him for himself. For me, that's the whole package. Also I'm not into things. I don't own much; I don't want to. It bores me. And even if I was an acquisitive soul I wouldn't accept anything from Cal. The man is a sweet prize in himself. Maybe you know that, maybe you don't. But get off that subject or talk to yourself. Your lousy money doesn't interest me."

Joan was disgusted with herself. Not only because of the insults but because of her own inability to read the gardener's wife. It was humiliating. She reached out and touched Tessa, softly, with her long manicured fingers.

"Again I'm sorry, Mrs. Bruno . . . Tessa. I don't usually make so many mistakes at one time. It's not like me." Joan then stared out the tinted window.

"Sorry to make mistakes in judgment or to try and buy someone?"

"Both."

"Okay," Tessa answered, "I guess I can understand. It's not every day a woman has to face this kind of thing."

A little charity from a husband stealer. Joan was gratified for this pat on the head. Amazed at herself for lapping up crumbs she watched the two boys bounce out of the wide glass doors laughingly. Tessa's eyes caught fire and burned with a steady glow when she saw them. She looked at Joan.

"If there's nothing more. . . ."

"No, there's nothing more," Joan smiled, as though from a sick bed. "That does it. I've seen you and I talked to you. That's what I wanted." She squeezed Tessa's hand. "Thank you so much."

Tessa could not think of a reply and left.

When they were all in the car Stephen thrust his face forward as his mother cleaned it with a Wash'n Dri.

"Who was that lady in the funny car?" Victor junior asked.

"Oh, just some lady who asked for a favor, puppy dog."

"And what did you say?"

"I told her nothing doing."

"Oh," Victor junior replied, then a thought held him. "Weren't you scared when you told her that, mommie?"

"Why should I be scared?" she toyed with him.

"Because she looks real mean, mommie, like my principal."

"I was scared shit, *goomba*, but she didn't know it from me. I hid it in my tree house."

After they had gone, Joan bought a cheeseburger to go and a large Diet Pepsi. It was her first trip into enemy territory, but she was famished and wanted to think out Mrs. Bruno and her steel wall while both were fresh in her mind. She ate in the car, unmindful of the curious glances from teenagers and laborers, who saw humor in the contrast of a fancy lady eating a dollar burger in a ten thousand dollar set of wheels.

It was surprisingly good and the Pepsi, too, since it also helped wash down that tart Italian tomato with the curly black hair. She's not bad at all. Very zesty and full of life. If Cal hadn't gotten to her first, I would have liked her for a friend. She chewed on a piece of ice. If the Nazi brought one home like that I wouldn't go to pieces. She didn't bat an eyelash at anything I said. She didn't lose her temper, blush, cry, or stick herself out at the end of a limb. And she's not a tomato. More like a cool cucumber.

What to do? Destroying her is out. It simply won't work because I can't do it. Well, I'm not going to go back to Cal with a her-or-me ultimatum. That's too emotional and too risky. Suppose he chooses her? I can't afford any more mistakes. God, I'm making them like crazy, of late. Suppose he chooses her? I'd die. To just give him up, to give up all this, all I've worked for for twenty years. No skinny shiksa with a cutie-pie haircut is going to knock me out of the box. I don't abdicate so easily. I've studied with him, stayed up nights waiting for him to come home during the lean years when he made house calls to drunks. Having babies alone while he was out giving enemas and delivering someone else's kids. And I'm not throwing it all away because he wants another shot at adolescence.

She dabbed at the sides of her mouth. Plans and ideas were coming in from all angles. Tessa won't make trouble, she thought. She said so and I believe her. She's honest. . . . Cal was right. Funny what honesty has become. Cal might be a big problem. Soft-headed Cal. I just hope his damned conscience doesn't force him into making a choice. To try and make an honest woman of her. She's honest enough for me. He's so susceptible to attacks of conscience. At his age it could be fatal . . . to us both.

The mirror showed her that she could use some freshening up. She went to work on it. If only he were more pliable. I'm afraid of him. I admit it. He's the only person in my whole life I can't mold. I trust him, fear him more than God. Oh damn it. He's so stinkingly honest with himself, with others. Hell, I only made it half way. I'm only honest with myself. That's enough for me.

Cal and Victor. Two victims. Not Tessa, she's a survivor. She may hate what she survived into but she survives. Not like me. I love it. I wallow in the scheming, the phone calls, the backbiting, the crises.

She sat a moment longer, idling her own internal motor. It was good taking inventory.

Okay, she continued, suppose I do swing it and he says, "You win, the party's over. I'll tell Tessa we're through." Does it mean that the patient's cured just because I brought down his temperature with a cold bath? Hell, no. God, no. I'd only have to face the damned enemy again. I know it. Another affair and another parking lot confrontation. And they'll get younger and younger. Tessa lets him alone. And best of all she's locked into a husband and kids by choice, by her own choice. That's good. So what am I so upset about? Considering everything, I'm pretty well off.

Joan laughed out loud. For the first time all day she felt pleasure.

If I had to hand-pick a mistress for Cal I couldn't find a better one than Tessa Bruno. She's no threat to me at all, except in the bedroom. And that doesn't mean a hell of a lot anymore either. Not enough to pull the whole house down. She's no schemer. No chance of her taking him lock, stock, and estate. Perhaps she's even doing me a favor. Providing a kind of immunity against a more virulent strain. Tessa is my vaccine. Tessa, I love you.

The path ahead was clear. The doubts and the stomach-sickening fears that had plagued her since Cal dropped the bomb vanished instantly. Let him play house with her as long as he likes. Just as long as I'm the one he comes home to. It's as simple as that.

110

The ice at the bottom of the container had changed to water. She drank it quickly and filled the cup with her napkin, stained with catsup and grease. As she opened the door to throw the garbage into the large white drum at the far end of the parking lot she noticed a catsup stain on her slacks.

"Damn, damn," she sang in a low voice, and changed her mind about crossing the lot on foot. She did not want to be seen messy. Yet stained slacks aside, she considered the day a great success. It was just a simple matter of intelligence, organization, and communication. It works every time.

8

Massive doses of people are no cure for anything. They get in the way, steal your air, muck things up. Wherever you turn you touch noses, smell garlic on their morning breath, see how badly they need a shave, a bath, total facial restoration. Their body odor is devastating.

Cal weighed the pro's and con's of people, as the packed ferry to Liberty Island began its journey. He was locked helplessly between a brillo-haired Puerto Rican boy who drank something from a brown paper bag that made him belch and a huge, handsome Negro woman who wore purple lipstick and a white blouse that promised to burst its buttons at any moment. Tessa stood, not ten feet away, in white sailor pants and a Mickey Mouse tee shirt, clutching the fire extinguisher, as if someone were trying to take it from her as the skyline slowly moved away. Tessa looked, if not entirely comfortable on the boat, then at least well acclimated. The smell of things rotting in the water and mulching in armpits had not insulted her nose and nervous system. She looked cool and highpocketed and serene though her sailor pants already had grease stains on them. The stains would have already spoiled the day for Joan, he thought. Tessa ducked down and saw the Statue of Liberty standing unperturbed between Staten Island and Brooklyn. Mrs. Bruno, just one of the crowd, taller, prettier, but still one of them and not terribly concerned about the very noticeable grease stains. While he felt exhausted, defeated, and as conspicuous as a gorilla wearing red gloves.

He had begun his essay on the people, much earlier as he nervously sought a parking spot at the very tip of Manhattan. Even the pigeons were too fatigued by the July heat to strut for peanuts from the bench sitters. By eleven it was close to ninety degrees. Cal grumbled.

"Never again, goddamn it," he swore as he and Tessa prowled the financial district looking for a small patch of free ground in which to dump the Electra. Finally they found a spot.

Tessa stuck her tongue out at him and said, "See? Calm down, cuckoo. We got a spot. It's a good omen. Now you close your eyes and count to ten and think nice things and *then* we'll head down to the docks. C'mon, c'mon. Do it."

"You think I'm one of your injured birds that you have to jazz me up like that?"

"Right now you're pretty neurotic, mister, over finding a parking spot. Big deal. So we cruise a little. I'm not such bad company, am I?"

He smiled and squeezed her hand and that sent his temporary insanity free floating in space. But then they stepped out of the cool car and he swore never again, again. The heat suddenly drenched him and he thought of other places they might have visited. They could have gone to Montauk with its coarse, brown sand and life-restoring breezes imported straight from Portugal. There was Lloyd's Neck, in the Sound north of Huntington. That would have been fine. They would have buried beer cans in the sand, planted a marker and walked from Target Rock west to Lloyd's Point. Instead they chose the center of hell. It had suddenly become important to him to see Ellis Island, slightly behind and to the right of Liberty, important for reasons that had to do with his origins and with the woman who was with him.

They held hands and she swung them freely, taunting him to follow suite as they disembarked in front of the enormous green lady with her tiara of spikes, who looked disinterestedly out beyond the ocean. The island was peppered with fresh garbage. It overflowed the steel meshed receptacles and littered the grass like daisies. It was as if the elevated temperature had caused the beer cans and plastic plates to multiply like bacteria.

"Hon, I'm sorry I brought you here. It's a horrible mistake and this is one lousy place. God, it stinks to high heaven."

She patted their combined hands with her free one. "Well, you

113

just think cool," she said with confidence. She looked as if the chilly winds of October were freely circulating inside her clothing. They walked to the base of the statue and looked up. It was awesome and inspiring despite the assorted feast of refuse that was left on the lady's pedestal. Someone said that you had to walk the last part of the way to see out of the statue's eyes. Cal jammed his hands into the pockets of his light gray slacks and poutingly said not me. And Tessa acquiesced good-humoredly with a shrug.

"Okay sport. You save your energy for where it really counts," she laughed. Making jokes that defuse was a house specialty of hers.

She sat on his lap on a bench that was not really well shaded by the maple tree close by. They were content to sit and watch the young Negro and Puerto Rican families (it seemed that they were the only ones still interested in American history) stroll the small paths that ran the island. Cal, as yet, was not far enough away from his discomfort to talk rationally to her and he knew it. And until he was, he would content himself with touching her, supporting her, and being within the sound of her voice. It had become quite clear to him that he had always known her and loved her. What was cloudy was the external fact that "always" had only begun in May. Her body pressed down on his genitals. It was magnificent to be in such a state of confusion. He could recommend it to all his patients.

They waited until one for the little dingy to take them to Ellis Island. Three other couples, elderly and time-twisted, sat in the small boat with them. En route they filled out questionnaires handed to them by uniformed National Park Service employees who had jurisdiction over the island. Tessa and Cal penciled in the dates (approximated) of when their parents or grandparents passed through this very small funnel. It was like a game, and Cal was feeling better already. She sensed it and it made her feel better, too. The small boat circled the island and landed at the back door on the Staten Island side. Ellis was being restored as a national monument and only the landing area on the opposite side had been shored up. The pier was rotted, its metal parts rusted to a dull orange. Clumps of reddish-brown steel grew out of the water in patterns resembling modern sculpture. A makeshift wooden path was built from dock to firm ground. Evidence of carpentry

114

was visible wherever they walked. The new vied with decay and neglect for control of the small island.

They held hands again and fell behind the three other couples who were soon swapping emotional memories of their own arrival here half a century ago. The years blew away as they relived experiences as immigrants when hundreds of thousands of European unwanteds, came in steerage aboard jam-packed steamers. The feeling of overwhelming helplessness re-surfaced in them even though fifty years of time had coated that memory with others softer and sweeter.

When Tessa began to look sad and far away, he knew it was time to end his own selfish pouting over humidity, smelly humans, and luxuriating garbage. It was out of love and shame that he cupped her shoulders and drew her close. She smelled of baby powder and roses.

"Funny," he said, "how we lost our old differences starting here, when we Americanized, then went on to pick up new ones."

She looked at him and wondered what he meant.

"My grandfather was a Rabbi in Poland with an enormous beard, a beaver hat, and a wife who wore a wig so that no other man might find her attractive. He lived by a discipline that's just barely understandable today. And yours, Tessa, what was yours? You never told me about your family. Who touched home plate here?"

She linked arms with him and they slowly ambled toward the end of the New York City side dock.

"Well, my grandfather never made it here. I never saw him. He died where he was born, in Reggio di Calabria. Do you know where that is?"

He shrugged.

"That's near the toe of the Italian boot. Real tough customers come from Reggio di Calabria. The Calabrese are knife wielders, with vicious tempers on short leashes. Grandpa, I was told by my father, when he had his rare moments of civility toward me, was a fisherman."

Cal nodded his contemplative nod. "So we have a Rabbi and a fisherman at the beginning. And now finally my family and your family. Different as hell, still. Even with the Fonz and the com-

115

puter. Miles apart. First we become assimilated, then we grow re-alienated."

"You are not talking about us, you and me, Cal. We'll never become alienated. Never." She sat on a bench, at water's edge, and immediately pulled him down beside her. While looking at the small clumps of weeds she turned her white tennis shoes in toward each other. It gave her a sad, hurt, little girl look that touched Cal deeply.

"Even if we ever call it quits we'll never be alienated, Cal. How could that be? We're so compatible. And sensible. How could you say that?"

"I wasn't talking about us two mavericks. I was just generalizing, waxing lyrical about the melting pot thing and what America was supposed to be. And is. We're in a special category. We don't follow demographic patterns and social trends. We operate in our own vacuum." He began building with his hands. "We have this fantastic castle on top of a high mountain, insulated, from germs and people which sometimes are the same thing." There was a small sad undercurrent that ran through the stream of his words.

Tessa picked out that sad note. "I think the heat is making you morose and lyrical at the same time. Don't be morose. Come, let's join the other couples or they'll think that we're making a baby someplace." She brightened. "I'm happy, very happy. And this, I want you to know, from a broad who almost died of starvation from lack of happiness. Come," and she extended her hand. "We'll walk and because I'm so happy and so liberated I'll tell you about a girl who used to be me." Something in her said that it was still too painful to retch up, but something else told her that the time was now or never.

"My father. . . . It's so unpleasant (she wavered, almost reconsidered, then plunged on), so damned awful, to talk about him."

"Then don't, Tessa. It doesn't change a thing."

"No, I want to. You've seen me with my clothes off. You've seen me in heat. You *think* you've seen me at my nakedest, but you haven't. You haven't. And you should. You're a crystal-clear man. I'm sure I know you. No dark corners in your life. I'll bet you've never even masturbated."

116

Should he feel belittled not having a dark side in her eyes? He wondered. "Tessa, I'm no angel, and I do have skeletons. Some day I'll tell you about the pettiness and the viciousness and the . . ."

She decimated his references with a wave of her hand. "No, not that way. You are an angel in some ways and thank God you really don't know it. But don't distract. I have the floor."

"My father was not a nice, loving Italian father. The kind that pats your head and takes you to feed the ducks on Sunday. He was deeply disappointed about something early in life but we never knew what it was. He drank. He drank a lot. He beat my mother. He beat my sisters. And to be consistent he beat me, too. In fact, he beat me the hardest, the son of a bitch. He really had it in for me. He had this pet name that he hung around my neck like a clove of garlic. *La bruta,* the ugly one. No, worse than that. The beast. And I *was* ugly, Cal," she confessed as they wove in and out of the small tiled cubicles that served as examination rooms for the newly arrived. Though at least ninety five by now, Cal felt chilled. The small rooms reminded him of pictures he had seen of Buchenwald and Belsen.

"I was really ugly, especially when you rounded up my sisters for a family portrait. I had to be sick then, or my father would tear them up."

"I can't imagine your ever being ugly. Even if I pushed it."

"You can't, huh? Well let me tell you, at thirteen I was five-four or five-five, and as straight as a plumb line. A bricklayer could level a wall with any side of me. All arms and legs. I couldn't have weighed more than eighty, tops ninety, pounds. Also I had pimples on my face larger than my micro-dot breasts. And don't think my old man didn't remind me of it. 'Pimple face' he called me, when he was feeling mellow. He was, as they say today, in polite society, a physical man. A very physical man. An Italian John Wayne." Tessa was locked into a cadence now where her sentences flowed like a snow-melted stream in April.

"Victor's father crippled by using his mouth. It was enough. Manny, bastard though he was, didn't beat the boys much. And when he did there was no pleasure in it for him. My father beat us to work something out for himself. Real macho. He used his palms, his fists, his feet, he threw things. And he had damned

117

good aim for a drunk. My mother's deaf in one ear from the strikes he threw and some day, when you're up real close and your mind is free I'll show you the scar on my scalp where I stopped a rock. I really hated the bastard and I went from the specific to the general. I was afraid of all men and I hated all men, especially the loud ones, the swaggering ones, the physical ones, the slick ones, the boastful ones."

"That's quite a roll call, but you turned out to be a swan, Tessa, a very loving black-eyed beauty of a swan. And you don't seem to have any trouble relating to men, now."

"Oh, bullshit. A swan," she scoffed. "Some swan." Going back to the time of pimples and dangling arms had suddenly robbed her of the solid confidence that was a large part of the Tessa he knew. She looked like a gawky kid.

"Another thing. I was raped when I was twelve. By a post-man. He must have been real hardup to stick it to an obvious bruta. Afterwards I was sick and ashamed, but I never told anyone, except you. I wasn't a sweet, shy kid, afraid to open my mouth. Friends and neighbors called me *la tarantella,* the spider. It fit. I was ugly and I had a mean sting. So after the postman held me down and pried me open I got mad, too. And I got even, if you can ever square away an account like that."

"You didn't cut off his waterworks, did you?"

"Only figuratively. I followed him home the next day and saw what kind of a car he drove. I remember it was a shiny fifty-four Chrysler. So at night I came back, filled his gas tank with moth-balls and his radiator with sugar. Somehow I knew that every true American man, rapist, drunk, and wifebeater has this love affair with his car. It's a symbol of his manhood. I don't know how I knew those things then, but I murdered his car and in-directly castrated him. They had to junk it after the number I did on it."

Her eyes glistened with the glow from an inner lamp as she spoke to him. He caught the glint from the small high windows in the passageway between buildings. Cal forgot if they were in the examining area or the administration offices or the return rooms where the stark drama of families wrenched apart by TB had been played.

"I was a smart kid, but you didn't have to be too smart to get

118

the message. And my father and my mirror re-enforced it, every breathing minute of the day. That since I had nothing beautiful to catch a man with, I'd better become useful. My only function in life was to become someone's wheelchair. You see, I could never be a subject, so I settled for being an object. God, was I dumb. Dumb, dumb, dumb." She slapped her forehead with the heel of her hand three short raps as if to teach herself the meaning of the word.

"Cal, I was content, even happy to become a tool, a pair of motherly hands, somebody's prosthetic device. It was all so easy. I didn't have to look at my pimples, comb my hair, or judge myself in a full-length mirror. Nothing. Just to go to school and become smart, useful, and stay out of my father's line of fire. It worked for a while, but then my father got sick and it looked like he was going to die. So, in front of the whole family I had to promise to marry Victor Bruno. So I promised and it scared me so that I skipped my period for two months. Marriage . . . and to that big Victor. He was a gentle boy, fine, but I never figured on marrying, ever."

They came out into a small courtyard and the sunlight caught them full face. Cal searched her skin for traces of the acne that shaped her life. The scars outside were gone. No holes, no bumps, just a suspicion around her left ear that volcanoes had once erupted. If anything, he loved her better for the act of becoming, for the journey involved in going from an impossible beginning to the present.

"But I was kind of happy, too. If I had to get married, what better than to a very unmacho type. And he was willing to marry me, the ugly . . . pimpled face . . . spider. I was so damned grateful I would have given him oral intercourse four times a day if he said the word."

Before he could frame an answer she continued and he decided it wasn't worth saying anyhow.

"We got married. Then my father died and about the same time my face cleared up and I didn't mind looking at myself in the mirror anymore. It was a revelation. I found I wasn't bad looking. . . ."

"No revelation," he inserted.

"I filled out a little, even grew a small chest and when I finished

119

being grateful as hell to Victor and finished looking at the swan (your word, not mine) in the mirror it became clear to me that now Victor needed my help. Manny moved his mouth and Victor said the words. That's why the dummy married me, because Manny said so. But he did save me from becoming a walking bedpan and for that I owe. I pay back, by being his crutch, his wife, his fetcher of the Bud, and yes, his balls too. Not much of a change from life with father? Wrong. I function, I grow and I have the boys. Okay so it's not enough to keep me from crossing the border into your bed, but it is enough to center me in my world. It is enough and it isn't enough."

"Gratitude is a bitch, baby," Cal said, "and a damned tough master." They were in the huge main room, their hands clutching the rusted railing of a catwalk that ribboned its way around the intimidating room. He could imagine how browbeating it must have been to the frightened newcomer.

Her hands covered his on the railing. She had to stress a point. "But I accepted the role, Cal. That boy did say yes. He did take me out of the house where I was afraid that any minute of the day my father would beat the shit out of me. Victor was my Lou Costello Prince Charming. I can never wipe that out." When she felt her point made she released him.

"Everybody said, in true folk wisdom: You get banged regularly the pimples go and the bazooms they grow, as if a man's tool was some sort of magic wand. But really busting loose, away from my father's orbit toward crippled Victor did it. I read a lot before . . . and since about my problem. It doesn't change much, knowing your problem, but it makes it that much easier to live with." She hesitated when they came to the exit and he helped her down the recently secured flight of steps that led from the central area.

"As far as sex goes . . . well, that was another problem. With the rape and the horrible father figure I was frigid. And he needed help, too. A lot of help. I couldn't do much for him, being broken up that way myself. Everytime he got up the courage to touch me I flinched. When he finally got together a head of steam I cried and cried and said Victor I don't want sex, please. If you want a baby go ahead and do it. Only do it fast and do it easy. Oh, poor Victor, he was so embarrassed and so unmanned by my ice that he zapped me fast like a whore in an alley. It hasn't improved much since, I'm afraid. I've outgrown my fear of men, you can see that, but I still hate the kind that have pieces of my father in them."

"The kids, you know, they're my consolation. They need me. All three of them need me." She stopped and faced him. "Let me talk to you as a friend. We are lovers, but as a friend let me tell you I've got kids that need a home and a father. That father. They adore him. He's one of the boys with them. So, I'm stuck. In spite of the books I've read and the lectures I've yawned through about elevating my consciousness. In spite of my feelings for you that came from nowhere. In spite of it all, past, present, and future. And future." The repetition of it made Cal feel guilty and frustrated.

"I'm not going to try and push you off center. I swear it," he said realizing that was exactly what he was drifting toward.

On the return trip to Battery Park they had become separated. Cal laughed at something she said and turned to look at someone causing a ruckus up front. When he turned to face her again, she was gone, carried off by a sudden surge of faceless bodies. His stomach suddenly collapsed into his gut as if she had truly drowned. She was here just a second ago and now she was gone. When the first wave of fear passed through him, he was left with an overwhelming sense of loss. For the first time in his life he felt what real loss meant and was just inches away from being inconsolable. What had happened to him, he wondered, in the time it took to light a cigarette?

He plowed into the crowd seeking her. Faces flew by like traffic markers from a speeding car. He pushed in total disregard of the rights of others, and against his inherent sense of decency. Tessa was gone. My God, that was unthinkable. One of the black men he pushed impersonally, pushed back and hard. He kept on pushing. So far he had stifled the urge to shout her name. He knew that the voice of the crowd would drown his no matter how loudly he called her. Perhaps she had gone upstairs on deck to look for him. He took the steps, three at a time and almost missed the top triad. On deck he stumbled into a Puerto Rican grandmother bent low, practically rolled into a ball. She was holding a sleeping baby with a huge yellow teething ring planted in its mouth. Cal ricocheted off her and she bounced, in turn

121

off the crowd on the deck. Without apologizing in English or Spanish he tore into the crowd who made way for an obviously deranged man. A wild thought, born of the fear of losing her seized him. He would mount the railing and tight rope the deck while looking for her. He would find her sooner that way. Two men who thought he had suicide in mind restrained him and threw him back into the crowd.

Sweaty and exhausted he gave up looking on deck when the ferry was about three quarters of the way home. Down the same steps again and into the crowd. A sense of hopelessness dug its hooks into him and wouldn't let go. She was gone forever, gone forever. He would never find her. Then his vision blurred and his heart sounded as if the ferry were bouncing off the side of the pier. Was he having a coronary or a stroke? He looked at the faces. They had become his enemies.

Then he saw her, her black curly head bobbing to the surface between the straw hats and the baseball caps. The raging storm subsided, and the sun inside him shone. They reached out, locked fingers, and finally he had her safely surrounded in his arms. And he held her in a silence born of the fear of speaking lest he give himself away. He interrupted his thanks to whatever ruled matters on the ocean to give her small head kisses. They left last to avoid another such incident. He might not survive a second disaster.

He took her to Ratner's Dairy Restaurant on Delancey Street, a block she knew only as legend. The lower east side went from Jewish to Puerto Rican without the usual pattern of going Black first. Latinization was everywhere save the small bastion of Jewishness where the children of Abraham savored their own soul food. The mixed joy of thick pea soup (first the taste, exquisite, then the heartburn) filled his senses. Tessa stirred and sipped while Cal held his breath for a verdict. She approved and they dug in.

"You know I panicked, Tessa, I panicked very badly. For that eternity of about ten minutes I just fell apart. Why? I asked myself. I was sure to find you. Why didn't I know that?"

"It was silly," she said. "Worse comes to worst we would have met back at the car. We parked near a Chock Full O'Nuts, right off Broadway." She put her soup spoon down and pressed his palms together as if she were teaching him to pray, then kissed them. "Just silly . . . but nice silly." She said it and felt it, but was not quite sure she really meant it.

"Okay, so it was silly. And I don't panic easily. But I did. My head knew there was no real problem, but my insides didn't. Now that has to be a first, honey. All my parts work together, always have. But on that smelly boat, when I lost you, I feel stupid saying this, but my first impulse was to cry." He looked at himself in the stained gold mirrors that covered the entire wall of the restaurant. He felt compelled to see the face of the man, who had just confessed the impulse to cry. It was him alright, slightly worn by July, looking hangdog and remorseful. "I can't believe that I'm saying what I'm saying, Tessa. To feel so lost and alone that tears become the only response. God Almighty, I'm no kid. Does this embarrass you, Tessa?"

"No." She didn't actually say the word. Her lips formed it and waited for the rest to follow. It didn't.

"Fact, plain fact. There was this overwhelming sense that you were gone and I'd never see you again. Last time I felt so swamped with emotion was with Mrs. Rizzuto." He attempted to float a smile but failed miserably. "I guess from now on I'll gag every time I eat pea soup, too."

"That's . . . that's so sweet, Cal. I guess I caught your sickness," she said and dropped tears into her soup. They both fiddled with it until it became too cold to enjoy. She knew reassurance was called for. And freely gave it, without measuring.

"Cal don't let it possess you, please. I'm not going anyplace. I'm here. About this panic thing. I was frightened, too, but I knew you'd be there. See, I have more confidence about you than you have about me." She looked at his image staring back at him like a sadder twin. "God, why didn't you tell me that I looked like a drowned rat." She talked to keep them both from thinking the way a magician distracts with one hand while the other does the work.

"I'll bet you thought some P.R. was boffing me in the engine room, or maybe the ghost of your Rabbi grandfather dumped me overboard. Silly." And suddenly her eyes filled with tears taking the rest of her by surprise.

"If those tears fall on the cutlet there's a chemical reaction. It turns to veal parmagiana."

"Seems I have my own ridiculous reaction to worry about," she said and turning her moist eyes away dabbed at the poppy seeds that had fallen from the small rolls. "Please don't shake me like that until I cry and stutter. I'm no good to anyone a weepy, stuttering basket case. Did I tell you that I stuttered a lot along with my pimples when I lived at home? Well I did. And by the way, Victor helped me with that, too. Seems I had to say everything slowly and deliberately to him to penetrate that thick wop head of his. . . ."

She nodded slowly and deliberately to him and dabbed at the poppy seeds. "In his own clumsy way, Victor saved my speech."

"Then I'm terribly grateful to Victor."

"Are you being a smart-ass because you're in your own ballpark, here?"

"I don't fit any place, you should know that, Tessa."

They checked into a small motel shoe-horned between two large catering facilities near Kennedy Airport. He began making love to her in the shower, then followed her to bed. Soon, much too soon, it was over. A short furious burst of passion that was unusual and suspect for such a fatiguing day. Given the unwanted present of free time she rubbed his back and filled in gaps (at his insistence) of her story of change from ugly duckling to graceful swan. This time she was freer with detail, franker with self-portrait. He listened until way past eleven and realized that they had found a second, though not secondary, use for a bed.

Sunlight broke through the foliage of the apple trees and spilled into the den where she sat serenely at the rolltop. Doing her monthly bills, she was aware of floating in a sea of sunshine. She had operated on solar power before the energy crisis, storing it in some secure place within. On her swivel chair she was in a state of grace as true as that experienced by saints, without the confinements that usually accompany their situations.

For a few delicious seconds she recalled the time when she had found her rolltop desk. It had been on its way to the garbage dump, site of great future archeological discoveries. She had spied it in the back of a fifty-seven pickup truck. The driver, poor fool, thought she was trying to pick him up, cutting in and out like that. He, no doubt, was disappointed to find out that she had only furniture on the brain. Joan bought it on the spot. Within a month she had nursed it back to health, hammer, screwdriver, and paintbrush the only surgical equipment required. An almost mystical relationship blossomed as it often does in life-saving situations. The desk was given a place of honor in her den and assigned duty as guardian of her economic and social interests. Her wooden eunuch.

Neatly (neurotically her family would say), she maintained a complete and cross-indexed filing system on every member of her organizations. She also indexed people she met, fixing them forever in her files like butterflies. It was an unspoken compliment to be assigned to her three-by-five world. Only the live wires, the movers, the activists were allowed in. She segregated solely ac-

125

cording to the ability to function. At a glance she knew who to summon anywhere there was a problem within the Five Towns. If the wild ducks were oil-logged due to a tanker spill near the Atlantic Beach Bridge, she made a few calls and a hundred volunteers carrying sacks of towels and torn shirts, would appear. If someone whose life she touched, however lightly, was suddenly widowed she made sure there was another someone, often many someones, to provide a shoulder against the pain. On Christmas Eve it was Joan who appointed herself a temporary employment bureau to provide enough trained Jewish bodies to relieve their Christian counterparts in the Police station, the firehouse, and the hospital. Father Kerrigan personally thanked her for the increase in attendance for that mass.

Like an artist at his keyboard, she sat in charge, every pore open to absorb the joys. The desk was the medium, the sunlight, the catalyst. She almost lost consciousness of self despite the turmoil of Cal and his steely mistress, despite the reckless pace she set for herself and her cavalry on their latest U.J.A. campaign. Peace balanced well with ambition. The inner light shone because she was now with desk, as some women are with child and radiate because of it.

Nothing in the entire gamut of her Jewish experience had ever opened the gates of her soul as this experience. Had a friend pointed out to her the spiritual quality of her experience she would have been shocked. What she could not touch and know she distrusted. Spirit, being without weight and form, was useless. The soul could not be indexed on a three-by-five file card. Yet sitting here with the sunlight exploring the cubbyholes and warming her fingers, she was deeply touched.

Paying bills. A headache to most, a pleasure for her. She relished bookkeeping as much for the solid satisfaction of a house in order as for the joys of having the local merchants on their collective toes. All her old bills, from the day she and Cal moved in, were at her perfectly engineered fingertips. Reviewing them gave her much the same pleasure as looking at old home movies. Both showed a journey between distances.

Her thumb worked through the fuel bills as if they were a collection of Peter's report cards (she saved them too in another

126

section). From ten cents a gallon to thirty eight. Will it ever stop?

Though absentmindedly wearing her saint's smile, she knew which tradesmen allowed the two percent for cash, which retailers sent statements with excess padding, and who the sly foxes were who ran specials in store and charged more for them when delivered. Often she picked out errors on their statements with the annoyance of a diner finding bones in his filet of sole. Not that they cheated, that is the nature of business, all businesses, but that they had the audacity to cheat *her*. Every dollar that the household spent paraded past her inspecting eye. It was a half-compliment when the merchants, out of respect, offered her a job as accountant. She was acknowledged as a tough lady when it came to getting her due. That she liked. Everyone likes his own self-image reinforced.

Her work completed she leaned her back against the swivel chair attempting to keep the nun's mood alive. The shades were up, the windows open, and the sharp sweetness of rotting apples occasionally wafted through the air. Sunlight, filtering through apple trees, seemed to pick up some of the greens and reds. Perhaps it is only an illusion, she thought.

Victor was not an illusion. He was there, shaggy and bear-like, raking up batches of rusty apples into little pyramids. His molasses movements annoyed her sense of the speed at which things should be done. It really came down to that with all the Victors of this world. Joan had many quarrels with the world, this one would have to stand in line. Now that he had gravitated into her orbit, as Tessa's satellite, he had become the object of her thought. Certainly he would never enter her three-by-five world, but his place in her solar system was enormous, at least for now. She knew that she would have to insinuate herself into his life. She felt a twinge of pity, like a momentary spasm of no consequence. Pity being a rare element in her life she had no tools to measure it. She just ignored it instead. To the melodramatic it might seem an act of seduction was called for. Not sexual seduction, which is of short duration and not trustworthy over the long haul, but mind seduction, a more insidious semi-crime with far reaching consequences. The physically seduced can rise again; mind pris-

127

oners are like rotting apples, just fit for a compost heap.

Ever since she had agreed in her mind to accept Cal's adultery it was clear that Victor had to be sequestered. He was the loose end, the weak link. Perhaps Tessa had weatherproofed her own house. Perhaps. But Joan's life wasn't built or maintained on perhaps.

She looked at plodding Victor, a study in the arcane technique of moving a rake handle from here to there. True, no smashed, souring apple escaped his green prongs, but at what cost? He paid in time, but, she reasoned, he was rich in time and could squander it. No adoring wife to spend it on now and probably with no worthwhile pursuit to waste it.

Actually Victor did more than just tickle green grass and fermenting apples. He didn't speculate on the gamut of human needs or on how to become a man emotionally. Victims' thoughts occupied Victor's mind. Why me? he asked. Why good-natured, friendly, home-loving, hardworking, easy going, much-abused me? These thoughts were strung out like firecracker tails, but they all ended in . . . Why me? I'm abused because I'm good, he surmised. To be good was what his mother and father always wanted of him. Especially his mother. She made no other demands. His father was another matter. Victor never got a specific bill of particulars from Manny, his father being the kind of man you don't question. Manny assumed he taught Victor by example; Victor assumed Manny told him once, but that he had forgotten the instructions. Now if Victor was good and he got a full helping of abuse it was only natural to assume that it was the rest of the world that was bad. An ironclad fact that flowed from the first principle of Victor's goodness. This way, despite the heartache of Tessa being occupied by another man, he was as blameless as the rest of the world was to blame. That at least was something.

A gentle rap on the Andersen window with her ring finger. No response. She rapped again, insistent, shorter notes trying to convey annoyance through a glass medium. The big bear, his head a swirling mass of black curls, looked up, startled. Were she soft of heart, that heart would have ached for plunging him into the world of adultery and action.

128

At last he saw her cut into a dozen squares by the den window. She beckoned to him, her index finger flicking like a snake's tongue. But he stood there surprised at being singled out from all the trees and bushes, pointing to himself, certain that she didn't mean him. His heart sank. Joan nodded forcefully. He dropped the rake. Then he picked it up and leaned it against the tree. Joan wondered if he had to do everything twice. She vanished only to appear again at the open den door.

Standing there all in white, like some souped-up nurse, she waved him in with a generous sweep of the hand. Some part of him turned white.

"Victor, my friend Victor, don't stand there like a statue. Come on in and take a load off your feet. I want to talk to you.

"Wipe your feet on the rug," she said.

Victor was braced for a tongue-lashing or worse. Last month she bitched about the ragged condition of the hedges. So he had come back on that Sunday and awakened the whole neighborhood with his hedge trimmer. And got hell for it from Tessa for lousing up the kids' Sunday.

Wooly head slightly bowed he stood on the rug and wiped his soles. If he had a hat he would have held it in his hands. He assumed that position anyway, hatless, but with his hands raised to his chest.

She smiled to soothe his fears. Without results.

"Victor, Victor, Victor, don't *stand* there. Come in please. Sit down on the couch. I want us to talk together. Like old friends. I know I can talk to you that way. You've been like part of the family, you and your father before you, for years and years.

"We suffered through lawn fungus, and remember when we lost that big pine in the front? My that was some experience." She tried to look as if the loss was only yesterday. "And the apples. Victor, do you remember two . . . no three years ago when the apples came out lousy? I certainly do. And the time you used too much arsenic on the trees, when you first took over for Manny, and we all got sick? Remember? Oh Lord, we've been through a lot together, haven't we Victor?" She purposely used Lord to refer to the deity. It was more ecumenical.

"We sure have, Mrs. Bernstein," he replied, not knowing what else to say.

129

"That's why, Victor, I know I can talk to you like a friend. And believe me, Victor Bruno, we've got something to talk about, you and I. Right. Hmmmm? You know what I'm talking about."

She knows she knows she knows she knows rang through Victor's head like the bees buzzing when he got in their way.

"Don't be coy, now. This is our moment of truth, Victor. We both have a bellyful of heartaches," she said, flunking anatomy.

"Victor, will you please sit down. I can't stand talking to someone when I have to look up at him. Especially someone as big as you, Victor. Sit."

Reluctantly, Victor sat on the wicker couch with the billowy cushions and sank slowly like a torpedoed ship. Rather than feeling less uncomfortable he was pushed further off balance by its lushness.

She pulled her chair up very close to him blocking his exit. Touching him slightly, she gave a few seconds of reprieve. Time to summon courage.

"Now Victor," she began, "we are two adults, two intelligent adults and you know and I know that we both have something in common. Right?"

Victor blinked and held a lobotomized stare. Joan was grateful for the blink. He was still breathing.

"And you know I know, and I know you know, right?"

He wanted to leave at once but feared she would stand up and block the door. What would he do then?

"Victor, listen to me. We are both married to cheats. And those cheats are fooling around with each other. Okay, so now I've said it and now it's out in the open. And now we're going to talk about it. See," she smiled, "it wasn't so hard to listen."

Shame stepped in and took control. Had he that hat he would have covered his face with it. Like the *Daily News* pictures of arrested Mafia bigwigs.

"Oh no, we ain't, Mrs. Bernstein," he managed to say. "It just ain't something you talk about."

"Victor, *shaina punim*, we have no choice. Don't you see that? Oh Victor, Victor, you foolish boy, listen to me. Let me tell you why," she said. "It's on my time anyway, and believe me, if there's a God in heaven, you will be glad you listened. I guarantee you'll walk away a relieved man. Scout's honor."

130

She squeezed his hand again while he sat there half buried in blue cushions. What the hell, it was only a minute. Besides, she was so nice and so insistent. It won't hurt to listen. He once listened to an atheist preach in Times Square for ten minutes and it didn't change his mind about God. As long as she didn't beat his ass about letting Tessa run around with the Doc. As long as she didn't blame him.

"You work very hard. I see your truck wherever I go. At all my friends. Sometimes on Saturday. Even on Sunday when you have to. You do good work. We all know that. For damn sure you have this whole area locked up. Even better than old Manny before you. It took two lifetimes and a lot of sweat, Victor, but you got a solid business." Her face grew dark and stormy. "I wouldn't like to see everything old Manny worked for, everything young Victor worked for fall down and break into a million pieces."

"That can't happen, Mrs. Bernstein. I worked like a son of a . . . I mean I really hustle to make the thing go."

"Oh, I know you do, but it can happen. It's a distinct possibility. But we, you and I, won't permit that awful thing to happen. We're going to make sure, right here and now, by our combined heads that it doesn't happen." She pinned him with her Joan Crawford look, a determined stare that promised concerted action through will power.

"Just for argument's sake," she continued, relieved that she no longer had to shove and push, "let me show you what might happen if I weren't around watching with my good eye. Say the word got around somehow, through no fault of yours or mine, because the two of us would never breathe a syllable to anyone." Seeing disbelief around the corners of his eyes she sought to erase it. "Listen, it could happen. Who knows. Life has its little surprises. It's a possibility. They're seen together coming out of a motel or a restaurant. Or maybe they pass by and one of your brothers sees them. You have brothers, haven't you? Well, it doesn't take long for something like that to travel. Like wildfire. And just like that every gossip in town knows it. Just think now, my friend, what the goldplated fancy ladies would do. My God, Victor, they would drop Bruno and Sons so fast you'd get dizzy and have a nose bleed. For sure, I tell you. I know these broads.

131

They are vicious. Right away they would picture their own husbands involved with Tessa. Dirty slimy minds. And your business? Well . . . you fill in the blank spaces. So help me Victor, you'd be left with zilch, zero, a truck-full of rakes and things and nowhere to go. You'd have to leave town in the middle of the night, or go on relief. Imagine a son of Manny Bruno on relief."

With horror Victor looked into her mouth and greedily gulped every word.

"Now, my friend, I'm not telling you what *might* happen, oh no, I'm telling you what *will* happen, if our combined heads don't come up with something brilliant."

Victor squirmed and sweated heavily about the armpits having bought Joan's picture, the one she couldn't sell Tessa. There are customers and there are customers. Coolly, dryly she watched his agony. Nothing to be especially proud of, the capturing of this large wooly bear. No feather in her cap, but it was an important conquest. And they would all gain from it. Of that she was sure.

"So Victor," she pressed on, "let me give you some good advice. I paid a lot for it and you can have it free. Because I'm older and wiser. Because I've been around a lot. But mostly because you need a friend's help."

Had he a bushel basket, a gunny sack, a hefty trash bag, he would have held them open to receive Lady Bountiful's largesse. She would save him from sinking, from welfare, and from Manny's beady Italian stare. Most of all from Manny's stare.

Joan leaned back into the cushions. "When it first happened, when you first saw that she was spending a lot of time away from home, or when she wasn't as . . . as . . . affectionate as she should have been, you should have hollered like hell at her, kicked the living daylights out of her, broken her face. Oh, look at me, telling you macho Italians how to kick a woman's rump in. Anything, anything, Victor, that would have kept her where she belonged. Anything that would have kept her from laying that fine business of yours on the line. But," and she shook her head and closed her eyes as if his pain and fear of bankruptcy were hers too, "it's too late for that. Entirely too late. For both of us."

"But Mrs. Bernstein, Mrs. Bernstein," he managed to eke out. He tried getting his hands in motion as if to use them in the process of explanation, but gave up. They fell lifeless back into his lap.

"Now don't be too hard on yourself, Victor," she said. "Look at me Victor. Me, Victor, not the floor. I'm supposed to be a smart cookie. A real shrewdie. Everybody says so, right? Right, Victor?"

He nodded.

"Well, I got caught with my pants down. Just like you. So I'm afraid that we're both dummies. Two of a kind. A pair of real jokers. But Victor, here's where the smarts come in. No one says that we always have to be dummies. Dummies once doesn't mean dummies forever. Now just because yours has the seven-year itch and mine has middle-age hots, we don't have to throw our life's work into the ocean. No sir. That would be stupid and wasteful, Victor. Everything we worked for in life down the drain because of them. Not us, Victor, not us. We're only innocent bystanders. We shouldn't have to be hit and run victims. Let's be smart, cookie, let's outfox them and take home all the marbles."

"But how do we do that, Mrs. Bernstein?" Victor asked, his eyes grown to billiard-ball size.

"The trick, my dear friend, is to do nothing, absolutely nothing. Let's ride with it until it burns itself out. And it will. I know it. I'm sure of it. I guarantee it. I know my husband, I know him damn well. Victor, he's no prize package and certainly no stallion. She'll get tired of him, and very soon, too." She smiled wanly, knowingly. "He doesn't make revolutions. He's used to good living and he won't break everything into little pieces and walk away, just for a fling. And I swear to you, Victor, that's how he goes, in little pieces, if it ever came down to it." She breathed a sigh, quite taken with her progress up to that point.

"The best thing for both of us, for all of us, is to just look the other way, put a lid on it, and keep everything nice and quiet and under control. Under *our* control. That, my friend Victor, is being very smart."

And Victor wanted so much to be very smart. Doggedly he did follow her reasoning for a short while, but got trapped in the maze at some dead end point. This absolutely dynamite lady was telling him that you put out a fire by pouring kerosene on it.

133

He lost her on that. He heard of fighting fire with fire, but with kerosene? By letting them alone? By letting Tessa take off with him to some motel? He wanted to be convinced because she was so sure of it and she was so smart and because no one in his whole life had taken the time and trouble to tell him things.

She caught him wandering aimlessly in the maze of her logic. "Victor, you look so confused. Don't be, and don't hold anything back. Talk to me. Tell me something. Anything. I'm a good listener, too. Tell me why you look so confused. You're not used to this cat and mouse stuff. That's it, isn't it? It's dirty stuff. But listen. Listen to me. Doesn't it make better sense (she bent over and half whispered) to sit and wait instead of committing suicide? But you tell me, I'd like to hear what you have to say." After that Victor would talk. She knew that. It was needed to seal their bargain. Once she had him talking, it was a notarized signature. Then she would know that her words were not just puffs of smoke blown in his face.

"What can I tell you, Mrs. Bernstein. I hollered a lot when I found out. I mean when she told me I hurt like a bitch. She just sat down, turned off the TV, I was watching the Yanks and the Red Sox, took two beers from the refrigerator, and said, like in the movies, 'I'm seeing this man. I thought you should know it and I have no intention of ending it and I'm not going to leave you either. And that's the last you'll hear of it.' Just like that. Imagine, Mrs. Bernstein, a wife should dump a load of garbage on your head and then tell you to live with it?"

His hands attempted again to rise in protest against his ill-treatment but they changed their mind again and fell back into his lap, defeated. "I can't handle her no more. I never could, but it's even less now. I don't know if I should be tellin' you all my troubles, but funny, it's kind of easy to talk to you, seeing how you told me your troubles." He smiled without showing teeth. "I hit her a couple of years ago. Don't think I do that all the time. She threw my best friend out of the house because she caught him fooling around with her sister in the back yard. I got mad and smacked her across the mouth and she went into the garage and came back with a rake, my best rake, and broke it over my head. She stopped the bleeding and took me to the hos-

134

pital. I needed fourteen stitches. Man, I was a mess." He held the spot that Tessa had ventilated as if the wound was fresh. "Well when I found out about her and the Doc, I smacked her again, but you know something, she just stood there and took it. Like she knew she had it coming. It made me feel like two cents when she just stood there with her jaw set like that." He couldn't look at Joan, telling about Tessa's reaction and lack of defense.

Joan merely nodded indicating she was on his side for the most part in the broken rake matter. She withheld an approving head motion in the case of the second slap, but she didn't chastise him either.

He looked at Joan with large sad black eyes, and almost whispered, "Tessa's too much for me. I say something, she says something better. I come up with an idea, she's been there before. Too much, too much, the girl's too much. It's like living at home with poppa, sometimes."

The dividends began rolling in. Victor finding that he had a tongue and she had an ear rewarded her. "You think you knew my old man? Well you didn't know my old man. He really treated me like a dog." His voice was rising and quivering at the same time, as if raising the pitch put quite a strain on it. "Beat me down. Ran everything. So I figured when I got married I'd be out from under. I'd have a wife and family and I could run my own show. Like him. But Tessa's too much for me. She takes care of the kids, the home, and me, sometimes, but Jesus, I can't make her happy. I don't try no more."

A quick glance from side to side, to make sure that they were not overheard. Never once had he said before what he had just said. It was in his mind, all cloudy thought, but never actually said. He suffered instant regret. Somehow saying it and hearing himself say it made it so much worse. Now someone else knew and rather than having the misery divided, it was doubled. Lucky for him that the somebody else was a smart, decent lady like Mrs. Bernstein. Anyone else and he would have felt dirty, stained.

Joan was almost touched. Had she felt at all close to him, were she able to surmount the boundaries of religion, class, and age, she might have been moved to tears. But what did float up was a silly blend of poignancy and low comedy. Victor was a silly sad

135

comic who doesn't know how sad and silly he really is. Why couldn't she feel his pain? she wondered. The questioned teemed with life, but was of short duration.

She leaned forward and tapped his knee. "Show a little patience and grit. Some wisdom, too. You can have her back, Victor. You do want her back again? You do love her, don't you, Victor?"

"Yeah, I guess I do love her. But the damn woman makes me wish I didn't. I get sick about it. You tell me to close my eyes and he'll go away. Geez, I'd like to believe it."

"Believe it, believe it," she intoned.

"And if he doesn't?"

"He will."

"And if he doesn't?"

"Then what have you lost, Victor? A little more time? As it is now you figure her lost. She can't get more lost than lost. Time works for us."

"Maybe."

"No, for sure," she said wondering how he had slipped off the line. " You just listen to me. You do nothing. And I mean nothing. No digs, no insults, no ugly noise in the house. And don't try to get at her through the boys. Don't rock the boat in your pond and I won't in mine. It'll be like a conspiracy. The four of us against the whole world. Really the two of us (really the one of us). Our partners will go at it until they're sick and tired of it . . . of each other. Then they'll come home like two runaways. If we only keep our heads."

She found herself straining, trying a bit too hard to convince. Usually she ended off as she began, smooth and quick, like a needle, not an axe. But Victor was a damned blockhead, without wit or culture. It was difficult for him to grasp the beauty of her logic, the base on which she built the conspiracy.

Victor thought. It was a tortured process. Then he brightened. "Do you really think Tessa will get tired of the Doc? After all Mrs. Bernstein, after all, he's a doctor and he's good looking and he knows a lot. Me? I'm just a *paisan*. I work with my hands."

She feigned indulgent annoyance, masking the pleasure of the catch. "Will you listen to me," she said. "He's past forty and he walks around in torn sneakers and he doesn't always shave. And he is a little crazy. Not a lot crazy. Just a little. All he cares about is playing doctor. Otherwise he's as boring as hell. Your wife is young and vivacious. She needs a young man to laugh with, to run with. She needs you, not an old bore. This is just a change of pace for both of them. In a month or so, two tops, he'll be glad to come back to peace and quiet. If we only keep our heads.

"Do nothing, Victor. That is the password."

"I think, I think," he said twice, unfamiliar with the process and the language, "you're right. Now that I wore it a while, I think you're right. Sometimes it takes a while for it to sink in, but now that it's sunk in tight I'll go along with it. I'm all set. And how! We're going to do it your way. See what happens. Gee, though I didn't think the Doc was like that. Sometimes it's hard to figure people out." They both nodded in unison over his weighty comment.

Finally, she thought. He's aboard ship. Now if his club-footed stumblings don't capsize us . . . maybe . . . maybe. . . .

Summation time. She always closed with a small review of what took place. No one could ever accuse her of fudging. "Okay Victor, we do have an agreement, don't we? Mum's the word."

"We do, we do, Mrs. Bernstein. It's going to be like you said. Give them plenty of rope."

"No, no Victor. We planned it out and it's *our* way. *Our* way, Victor. We're a team now, with team goals."

"Okay, our way, just like you say, Mrs. Bernstein."

She settled for that. "Good, Victor. Now you finish your work. The fancy ladies are coming for bridge and gossip. The noise of the mower might mess their little minds."

Victor left a bit straighter than when he entered. For now, at least, the bit of expended air had puffed him up so that he felt a degree of strength new to him.

She sat once again at her desk watching him work at a slightly increased speed. Dumb ball-less son of a bitch. Poor bastard. We'll see how long the treatment lasts. Maybe he'll keep his mouth shut. I hope to God he does.

Damn it, she almost vocalized, forty is a tough age for a woman. Between a kid and an old lady. A place where all the mistakes explode in your face, where nature gets even. Then she looked out the window at nothing and clenched her fists. I won't give up because he has doubts. He's grown cold and I've grown cold and what of it? Something died a few years ago, or longer. So what? Something's left. You don't throw out everything just because part of the system fails. She unclenched her fists and looked at them turn into palms. So I love him. And I'll hold him anyway I can. For love's sake, for comfort's sake. For God's sake, who else do I have? My mother with her bellyaches and her scheming? My sisters who only think of inheritances? The kids who'd like to float me down the river on a cake of ice? No, he's still the best friend I have. The bastard.

**10**

"Is the Nazi coming down for breakfast?" she asked in a combative tone. Cal heard the call to battle on the fields of dirty socks and bathtub rings, but he refused to fight over Peter's primitive hygiene habits. Having just lost a patient, a night's sleep because of it, and the keys to the car, he was hardly in a mood for war over interfamilial differences. "How should I know? You ask him," he answered. "I'm not his keeper."

She either did not see the posted warning or ignored it. "That, Cal, is exactly what I am. The keeper of his cage. He lives like Tobacco Road up there with his betting slips, pizza boxes, and beer cans. It's a disgrace. And you encourage it."

One brush, two tarrings. Another of Joan's techniques. This classical American play was as styled as Kabuki. Rotten kid versus long-suffering mother. It made Cal edgy to see television reruns. Real life reruns were unbearable. When she became the shrike he became the shadow. His role, played unwillingly, was kept low profile to let her absurdity fall of its own weight. When it did, it was seen by the entire household, save her.

Sometimes he was the buffer, a role that required a master's skill. Duck when each side was shooting, negotiate when talk was high-pitched, carry messages like Gunga Din bearing water. Never the star, though. That was Joan. The children were supporting players; Cal had cameo roles. Not atypical in the Kingdom of the Five Towns, but numbers were of no comfort to the bit player.

Not content with great skill in bit roles, he added to his bag of tricks concentrated one-word replies that communicated worlds.

Words like "wrong" could be devastating when used well, "So?" applied on more than one occasion brought the family back from the edge. She: "Star Cohen is going with an intern." He: "So?" She: "The Bitch has no idea what she wants to do in life. She's a sophomore and my mother asks her what she's going to be and she says a parasite." He: "So?" Of course what can one say after "so?" It is the ultimate last word.

A thunderous stampede on the steps. The animal was loose. He breezed into the kitchen, delicately sniffed the air for enemies, then sat down at the table. A tall, narrow-hipped, broad-shouldered boy, with a sensitive-faced head bobbing on a long, slender neck. A mat of dirty blond hair, or a dirty mat of blond hair, depending on his mother's disposition, was worn loosely over mocking eyes and lips that curled eagerly when sarcasm did the curling. His gut response was the put-down. He threw rocks easily; hitting targets was secondary. Peter the Nazi knew things: Letters to the editor of Penthouse were all self-generated, written by the staff writers themselves; all politicians stole; God was a put-on; all businessmen were crooks; and his parents were clowns. He knew. A star athlete, a scholar in spite of himself with a large female following, he knew everything and did everything well, with little reticence to advertise himself. Grandma Pearl hung his nickname around that long giraffe neck one day when he proved conclusively (for him), arrogantly (for her), that Nixon was controlled by the Mafia.

Peter considered it a form of detente to keep to his room, obviating the need to expose his parents' silly little frauds. Her with her gavel, he with his stethoscope. He gave Joan nightmares, this enemy from within, while Cal only recognized something of himself in the boy and had faith that once the high waves of the glands had receded, a decent man might emerge. He had the tools: intelligence and common sense. When he and Cal did talk, quietly alone, there was reason for hope. Someday. But still, then there was Joan's well-modulated invective, Peter's return serves, and Cal's simulation of the net between.

The Tropicana slid down his long throat. He was unusually spirited and friendly. Arrogance and insults were left upstairs, as the Nazi appeared human. Cal and Joan both sensed a charged state the way an epileptic presages an impending seizure. The Nazi smiled and looked full-faced at his parents.

"I'd like you both to know that I'm giving up cards and betting for the week. No promises," he promised, "but maybe a new start." He refilled his glass with orange juice and did the giraffe swallowing trick again. A slight gurgle this time.

"The sharpies clean you out this week?" Cal asked over his Rice Krispies, his grin spreading like ink on a blotter.

"No," he answered, remaining calm in the face of provocation. Never burn bridges, his mother once said. Today he was listening to dear old mother. After all it was her kind of situation he was in, requiring charm and tact.

"You know, dad, I never lose. That's like expecting a river to run upstream. Nothing like that. Just that I'm getting into better things." The Nazi smiled with difficulty.

"Better things," Cal echoed to keep the thought alive.

"Yes, and I think you ought to cooperate on this one."

"You know, son," Joan said, "we are always ready to cooperate with you. You are our pride and joy . . . when you want to be."

Peter thought, here she comes, a little late but ready to make up for it. Who asked her in? *She* asked her in.

Joan was more than willing to overlook, especially with her son. Peter could blind her, steal the fillings from her teeth, even carve his initials in her desk, and she would still feed him more line. His mother: In like a lion, out like a lamb.

But it was Cal who always spotted the snow job first. Peter's fancy foot work meant little, Cal was immune to the dance. The boy was often surprised by what he could or could not get away with as regards his father. The constants of love and merit were variables to the boy and that was the secret of his failure.

"Then you shouldn't object to doing me a favor," Nazi said obviously pleased with both his logic and delivery.

"What favor?" Joan asked.

"Well," he said, attempting to sound serious, "this girl I met, a nice girl, a nice Jewish girl, wants to see where I live. She heard what a fabulous house we have."

"So?" Cal said.

"So?" Joan said.

"So, I'd feel uncomfortable showing her the place with the two of you around. I'm not ashamed of you, of course, but you know, you'd sort of cramp me."

The spoon sunk into the bowl of milk. All the Rice Krispies were gone while the milk remained. Just a total lack of planning. Cal gazed into the small white lake as if he were searching for answers. "Hold on to your socks, Joan, he's coming in for the kill," he warned. It was a friendly warning, not unkind to Peter, not hysterical because he sensed the point.

"Now Dad, let me finish before you shoot me down."

"You were never up, kiddo."

Joan finally found the current. "Wait a minute. Wait a minute, Romeo. Are you asking us to leave our own house so that you can bring some tootsie. . . ." Her eyes widened as the parts began fitting, as she joined in unholy matrimony the Nazi's good mood with his plans for a *Jewish* young lady.

"Not a tootsie and not a hooker. A nice girl that I know from school. She's in my Spanish class."

"To do what?" Joan pressed.

"To show her the house, the lawn, the garden, and . . . the rooms."

"Your room?"

"Yes, my room and yes my bed. Okay, you want to know. I'll tell you. I don't deny it. I'm no liar," he said wrapping himself in a flag of truth as if all men saluted it.

"No, you're no liar," his father said, "just pretty fast on your feet. And I guess pretty arrogant, too. You want to evict us old folks from our own house so that you can shack up for a few hours. That's gall, kiddo," he said, trying hard not to assume a staid Republican sense of outrage at being locked out by a son who preferred sex in a familiar place.

"And cheap, too," Cal added while he was being outraged. "If you're not satisfied with the back of a car or someone's garden, check in at a motel. You can pass for twenty or so. You can do that. My God, you can do anything, Herr Gauleiter."

Peter's snarl returned to his face where it belonged. "Don't you think I would, if I could? They'd let me in, but they'd never let Mindy in, too. If anything happened a guy's father would never

142

push it, but a girl's would. Especially Mindy's. He's running for judge or something. She's afraid of being seen."

Disappointed at Cal's lack of true indignation, Joan's face displayed horror, amazement, and shame. (A bit too thick around the mouth, Cal thought.) "You'd bring a young girl into *my* house and fool around? Peter, what's gotten into you? At your age you want a honeymoon without obligations?"

"What the hell are you talking about?" he spat out. "I only want to do what the two of you do when you close the bedroom door. You're not fooling me, you know." He was puffing up like a blowfish, puffing and growing agitated. "I know what's going on. You think it's a big secret, but I'm wise to you."

Cal looked up over his glasses, owlishly and determined not to flatten the boy by laughing out loud. He certainly deserved to have some air punched out of him. Not for the sex part, that would be childish. For the disrespect (it was disrespect, wasn't it?) that had engendered Peter's transparent request. For that alone the Nazi deserved . . . whatever the hell he deserved.

"It's no secret," he said, "that I sleep with your mother. We close the door for privacy, not to keep it a secret. You're too young for wisdom, and obviously you haven't as yet developed any sensitivity."

Joan had removed herself from the war zone to make coffee. She could discuss sex with family, friends, strangers. Not, though, with the Bitch or the Nazi. It was uncomfortable and she lost her tongue. For the life of her she did not know how Cal could blandly discuss the most sensitive of areas. Orgasm, masturbation, fellatio, their personal sex life (that wilting flower) were bandied about with the kids as if it were political science. Being a doctor helped, she supposed, but only to a point. Frankness ended at her bedroom door and her children's. It was not the worst thing for a mother to confess to.

As he had always done, since the day when she first met him in Flower-Fifth's cafeteria, he warmed his hands on the coffee cup. Somehow he received encouragement through his fingers by the act. "Don't get me wrong, Peter. What bothers me is not that you're gung ho about sex. Good for you. Start early and work at it the rest of your life." (That did not sit too well with Joan, knowing how truly he was now following his own advice.) More power to you, son. What I don't like is the little soft shoe number to get us out of our house." He took two small sips and savored it all the way down. "That catches me in the pit. That hurts."

"Bullshit. That's bullshit, dad," he exploded, finally triggered into vocal violence. "I'd think a helluva lot more of you, both of you, if you were really honest. Other parents. . . ."

Cal cut in. "No such person as 'they' or 'other parents' in this house. There's you, your mother, Laura, and myself. That's our world. Also, I'm not interested in buying your respect. Not that way, at least. We all pay for respect, one way or another. That just ain't my way."

Peter's anger grew. His mouth became an ugly gash. "Damn hypocrites," he shouted. Cal looked at his wild flaying and thought that Jeremiah might have looked like Peter if Jeremiah were a matted blond giraffe. "Jewish hypocrites. I thought you were different, especially you, dad, but you're all alike, all hypocrites."

Cal side-stepped the appeal to his sense of individuality. It wasn't worth a nickel of his loose change. "Why hypocrites?" he asked. It was like trying to talk a potential suicide off a bridge. Peter was out there on a limb. It was always better to coax him down. Sawing him off would be faster, even more satisfying, but so dangerous. He loved the boy and wanted him in one piece spiritually when adulthood came, if it came.

"Just because you can't get your way? Get used to it. Life ain't no tunnel of love." Cal cut himself off before he had a full blown lecture going. No surer way to set the boy adrift.

To no avail. The Nazi stormed out of the house, the yellow paper napkins floating off the table as he slammed the front door. The bolt of the giraffe almost caught the Bitch in its path. She giggled, "Mornin' lover," with head turning, gaze following him out the door.

Without looking back he spat out, "Fuck you, creep," instead of the civil exchanges that characterized their relationship.

She strode into the kitchen as if clad in an especially revealing bikini with full knowledge of the sensation her magnificent figure would create. A good figure, but not all that great. But it was her

144

ace card and many times in her short life she was forced (her decision) to play it. Tall, willowy, attractive, she looked and acted dreamy and contemplative. She was also a terrible hypochondriac. Kvetch, her grandmother said; Bitch, her parents corrected. They were both on target.

"Ooooooh. I feel awful, just awful. My head, my nose. These sinus headaches."

"Are you doing a commercial?" Cal asked hugging his second cup of coffee.

Bitch sat down and stared at the black formica table top. She was seeking answers to why the world ignored her. The world was the pits. That was the latest term making the castle rounds to describe the absolute bottom. Life was the pits. Her life.

The day was predictably falling into place. First the Nazi's attempted coup, now the Bitch and her computer printout of all possible ailments. This cool August morning, a pilot film for the fall, she was even more dissatisfied, even more fatally ill than ever. Cal delayed surrendering his soul to her until the last drop of coffee was gone.

Joan was struck stone deaf the minute her daughter began peeling off her symptoms, having long ago decided that her maternal obligation to Laura began no earlier than twelve P.M. By the post meridian the Bitch was just barely sufferable. By no more than a hair. Cal must bear the brunt of her personality until the noon whistle blew.

"Daddy, I think I have a brain tumor. It must be as big as a grapefruit by now. I'm probably dying." She had discovered Bette Davis, he guessed, by the thick slabs of bravery in the face of certain death. And the rat-tat-tat of her delivery.

"Do you black out?" Clinically, seriously, while fishing the milk bowl for Rice Krispies stragglers.

"No."

"Do you get dizzy spells?"

"No."

"How about nausea?"

"Most things make me nauseous. People, things. . . ."

"I mean physically nauseous."

"No."

145

"Do you put your shoes in the refrigerator?" His eyes in a holding pattern not to tip his hand. He thought of sorrowful things to insure a stone face.

"No, none of those things, daddy, but I know, I just *feel* it growing. When I'm very still I can almost hear it."

"Final question. Has anyone proved for certain that you have a brain?"

"N . . . oh, you. You make sick jokes about everything. (They smiled together.) You're serious and you're funny at the same time. But no fooling, daddy, I have symptoms. It hurts here (temple), and here (behind right ear), and especially here (back of eyes).

Cal was hooked. Where the Nazi attacked in the open, stormed his door, with rattle and thunder, the Bitch came in through the basement and had him bound and gagged before he could shut his peephole. She said, "daddy" softly, her brown eyes moist and clingy, and he was in knots.

"What symptoms, miss? What symptoms? Don't be vague now. Give me definite, legitimate symptoms. Not a general dissatisfaction with four thousand years of history."

"Big joke. To you it's a big joke. I feel . . . I don't know . . . achy, restless, bored . . . you know . . . uneasy. Yes that's it . . . uneasy. Like something bad is going to happen to me at any second. Is that indicative of anything serious?"

Hooked, yet playing with his captor, he said, "Gee, baby, I didn't know it was *that* serious. We'd better take tests."

She brightened. Joan, from the den, took no sides, which meant she sided with Cal.

"We'll have to start with an angiogram. That's a must. You know how that works. We take a six-inch needle and inject this colored dye into your spine. It makes your whole system visible under special light. Then the procto-vue master. We have a look at your intestines through your rectum. (She lit a cigarette, shaking, and inhaled greedily as if to catch up on her smoking.) Keeping up with me? Good. Finally the needle test. That one's a little more extensive than the other two. We plot your nerve endings by sticking you with little gold pins. Your nerves stay green for about a month, you know, from the angiogram. You look like a roadmap of Long Island. But it's all part of the test program

146

and goddamn it, Laura what the hell's the matter with you?" His about-face caught her between puffs. She coughed, belching smoke. "This nonsense with tumors and cancers. Last week it was accidents and operations. Leave it alone, Laura, you have time thirty years from now." Left hanging, suspended between a soft daddy and a hard one she puffed again as if the smoke could be braided into an escape line across the chasm. Finding she was no spider, she plunged her Kent filter into what remained of the cottage cheese and cinnamon.

"Well Jody Kleinmann died of cancer. I'll bet her father laughed and laughed when she complained."

"But all you have is a mild case of astriminosis, a very mild case." He played her game, to waltz her away from the edge with a sickness concocted just for her. An exclusive, fit for a princess. Because she has no right thinking of death at twenty. And it wore well, she was quite happy with it. It was something Bette Davis might get. She didn't even ask for a description.

Joan looked at her watch. Twelve thirty. "God almighty, Laura, let's not spend your last week in the doctor's office. Move yourself if you want to have something to wear this fall. You're late, as usual, for that, too. Probably nothing left in Lord and Taylor but oddballs." The girl needs pins up her ass not in her nerves. She chuckled over Cal's shell game with the Bitch. Good show.

Going shopping. Japanese tea serving was easy by comparison. Shopping, their style, was a complex and highly stylized cultural phenomena. After food and sleep came shopping. In time of tragedy, when the heart ached with an irremediable wound, when the spirit sagged like the belly of a pregnant elephant, and sex and alcohol had no effect, shopping proved to be the magic potion.

Joan loved it. Loved it though she was not a heavy spender. Shopping and spending, related as they are, are not the same thing. In Cedarhurst and its four sister towns she was quick to assess what the latest was, where the supplies were best, whose prices were the lowest, and which stores had the brightest, politest clerks. Head-hunting, too, while shopping. She could always fit another three-by-five into her file. As a seasoned retail veteran she knew that the A and S parking lot in nearby Hempstead was always filled, that Korvettes' lots in Green Acres had car thieves who preyed on shoppers like cattle rustlers. That the more Jewish an area, the better the prices, that shopping in Garden City, a tight Christian town across the Southern State Parkway was a treat for those who wanted it all in one place. Peck and Peck, Lord and Taylor, Bloomingdales, and A and S, row after row of giants that stood like the pyramids along Franklin Avenue, cold and imposing from the outside like the Christians, warm and bustling inside, like the Jews. And the parking was easy.

If she permitted herself, if the real things in life had not so absorbed her, she could spend every day haunting the Judeo-Christian pleasure palaces in Garden City. But bound by priorities she limited her reserves to the business of life in her own kingdom.

Today was border-crossing day. A and S had a marvelous room for young willowy college girls that leaned toward plaid skirts and bulky sweaters. The Bitch didn't, but her mother did. They had words and Laura, as usual, acquiesced. It was easier, having no strong feelings about anything, for the daughter to tag after the mother. After all, Joan reasoned, she might as well learn to shop. God knows, she isn't learning a damn thing in that fun factory taking courses like horseback riding and music appreciation. (Did you know, mother, that Chopin was an anti-Semite? And that Tchaikovsky had epilepsy?) Those bastard professors could make a course out of nose-picking if they could fill up a class of nose-pickers. Call it Internasal Exploration 303 and build a whole department of study around it. That girl. The Nazi, though, that's something else. He's got a brain. His father's brain. Now if he has my sense of life we'll see something great. Maybe like Arnie . . . minus the death wish, minus that streetwalker yen of his.

Laura is just a body consuming. Might as well teach her consumption so she can trade her body for an earner. Make her a perfect match. One who rakes it in joined to one who spreads it like manure. Cal disapproves. He wants her as educated as she can be; thinks it's great for a woman to make it on her own. My Laura will have a survivor's education, dear husband, we don't need any more victims. But who knows, he may be right. Maybe she's a late bloomer. I wouldn't want to live with the idea that I stood in her way. So it's on to basketweaving and Martin Buber

148

or Internasal Exploration, if it must be. But smarts I'll try to give her, anyway.

Their caravan of two wandered for hours, buying much, sampling more. Joan stopped at the cruise-wear displays, thought for a moment about a mid-winter sailing and moved on. Sadly she wondered if she would still have her first mate by then. The United Fund thing this winter. A big responsibility. A cruise was out of the question.

Lunch at Stouffer's, at the very center of Christiandom. Once in a while they pretended to be rich horsey Old Brookville matrons. Churchgoers. It felt good, on occasion, to wear another skin. The menu was not very appetizing. No pizzazz in it, Joan thought. The place needed a little life. She polished the silverware while waiting for service. There were spots. She looked at the knife as if it were a mirror showing her crow's feet and frowned. Spotted silverware was insulting.

Laura feared an incident. She held her breath and read her mother's face. Waiting for service was all the incident needed. Finally the chopped liver came.

"Abominable. This chopped liver is abominable. It's sour. Can't you taste it?"

"Mother, it's alright, it's a little tangy, but it's alright. Please let's eat. Not another scene."

"No, not another scene, but I'm paying for decent food. I *want* decent food. That's the right way. I do things the right way. They should, too."

"We can't all be Mrs. Perfect, now can we, mother?"

"Oh, sir," she summoned the waiter with an undue amount of respect.

He was not a young man, perhaps that was why he walked so disinterestedly. A smirk was the easiest pattern for his face to fall into. She decided to be rather unkind about the appetizer.

"The chopped liver," she said to Smirk and pointed to it as if she had found something he had been seeking for years.

"Yes, you are correct, madam, it is chopped liver," he said with an extreme courtesy that was clearly impolite.

"Wrong," she said, "that is sour chopped liver. Taste it yourself."

"I am not permitted the luxury of dining with guests, madam," Smirk smirked and looked past her.

"Please bring me either a fresh plate or a piece of melon."

"Very good, madam," he answered and left like a proud, bleeding rooster. He soon returned with a different plate and the same disdain.

"This is fresh," she announced, "however, I ordered Russian dressing not French on the salad."

Smirk's nostrils vibrated and opened to maximum aperture. He was unnerved and so was Laura. They were both suffering, he in silence, while she twitched uncomfortably in her seat like a child with bladder trouble.

"Mother, you definitely said French," she whispered loud enough for Smirk to hear, sort of a back door apology.

"Laura, I said Russian. Now I am not an idiot and I am not losing my mind. I run very large organizations. Don't tell me what I said." Her eyes discharged large white sparks. Laura turned away to protect herself.

"You did say French and you are embarrassing the hell out of me."

"Then leave."

"Give me the keys."

"Like hell I will. Call a taxi."

"Fod God's sake, just behave, mother. That's all. Just act like a Christian."

Joan concentrated on the soup. It was cold and she hated cold soup. More than the Bitch's provocation. The waiter across the room tugged at his collar and drank water. He tried avoiding her glance, but like Lot's wife, he gave in to curiosity. He was a pillar of stone by the time he returned the soup to its maker.

"Like shoe leather," she stated and dropped the knife and fork in disgust. She summoned him back for round four as he was about to leave on a life-saving mission. His own. Leather steak in hand, spirit broken, his smirk reduced to a sickly smile, he nodded in resonance with her every gripe. Had he a tail it would have been dangling between his legs. It wagged when she summoned the Maitre d'.

A very dark, very small man, who looked as if he had to shave on the hour, fielded her complaints, smiled, nodded and promised instant satisfaction. He left, his heels clicking behind him on the oak floor.

"God, God, God," Laura softly wailed. "This is *not* the automat, mother. And Deidre Jaffee's mother is sitting in the corner. No don't turn around. Must you compound this comedy? Must you subject me to a touch of Old Brownsville? Oh, this is so mortifying. If you were so dissatisfied the proper thing to do would be to pick yourself up and walk out. Not create a scene."

Joan fizzed like an Alka-Seltzer. She tattooed the table with her fingers in march tempo, glaring coldly at her daughter. "Listen, you dumb Bitch, listen and learn," she hissed. "It's semi-aristocrats like you that get shafted all the time, that permit bugs like that waiter to get away with murder. You fancy-asses swallow a lot of guff from a lot of shitheads and call it good manners. Not me, I'm no lady in your sense of the word. Big deal. Who cares? You just shut up and learn. Learn to give the rest of the world that fat lip you give me."

Her lecture, simmering since this morning, was interrupted by the flare of silent trumpets. The Maitre d' approached the table with two waiters riding point, pushing two food carts. It looked like a crowning ceremony. And so they dined with three waiters flitting in and out. Everything was done to perfection, to almost a parody of excellence. Joan adjusted well to being served by three while Laura seemed to grow smaller each time a waiter helped her.

By coffee time the charade was over. They had full possession of the table again. The Bitch looked at the ceiling and offered thanks to the chandelier.

"Those toads. Do you see what hypocrites and fools they really are? I only wanted what was due us. As patrons. I bitched like hell and they put on this act for us. I really didn't get what was ours. I got a lot more. That's why they are toads. One harsh word and they fell all over themselves. Like cowards. A lesson, Bitch," she said dotting i's with her after-coffee cigarette. "If you're right, demand what's yours. The true aristocrats do. Be like me . . . a little?"

What began as a lecture ended as a question.

"What makes you think I want to be like you? No, don't ask me what I want to be like. I don't know. I'm a slow learner. But you're *not* my ideal. Oh, don't get me wrong. You're my mother and I love you. You know that. At least I think you do. But I don't want to be like you."

Softly, knowing that danger lay up ahead, she asked, "What is so wrong with me, dear? In your eyes, at least. I never neglected you, in spite of all my other activities. You've always had the best, the very best of everything. Like I did, like my mother did. I'm not a tramp or an alcoholic. Nothing really to be ashamed of, even if I badger your friends' fathers for donations. I was always there when you needed me. We did your homework together, took care of you when you got sick. My God, you always come to one of us when you have a problem. So why do you have such little regard for me?" She knew she had to be careful not to appear on her knees. She lit another Dunhill. Funny, she still enjoyed the first puff. Life should only be first puffs.

Laura played with the cream pitcher. "Oh, I don't know, it's not the kind of thing you have on the tip of your tongue. Sure, I've thought about it. But I never really *said* it."

"Say it now."

"Well, mother, you're a streetfighter, a real tough egg even though you've had more than most. What I resent most, though, is the me-against-the-rest-of-the-world thing you have. About everything."

"You need that, Laura. In every situation someone's waiting to cut your throat. It's that kind of world. And let me tell you something about you. Something valuable." She stopped to remove a small cut of tobacco that caught between her teeth. "You are not a survivor and I've got my work cut out to make you one."

"Is that what you call what you're trying to do to me?" She had three ways to respond to her mother, sardonically, sarcastically, and caustically. The mildest of the three was employed here as they conversed on a less than bitter level.

"Shut up and listen. Let me tell you a bit about yourself. You are a follower without conviction, an aristocrat without a fortune, a weakling without the saving grace of charm, and in Grandma Pearl's terms, a lazy good-for-nothing. But above all, basically you're a good girl and a first-class Bitch. There's hope. Don't worry, I can still do something with you."

152

"I do worry, because I know what you mean," Laura said, attempting to salvage a few drops of pride.

Joan rolled over her. "Your mother wants to educate you despite your college background, despite those other bitches that mirror and infest you. And when I hand you your diploma from *my* school, sweetie, you'll be solid. You'll rise to the top like cream, when cream rose. Not like your gooney friends with their organic food and colored boyfriends, their uppers and downers."

"Unfair, unfair, mother. I never. . . ."

"Yes you did but it doesn't matter. Let the others sleepwalk through the next fifty years. Who cares? You won't and that's as sure as sunrise. Your father can walk around with stars in his eyes. I can't. Maybe he thinks healthy neglect is going to work in your favor, in Peter's favor (thrown in for balance). I don't."

She had promised herself, driving to Garden City, that it would just be the two of them. Now he was pulled in, Laura's unseen, silent ally. (Did she do that?) It would be geometrically harder to reach her now with her forces doubled.

Laura reacted in textbook fashion. "Now, why is it, that daddy sees a lot of things differently without all the brass knuckles and razor blades? He's struggled, too, but you don't hear him talking about life as if we were back in the Stone Age."

"Oh, Laura," Joan said wearily as she surveyed the mounting work load, "we all love daddy, but can't you see that he's a hopeless victim of everything, everyone? If it weren't for me we'd have nothing, nothing."

"By nothing, you mean money?"

"What else? Money and what it can buy. Grandma says that money is the world's sunshine. It brightens everything it touches." She knew it sounded silly, but sometimes silly things are truer than sensible ones.

"Well, I won't spend my life worrying about those things."

"Then you better find someone who will."

"I guess I can do that if I have to. I have the equipment."

"Acquired, in part, with my money."

"Yours and daddy's. You seem to forget that it all came through his hands."

"I guess so, baby, but without me it would have kept right on

153

going. But when did you become an expert in economic matters?"

"I'm not," the Bitch said, happy to confess her ignorance. "But I love daddy a great deal. It hurts me when he's belittled."

With her will-o'-the-wisp voice she painted Joan into a corner. Clearly she would have to be defensive for a while. "I do, too, Laura. This talk is just between the two of us. Forgive me my little delusion of economic power. I got carried away by the fact that I'm a good money manager. And I am, you know that. And you know how many people owe daddy money and he doesn't press them for it."

"But there's plenty left over for us. We're not on the poverty level yet."

"Well, it could be better. It could be a lot better."

"Everything could be better, mother, my life . . . your life. Don't think I'm not grateful for what you've done. Not as grateful as you expect, but grateful enough. You show interest, that's fine. That's great. A lot of mothers don't. I'm slow, I'm creepy, but I'm not dumb. I see things, I know things, and I don't want to be created in your image, with my head screwed on right, pointed toward the land of milk and honey. I don't want your wonderful life. I want my life," she said as she crushed her cigarette into the ashtray, "whatever it turns out to be."

"Laura, I'm doing the best I can. I never said it was perfection or the top of the world. That's one of the things I'm trying to teach you, you make the best of what you have. Adapt, adjust. Now your father and I are two very different people. Not my fault, not his. But we have an understanding. We get along."

"Some understanding," said the Bitch, unable to resist the opening. "You have your clubs and the beach and he has his Italian connection."

Suddenly Joan grew deaf. Noise of the trucks passing by, diners clinking glasses, was suddenly shut off. She felt very old, very weak, like some trapped lioness with a dozen poisoned arrows sticking out of her.

"You know?"

"I know."

"How long?"

"Not long. I overheard a few sentences. I put together the rest. What are you going to do?"

154

"I'll do something . . . I guess."

Laura thought that she would soar like an eagle, float and gloat over her mother. And she did for about five seconds, falling earthward due to the unguarded look of ashes on Joan's face. But it was gone before her mother lit the next cigarette, absorbed, detoxified and eliminated through her pores.

"So we're having problems," she admitted. "Everybody has problems. We'll work it out though. You can put money on it.'"

They smoked in silence, encased in their own smoke screens. Still after years of sharing the same bathroom they were sizing each other up, tallying strengths and weaknesses.

"Mother, if it makes you feel better, understand that I'll adjust nicely, too. So many of my friends have divorced parents. I wouldn't feel out of place."

"Screw you, sister," Joan said. "I'm not in the least interested in your trauma right now. Right now we'd better get going. Grandma Pearl is on the 6:02. Be nice to her. She's going to stay for the weekend."

Laura groaned. Joan paid the bill and they left.

Grandma Pearl waited at the station like an aircraft carrier at anchor. A solid man-of-war, armed to the teeth in furs and diamonds. She wore her famous ten thousand dollar mink. The Nazi originally thought the name of the animal who died for Mrs. Fialakoff was the ten thousand dollar mink. Even after learning the truth he still called the coat by its price, as did his father for the same reason.

As always, two shopping bags that announced to the world that Judy Bond was on strike, were at her sides like harbor tugs. Though the strike was settled years ago, the imposing Mrs. F. wore the bags with the same elegance that she wore her diamonds. She never came to Cedarhurst without her two sidekicks for they contained the cream of Wolff the Butcher's crop of fine meats, cookies available only from her bakery, and peaches the size of oranges.

The Bitch giggled seeing the small navy.

"Oh stop that," Joan said as the Mercedes pulled into the small station. "She's my mother and your grandmother. Be kind."

That word bounced off the walls in Laura's mind. Kindness

155

never characterized the relationship between her father and the large gray-haired lady who waved to them. She had heard stories of the sharp clashes between the soft spoken doctor and the diamond-studded dictator. By now, though, both combatants were tired of struggle. If she wanted to be an authority on cancer (and why not, didn't her own husband and brother die from it?) the doctor permitted the lady her degrees. Let brother-in-law Sidney stand up to her on insurance, if he dared (he never did). All he had to lose were the premiums on her houses and diamonds.

She seldom spoke to the Nazi, especially after he had called her a schmuck during one of their dialogues. A battle of the giants, under one roof, the world's two greatest experts on everything. A real happening, Laura called it. Peter uttered his curse as they (neither of them drivers) argued as to which was the best car ever made. She stood there with her injured-woman-of-great-nobility look and demanded an apology. And was told to go shit in her hat, complicating things for weeks.

Laura stole side glances as they drove home, comparing, studying. If the waiter at Stouffer's was smirk, Grandma Pearl was suspicion. Permanently arched eyebrows, on a collision course with each other framed the coldest, most suspicious eyes Laura had ever seen. A slightly hooked nose and sallow skin gave her a look of oriental cruelty. Her hair, jet black at one time had turned partly gray. She was heavy, but that had little to do with the fact that she was an imposing woman of substance. Where Joan struck with a rapier, her grandmother used a bludgeon, hammering into blood and gristle anyone, genius and idiot alike, who dared oppose her.

Mr. Fialakoff, though many doubted he ever existed, had contributed a certain gentility and tenderness but only Joan had received the genes. His other two daughters were emotional basket cases. Papa also left quite a flourishing fur business and a few pieces of property. Pearl sold the former and enlarged the latter, but this all took place before Cal came "into the family," a term that implied a certain degree of condescension on the part of the family Fialakoff in permitting the grocer's son entrance.

Grandma Pearl had things to do this weekend. She was still a mother. That condition did not end on the borders of marriage. Laura (a funny name for a Jewish girl) was an alarmist. Very likely the noise about an affair with a shiksa was just garbage. And Calvin, for all his nuttiness, was not a skirt chaser. Well, by the time the weekend was over it would all be love and kisses again. If it wasn't, then first thing Monday morning Sidney takes her to O'Brien, the lawyer, and we change the will. On third thought, a meaningless approach, an empty gun. Money and that man weren't the best of friends.

They talked. With two such iron wills there had to be rules. One speaks, one listens. Otherwise chaos. Mrs. F. who only remembered others' failures listened as Joan, emotionally drained from lunch with Laura, talked as if Pentothalized. She began with Cal's confession over tea and graham crackers and concluded with Victor leaning on his rake and asking, "Who, me?" Pearl was not a mother in whom to confide. It was like sticking one's finger in a live socket.

"Never heard such a thing. The bastid wants his cookie and he wants to eat it, too. The dirty bastid." Her head rocked back and forth like the sages of old. "Vey, vey, vey, we got a problem. Why you married that schlemiel instead of Arnie I'll never know. At least with Arnie you know he's a skirt chaser. So you make him pay for it. And he's some provider with the Medicaid. But this bastid tells you to your face he's playing around and he likes it just the way it is. The quiet ones. They're all the same. Like thieves in the night."

"You know," she said after careful deliberation, "he's worse than a nigger, Joannie. I wouldn't take it, I tell you. I wouldn't take it no how." Her eyebrows arched to a meeting. "You tell that story to a judge and he'd die. He locks up the bastid and throws the key away." She began building a case for the judge. "You worked, you sweated, you made him a doctor and now he tells you to go screw yourself." Pearl walked the kitchen as if it were the Jewish stage on Second Avenue. All her creative hate was flowing, small streams of it joining the main body.

"First thing Monday morning we go right over to the vault and clean it out. Stocks, bonds, jewelry, cash, the whole schmear. You hear me Joan? (She was only five feet away.) We'll put it in my vault for the time being. Not even a rubber band we'll leave the bum. Then we'll take the bankbooks and hide them." Pearl was loving her scenario. "Then, we'll throw the bastid out on his ass. With his whore."

Joan began to swim for her life. "Mother, calm down. Don't say such nonsense. It's all half his. The house, the money, what there is of it, everything. It's all half his. You're not helping. You're looking to castrate him."

"Foolish child, don't talk that way. It's yours, all yours. Didn't you struggle with him getting started? You didn't have to. When all the rest had cars and babies and houses you had nothing, nothing because he was struggling. And that bastid had the nerve to tell me to stick my money in my ear when I wanted to buy you that Buick. His pride. My Joannie suffered without a car and he had the nerve to talk about pride. Now I ask *you*, my darling daughter, where is *your* pride?"

One of her weapons. Taking someone else's words or characteristics and turning it back on him. Like a bent thumb. A powerful tool. It took from the enemy's arsenal and added to her own.

If it were not too late Joan might salvage a bit from the flood. "Don't talk to me about throwing the man out into the street and about pride. It's very easy for you to point a finger. Where was your pride when you talked papa into buying that load of stolen furs? Remember? I remember. He said no, never, and you nagged and nagged and nagged until you won out."

"Oh, that was business."

"And that makes it okay?"

"Of course that's okay."

"Well those furs were stolen from somebody. Somebody had a bellyache."

"Well papa didn't steal them. It's not my crime. Somebody was going to make a bundle. Why not us?"

"It's the same thing as stealing."

Mrs. Fialakoff felt uneasy. Joan was not like the other two. Barbara and Carol would listen to reason. This one had her own ideas. This one was always a heartache. Like her father. She doesn't listen. She wondered where in the entire orchard of their family trees did she inherit this rotten apple. "Still you ought to throw him out," she insisted.

"Why, because he's become a little sick, a little confused? What

158

he's doing is a kind of sickness. I'm sure of it. Did you empty the vault and throw out papa when he got sick?"

Mrs. F. put on one of her scornful faces. She had that number in different styles. This one was haughty scorn. "How can you compare? My God. Papa had cancer, a decent disease. Not hot nuts. Can't you see the difference?"

"Well, regardless of what you say, I'm not throwing him out. I'm going to stick with it as long as necessary, that's what I'm going to do, mother."

"So what you're telling me is that you're going to encourage Calvin to fool around with the shiksa."

"No, mother, but I won't forcibly discourage him."

Pearl threw her hands up to the heavens and spoke to its Tenant. "Listen to her, listen to her, will you. I don't believe it. She's telling him 'go ahead, fool around . . . but keep it quiet.'

"Yes, yes," Pearl told the heavens. "That's what it is. Oh, if papa were alive he'd beat the hell out of that punk, that bastid."

If Joan dared to smile she would smile wickedly. It was so difficult to love this woman. "But you said you loved him like a son. Now you want him dead or stripped naked, mother." She felt strangely like her own daughter earlier today.

"Sure I love him. As long as he takes care of you the way a Jewish husband should. But this? With the two of you acting like goyim with fancy new house rules? Poo, I'd like to spit on that damned shiksa housewrecker."

"Well, mother, I'm sorry you found out. I am certainly not leaving him. Period. I love him and if I can hold him this way, and I don't mind his little friend, you shouldn't mind either . . . mother."

Mrs. Fialakoff refused to face her daughter. Afraid perhaps of saying something that might sever the ties that bind. Cal would love that.

"That bastid, that bastid," she continued to mutter as if by these magic words alone Joan's spell might pass.

159

There was no such place as Greenport; Cal was teasing her, toying with her love of myth and folklore. She knew of Montauk and the Hamptons, elegant strips of beach where southeastern Long Island branched off like a lobster's claw past Riverhead. Sutton Place East, Cal called it. Some of Victor's customers had fifty thousand dollar shanties planted like mushrooms in the dunes around Amagansett and East Hampton. But she had to be shown the North Fork as proof of its existence. Maybe *then* she would believe it. She was quite selective about reality.

They cut a week out of August's end, a reward for enduring summer's oppressive blanket, and went away together. The timing was perfect. Stephen and Victor junior went to summer camp courtesy of an Italian Benevolent Association that Manny half-heartedly joined when his own boys were small. Cal felt the time was a debt due them. Hours plucked from the week, when they were together, were like a rich dessert to a starving man. Quite delicious, but hardly sustaining. Cal wanted a full meal . . . and the time to savor it.

As all feasts begin with a look, he repeatedly glanced at her as they changed to State Road 58 when the Long Island Expressway ran out of concrete. "I just want the pleasure of going to sleep touching you. And I want to wake up and see your scrawny neck first thing in the morning. I want that for one week or I'll go bonkers thinking about it. That's not too much to ask, is it Tessa?" They were on Route 25 now.

She touched his inner thigh and stroked it encouraging him,

strengthening her. A promise of wild things in the night while the Sound roared below. He knew that he could please her and that in turn pleased him. A delicious cycle.

August had turned warm again destroying his hopes for an early fall. He hated summer, viewed its sultry omnipresence as an invasion of his privacy, an attempt to steal his strength and make little puddles of it at his feet.

After half an hour of roadside stands that overflowed with tomatoes and peaches, of quaint New England-type houses where old ladies sold homemade pies, they found a motel almost drawn to his plans. At a bend in the road, where the Sound broke through like a river of quivering mercury, set back to where the cliffs began, was a two-tiered railroad car of white motel built over a row of parking spaces. It had a joyous symmetry, but at that moment he would have found joy in a bolt of lightning.

"Here?" he asked hopefully.

"Here."

She casually undressed before him and put on a white bikini. "No," he said disapproving with a slow nod, "I like you the other way, without those two handkerchiefs." She obliged. They made love with a chair propped against the door knob, an angled sentinel against overzealous chambermaids.

"I didn't see the point in waiting until the sun went down," he said as a half-apology.

"No reason why we have to," she softly whispered and opened her arms to welcome him. Her body glowed with the sun. No beachgoer, she trapped the great bestower of life in her backyard, clad in shorts and a halter.

He wanted desperately to slow time to a crawl, but he was forced to surrender to a lust older than his will. Too soon. It was over too soon for them both. Dr. Bernstein had lost another battle with Nature as he tried to extrude his passion, to dole it out in barely measurable units. The starving man won out over the miser.

Tessa, rolled to meet him, became glove to his hand. When her body commanded she surrendered, kissing and caressing him, begging him to surrender, too.

Pleasure evanesced drop by drop; they separated and lay like sunbathers on their backs, silent and tender with each other. Cal

161

thought of Oscar Wilde's line about not knowing what enough is until you've had too much. He hoped, ecstatically, to overshoot (he grinned at the pun) his mark. If his body were good to him. She was too much, lying there, her long, firm unmarked body, breasts saggy a bit, vertically, but fine, very fine, prone. Her bright dark face was too much, also the crown of black waves shiny as a crow's wing.

She interrupted the silence. "I have small breasts . . . or didn't you notice?"

He kissed them, half-answering her question. "Tessa I don't care if they're large or small. If they stand at attention or hang like eggplants. They're attached to you and that makes them lovely. They give me pleasure because you give me pleasure. You're not supposed to be a centerfold."

She kissed him for that, spontaneously yet without passion.

They showered together like friends instead of lovers and quickly dressed for beach strolling. Cal assured her that the hundred-foot high cliffs, the vermillion sand, and the shoreline that twisted and turned so that not more than a mile of it was visible at any time, would give her a sense of lower California. Neither of them had ever been west of the Mississippi. She walked with a stride, he noticed for the first time, that worked her hips to greatest advantage. Clothed, that is. Already he was seeing things he had never noticed before.

He began making presents of everything they saw. Odd-shaped boulders, pockmarked and shiny with sea spray, sat in the Sound like cows in a meadow. They became hers. Seagulls buzzed them and flew off to keep other appointments. A gift. Orchards of driftwood with their fingers bent to palms, like beggars . . . for her. She accepted each present with a smile that suddenly turned inside out when he promised a tomorrow certain to be better.

One hand shading her eyes against the sun, the other on her hip, she said, "Look darling, take that word out of our conversation. I don't want to hear about tomorrows. I love it when we don't talk about tomorrow."

She found a large rock built for two, took her place and he took his. It shone in the dying sun because of the thousands of tiny glass chips embedded within. They faced the Sound and threw

162

small pebbles into it as if they were feeding monkeys in a zoo.

Tessa reached for and found his hand . . . "Baby, we *have* no future. We have no past. Every day is a gift, like the ones you just gave me. Once we start talking about tomorrow, or plan for it, we're only lying to ourselves. I don't want that. I don't need it. It's like using a credit card when you haven't a damn cent." She scratched the rock, loosening a few translucent flakes. "I love you like I never thought I had it in me to love. Like a corpse come to life. And you feel the same way. I see it. I know it. You don't even have to say it anymore."

"Even if I want to?"

"Say it whenever you like. All gifts cheerfully accepted. But it doesn't matter. What we have is one thin strand across the Grand Canyon. No more. Maybe less. So every day we have is pure profit. Victor could decide tomorrow to blow our heads off. Today we're alive; tomorrow we could just be photographs or a headstone. Tomorrow Joan could just say, 'Cal, old boy, your free pass has been cancelled. Either kiss the broad good-bye or it's curtains. I got the phone number of a hit man.' She's a smart cookie. She's got it all figured out, but she's also human, no matter what she's agreed to."

"All things are possible, Tessa," he said reclaiming and examining his fingers almost medically, "but not probable. Don't take the worst alternative. We have more room than just a day at a clip."

She took his fingers from him and kissed them one at a time. "Oh, I wish I could believe that Cal. But even if it were true, look, I take each day as it comes. Then I go to the next. Hey, that's not so bad. I get a full twenty-four hours worth and if there's more . . . that's great. If not. . . ." Tessa turned away.

Cal pawed at the red sand to see how deep it went. Her words cut into him. "You know, Tessa, so much of my life, almost from the beginning has been lived in the future. It's hard to get used to now, this day. *When* I grow up, *when* I become a doctor, *when* I set up practice, *when* the kids are grown. I don't think I ever said a paragraph without a when in it. I almost let a whole life slip away, preparing, planning. Some of it has been beneficial, sure. I'm someplace up the ladder. And I'm lucky. The mortgage has

163

been paid and I'm alive to cash in on my whens. But you want to do it whether or not. Okay, we'll do it on a pay as you go basis. We'll throw out the tomorrows and the whens."

They sat watching the sea birds, bobbing like corks as they rode out the waves. Then they turned eastward and began walking back to the motel. Retracing their footsteps, happy to reclaim the small part of themselves left behind, they yelped like puppies and dodged the rising tide that reached out to nip at their toes.

Cal said, "Joan is, was, more like me about time. A future liver. I guess part of our . . . estrangement is due to the fact that she's happy to exchange now for later. I did it, sure, but I wasn't particularly crazy about the idea. We developed a time lag and I guess a language barrier, too. I don't know what the hell she's talking about any more. It's the twenty years that keep us together . . . and apart, too. There's some love. The three of us know that, but it's not really love." He turned to her and diagnosed. "You know love, like cancer, covers a variety of similar conditions."

"Oh, Cal, how can you talk about those different things in the same breath?"

He shrugged it off. "There's the love I feel for you. Really a blend of lust, tenderness, respect, other things. A grab bag of things. You love your parents, but that's not the same love you feel for a brother, a friend, Joan Bernstein. There should be about ten words, different words where one is used. It shows, I think, a lot about this loveless society of ours that we have one lousy four-letter word for different worlds of feelings."

She covered him with her honey-brown arms, her eyes glistening like the silicate-speckled rocks. "Now, tonight think about the first variety on your laundry list, mister. That's where the money is. Maybe, just maybe, we'll get away with it. Maybe we'll be lovers until we're too old to enjoy sex. Maybe. Till then I'll love you as as hard as I can in twenty-four hour segments."

"Like *The Perils of Pauline?*"

"Never mind. Like Ecclesiastes and The Song of Solomon."

As they strolled, a spot in the distance grew into a man. He scavanged the beach for what waste products of industry he could salvage. They stopped and chatted with the grizzled old beachcomber who seemed more confused by them than surprised. They praised him for keeping America beautiful and free of Schlitz cans

164

while gathering old Clorox containers and boat flotsam with him. When the man departed she convinced him to strip nude. Cal, at first very reluctant to strip completely (a novice at spontaneity), did so after a coax or two. He wondered how she could be so relaxed with her nudity. They lay on a bed of warm rocks and surrendered to the heat above and below. When ventral and dorsal currents met he sighed "ahhhh" and stroked her knee. She was at a loss as to what the source of his "ahhhhs" were, sun-centered or Tessa-centered.

Back in the room they made love again using the chair as their first line of defense. For years it was medical fact that he was incapable of more than one sexual encounter a day. So he made personal medical history. The first rewards of using Tessa's way of measuring time. He napped comfortably, enveloped by the sensation of crumbling walls and shattered truths.

The balance of the week, enjoyed in units of one day and night, floated by with the super-heightened vividness of a Cezanne painting. Cloudy mornings were spent walking the main street of Greenport where shopkeepers spent minutes with them discussing everything but the wares that brought them together. In parts of the town where the whites lived, everything was painted white. White storefronts, white homes, white hospital. All took the sun in and threw out a shine of great intensity on a cloudy day. Rural solar energy at work.

She wore her yellow floppy hat, renamed The Bayville Bonnet, after that day of a month ago, a tee shirt that said "A woman without a man is like a fish without a bicycle," bleached dungarees, and stringy sandals.

He, to sustain that silly sartorial mood, matched her with an inverted sailor's hat, corduroy pants, shiny in the seat, and a sweat shirt air-conditioned at the armpits. But they were scrubbed clean inside, the combination of sex and salt air acting as abrasives. Though they spent some time laughing at each other, a sort of easiness developed, initiated by the sharing of the same bed, perpetuated by a carefree pattern of dress and life.

In mornings they walked the defunct piers, black skeletons from the past when bootlegged whiskey and seafood kept the town humming. Unused appendages of a once active seaport, they were now useless and sad looking. A ferry boat from Shelter Island tooted and discharged its cargo of Volkswagens and Hondas. Then a new supply of Fords and Chevelles were taken away by the same host. A couple of beers, salad, and fried shrimp brought them past noon, they thought, since he carried no watch.

They were each other's world, these adult ragamuffins, for seven thoroughly lived days, seven ecstatically spent nights. No boring gaps despite the deserts of silence that spaced their time together. Silence has many meanings, contentment being one, restoration a second.

When it was too cool to swim and too windy to sun they walked the roads. A bronzed doughboy frozen forever with fixed bayonet, stood at the north end of town, oxidized green with age. She posed with invisible fixed bayonet for his invisible camera beside the silent soldier, mocking the foolishness of war until a black-and-white patrol car stopped short. A large rawboned kid, recently off the land, wearing an enormous gun only slightly smaller than the doughboy's, sourly asked them to move on, please. Which they did and the policeman wished them a good day.

"That must be some kind of magic incantation they use out here to ward off evil spirits, Tessa. Have a nice day. It just can't mean that. It's too simple, too obvious. Maybe the first letters give the meaning like in Kabbala. H, A, N, and D: it spells hand. The Black Hand. The Mafia." A false glow of discovery. "Mafia, that's it. What do you think, baby?"

Her voice sounded tired. "Hell, all it means is what it says. Have a nice day. Accept it, Cal. These farmers lead a nice, simple life. That says it all."

He let it die there.

They passed a duck farm. He yanked her in. And once in she was fascinated by the waves of orange-footed, low-bottomed fowl who moved like an armada of rowboats on a calm lake over the spacious grounds.

"Okay, hero, a test," she said enticingly. "Let's see who can drink the most raw eggs."

He screwed up his face and begged off. "Raw eggs?"

"Aw c'mon, to hell with the cholesterol."

"It's not the cholesterol, love. I just can't stand the thought of it. It looks like a slimy orgasm."

166

"But look what it'll do for your libido."

"Do you think I need it? Am I failing you, my dear?" All theatrically said within earshot of the goggle-eyed farmer who was sorting jumbos distractedly. The strangely dressed pair of New Yorkers only confirmed his opinion about the depraved life in the city.

Tessa declined to answer and began the contest alone by piercing the small end of a large egg. She held it high, as if she were using eyedrops. A soft slurping and the egg became a shell. He followed her suspiciously. Then they quit without keeping score, paid the farmer who almost forgot to charge them, and left holding hands. It had no meaning, the egg contest. One began, the other picked it up (after some reluctance). Spontaneity was the meaning.

"You didn't answer my question," he said and waited like a first-grader for his gold star.

"You know the answer, sonny. I don't pay compliments to insecure little boys." She reconsidered. "But as pure fact you do lay me well, lover." He got his gold star.

By the end of the week the sun returned to the beach and so did they. Cal took a long branch and with both hands plunged the pointed end into the soft sand. She was right behind him, close at hand, to see what the nut was up to.

"I claim this land for Princess Tessa," he said in Ponce de Leon fashion. "I will call it Kingdom of Caltessa. Any man who disputes my claim shall be sent to his maker forthwith. One small step for mankind, one large pair of blisters for the Senor."

Tessa kissed him and laughed in one messy motion. "Oh, thank you Senor Calvino. When will you erect my splanch on it?"

"As soon as you've submitted one thousand times, dona Teresa," he replied.

"Oh, goody," she squeeled. "I think we passed that point last night."

Images of Oscar Wilde.

"Don't sass me kid, or I'll take back my country."

"You do that, big boy, and I'll take back my lays," she threatened.

"Drats, foiled again, and by an Iap. That's Italian-American Princess."

They splashed each other until their clothes were soaked. It took some time for them to dry, hung on driftwood like scare-crows, in the fickle sun. Time well spent talking, talking, talking. He told her more about his parents, those elfish doctor-makers who died only weeks apart once their one job was completed. Their great tragedy, he told her, was never really knowing the person to whom they were in perpetual bondage. And vice versa. But such things happen he said, to Jews whose one fixed star is everything for the children.

Tessa's turn. The oldest of six girls, she had a major role in their upbringing. As with all her burdens she accepted mother-hood by proxy with resignation. Occasionally with joy. After they dressed, they went to visit country churches, all of them Protestant, on the North Fork. Most of them were wooden and Greenport white, with tall spires that pointed rigidly at God. All over one hundred years old but standing stiff-necked and skeletal. Tessa and Cal sat on flat plain benches and spoke in unnecessarily hushed tones while sunlight speared the floors.

"Certainly didn't let you get too comfortable with God," Cal remarked.

"We got plush and comfort at St. Ann's and I'm still not comfortable with Him," she replied. "Most of the time I feel He's not too proud of the mess He's made. Oh, that's silly. I rarely think about God, one way or the other. I just wanted to add something smart sounding. Something chic."

"It sounded good," Cal assessed. A salty breeze whistled through the open door. His stomach groaned with hunger. The taste of the skin on her neck was still fresh in his senses and he grew unbearably hungry for her, too. He felt so well that there was no time to think, to weigh life and come up short changed. Finally, finally, to be alive, here and now, and think of nothing else except how good it all felt.

The nights. Cal and Tessa were content, anxious, to retire early and either make lust-love or tender-love (without sex). Talk ceased when one of them fell asleep.

A few times they ventured out to study the night people of the North Fork. Once to see a science fiction movie that was as entertaining as it was unbelievable. The other time, their last night as an old married couple they ate an enormous lobster for two, almost as large as the table. Too full to go upstairs they

168

looked for a bar. Nothing fancy, nothing noisy. Just a quiet place to slosh a few ice cubes around in a glass. *Nimrod's* was just the ticket. An intimate log cabin-type of saloon, slightly frayed around the doors and windows, not too well-lit, but where a few Tom Collins would eat up the minutes before he would taste her skin again.

The booths were taken so they sat at the bar and ordered from a squat beefy man whose face showed a history of acne. Cal and Tessa looked around. A pleasant enough, young married type of gin mill. The drinks were large and Frank Sinatra sang "As Time Goes By" as if it had happened to him. Then Cal remembered. Sam Goodstein. He was trying out a new anti-spasmodic for Sam's rampaging colon. It had required a few days before the full effects could be gauged. That would have been yesterday.

"I'll be back in a few minutes. I have a call to make."

She kissed him, she didn't know why, when he left to find a phonebooth. The call was short. Sam's colon had declared a truce, the drug was working. Cal felt relieved since Sam was a dear friend as well as a patient.

Someone was sitting in his seat. A tall blond man, thirty, thirty-five. He had long side burns, a head full of obedient straw-colored hair and a wandering, bushy mustache. Obviously quite taken with himself, he was trying to sell the idea to Tessa.

She extended her hand limply to Cal as he approached, a devilish gleam dancing in her eyes. She couldn't wait to talk.

"Cal, I think this joker's trying to make me," she said matter-of-factly. "And he's so persistant, too. Won't take no for an answer."

He tried to stare the man down, flat-faced, squinty-eyed. The blond man had a slight scar on the bridge of his nose. Cal liked him even less up close. "I admire your taste, pal," he began in a monotone, matching voice to face, "but the lady already has a partner."

The man seemed to back up a bit before offering his defense. "Hey, dad, why not let the lady call her own shots. Women's lib, you know. You don't own; you just rent."

Cal's eyes became points as he responded. "Want to tell this young man the facts of life, honey?" he said to Tessa without looking at her.

169

She spun around on the red barstool, playfully, until she and the blond man were too close. "Go back to your sandbox, sonny, before your mama knows you're missing," she said.

"Okay, okay," he said backing away, drink in hand. "No offense intended."

"None was taken until you opened up your yap. Now back off nicely and I'll forget your face," Cal said.

With hands raised in mock-surrender he stepped back as if dancing, then, at the right moment he whirled around and left. Smiling, with glass in hand. They left soon after, scattering small jokes about the incident.

He wanted her very much that night. She encouraged him with everything she knew as they alternated leadership in their small room. This time no chair jammed against the doorknob, this time. . . . His gentleness with her was a powerful aphrodisiac. And her response was greater, deeper than at any time in her entire life. It frightened her. At one point, immediately after falling off the mountain she thought it was a great error to come with him to Greenport. Knocked at too many doors she preferred nailed shut. Had he taken advantage of her and asked questions about tomorrow . . . well, she wouldn't vouch for the answer. But doubt passed, carried by the strong blasts of sea air that rattled the screens.

He lay on his back breathing heavily. "My God," she told him, "that was super, really super. But look at you," she added, reading him by the light of the bathroom neon. "You're all sweated up. Here, let me dry you off, poor thing."

He felt like a baby during a diaper change. "Jesus, I didn't come out here to kill you. I couldn't even give you mouth-to-mouth. Did that guy at the bar cause you to . . . carry on so? Did you think you had to prove something to me?" she asked, ready to accept guilt.

"I think so. Silly isn't it?"

"Silly, yes, but I'm quite flattered that you try to impress me. Even after you have me. It shows you care a great deal. But I told you before, it's not necessary."

"It wasn't all insecurity. You looked very lovely tonight and I have this backlog of a week's marvelous experiences, pressing down . . . or building up. Like spontaneous combustion. You see, I'm finally getting some spontaneity."

They took the ferry to Sag Harbor early Sunday as the sun cleared the horizon. Cal wanted to explore the old Jewish cemetery on the South Fork. Tessa loved reading the engravings on the tombstones. It gave her, she said, a greater sense of history than the history books.

If he lived to be very old, if somehow enough of his brain remained to sort things, to arrange his life in descending order of beautiful memories, this week that just was would stand out well ahead of whatever finished second. It was the week that he first discovered Tessa for the second time.

He drove slowly back to Nassau. He took back roads expanding a two hour trip into four. In a trade off he would gladly give five minutes of any other week (and more) for one minute of the past one. But there are no traders in time, so it was up to him to pack his suitcase so that this week was always on top, available for instant wear. Memories are like good clothes; they always fit well and they never go out of style.

**12**

The lush smell of tomatoes ripening on the vine came to him in waves. Mingling with the odor of a long-dead DiNobili cigar it filled his nostrils, rendering him incapable of anything save reflection. Manny sat back on his rocking chair, white hair on pink skin. The aromas soon flooded his brain until he could taste the tomatoes and see the fruits' pink taut skin, plump and luxurious as a young woman's breast.

Surrendering to his senses was one of his life's last pleasures. (They were constantly leaving, one by one, like guests at a wedding.) And the garden was the only place in which it happened. He was a profoundly unhappy man, happiest in his reflections on it. Like many unhappy men he found refuge in his own senses. Manny, who scorned handouts, took only what he himself made with his own hands. Even in misery he refused to bend to the almost natural impulse to whine. He drew back into himself and fed off what his tomatoes, his roses, and the Italian cigars gave him.

Events of the past followed him into his reveries. One wife, two countries, three homes, and four sons added up to ten blunders. Wherever he went, whatever he did . . . blunders. Even when disaster arrived at a rendezvous before he did, Manny kept the appointment. He had come green and eager off the boat, to Canarsie with its black river bottom soil like home in Fiorenza, with a brand new wife. When the city had condemned his house (like Mussolini back home in Italy), he took Rosa to Cedarhurst and tried again for land and sons. After ten years of marriage both came. The bouquet of roses, of hope, was only to become a bunch of wilted flowers.

The Great Depression in the United States was like depression in Florence, only worse. When he left Italy, in the thirties, to escape hunger, he found breadlines and soup kitchens in Paradise. The gold in the streets of New York was made daily by policemen's horses. A rose died when he saw a protestor fall under pumping black hooves and become a pile of rags. Manny was in flight not only from hard times, but also from *them*. He had committed a political, nearly fatal, sin of omission in not showing the proper respect for some petty middle management Mafioso. It was and it wasn't a serious crime. The issue was debated. They settled their differences with a compromise that satisfied everyone but Bruno. They cut off his right pinky. This cut short a not-too-promising career as a clarinetist in an orchestra that played the local Florence music hall circuit.

In America, where beggars often turn into millionaires (just read the steamship ads), he became a gardener. Not even crazy, wonderful, miraculous America was looking for a nine-fingered clarinetist. But there were always rich people; and rich people had houses; and houses had lawns to cut, hedges to trim, appearances to maintain. In America he could live, free from Mussolini's gangsters, free from the dons. He had not improved himself over his father's lot, he had just changed the location. His disappointment was to multiply tenfold by the time he was weary enough to lean on his rake and look back.

Sometimes, when he began to stack his failures in neat rows like firewood, he would sit in the toolshed with rusty shears and edgers, and listen to Mozart's Clarinet Concerto in A Major, the one the genius wrote for his friend Stadler, the one Benny Goodman recorded. And mercifully autobiography would cease, anger would cease. He was content to listen to Benny. It was no good to dream when there was no future to tie the dream to, when the past neutralized the future.

His boys were good boys, if by good you meant harmless. They had their mother's disposition, soft, pliable, like Canarsie earth, like pasta without sauce. Girls they should have been. There

173

wouldn't be this bad taste now. No one should go to the grave holding dead flowers.

His oldest, Vinnie, as the boy preferred to call himself (what's wrong with the name he was given: Vincenzo?), was a watcher of paper for the State. Less than nothing. A cog in a wheel, a stitch on a coat, a leaf on a tree. He worked five days a week and drank beer two. Manny could never decide which of Vinnie's two vocations he hated the most: The Babysitter of the Paper or The Guzzler of the Beer. The next disaster in line, Thomas, worked in a hardware store. He sorted nails, also smiled at the Jewish ladies who came in to buy light bulbs and chisel on the tax, and maybe smiled back, promising. Women's promises. Like women's brains . . . now you see them, now you don't. Poor Tomaso, who hopes one day to seduce a fancy Jewish lady, wears a white shirt and tie to work and rings up nineteen cents sales, who makes him grandchildren left and right like he was counting nails. Manny rejected most of the grandchildren as damaged goods with their running noses and colds all the time, and special shoes for one hundred dollars because the feet weren't right. But what can you expect from a mother whose maiden name was O'Connor?

Next in line to inherit his Victrola and ten records was Peter. Mr. America. He lifts weights for pleasure and drives a bakery truck when he's not under a dumbbell. He's a dumbbell. All he has to do to lift dead weight is jump up and down. When the Comedian (Manny always called God by that name, it explained so much) put Pietro together he gave him an extra portion of muscle. To fill the spaces between his ears.

Which leaves Victor, his youngest, his biggest disappointment. Named for Victor Abruzzi, a very dear friend and left-wing newspaperman whom Mussolini murdered on his way to making a worldwide imbecile of himself and Italy. The one last hope that would make dying easier, son Victor, a clown. The best grandchildren though. And the worst wife. A real *mala femina*. A tramp with a big mouth. He had filled in her picture from the very start when she answered him back fresh in this very garden, years ago, the day he tried to find out if Victor was getting a pure girl. It was a mistake, but it was done, this agreement with Stefano Costa, his friend he met on the boat that brought them here. An offering to the Comedian for safe arrival. Two offerings,

174

really. Stefano's first with Manny's first. But his boys down the line objected. They found bloodless Irish scarecrows. Only Victor consented. But the mama's baby was no match for the alley cat. She walked up and down him like he was an escalator. All the answers she had, and she was too quick to throw them in Victor's face, in *his* face. The other daughters-in-law, those three washed out monkeys with curlers always in the hair, turned their eyes to the floor when he stared at them. Not the big mouth college girl. She paid back look for look, insult for insult. With interest. Not a nice girl for Victor. If she were his daughter she would be quiet as a little mouse. Guaranteed. Like Rosa, stupid Rosa, who crosses herself, on the hour, like she was a cuckoo clock.

Manny looked for a match to ignite his DiNobili. Not finding any he had to content himself with chewing on its frayed end. He rocked slowly in complete surrender to the invisible clouds of perfumes that washed over him. How to get through the winter? He could practically live in the garden until November when frost would steal into his gloves and socks, numbing his extremeties. Play boccie, without spirit (what good is the game then?) on Saturday and Sunday afternoons with some of the other walking dead men who interrupt the game to show pictures of the grandchildren. He carried no pictures, he told them, because he carried no wallet. Men who only hang around until someone taps them on the shoulder and says "Hey, *paisan,* you're dead. Come with me. A little faster, huh, a little faster." Then, when the winds got angry and cleared the world for the snow to come, his bones would ache. He never learned to drink well and couldn't count on alcohol to dissolve the days and most of the nights.

Winters were getting to be as cold as Caporetto, again. The long river of time permitted him to smile at the horrible winter of 1917 when the Austrians sent them in panic down the mountain. But he stood his ground and worked the machine gun and the snow around him was always red that winter, before the retreat. In that season of intense suffering he snatched Victor Abruzzi from death by shooting an Austrian officer who sliced off his friend's ear with a long, curved saber after puncturing his lung. Manny shot the Austrian with his pistol. How the slight machine gunner ever did it, he, to this day cannot understand, but he carried the two-hundred-pound Victor, in two parts, a

175

mile to the medical tent. On his shoulder most of Victor and in his hand the rest of him, his bloody ear, cupped as if he held a baby bird. The bald little doctor with the brush moustache and a permanently surprised look sewed the ear back as if it were a button on a coat. Unfortunately Il Duce's men did a more thorough job on Victor than the Austrian. Italy's trains, then, ran on time and its gunmen left no ears to be sewn back in place.

Victor Abruzzi was dead; his namesake was partially dead, being without backbone or testicles and soon Manny, too, would just be bones. Probably very soon, he thought, treating himself to a dish of self-pity. But what the hell to do this winter? Listen to Benny Goodman? Listen to Rosa crying in her pillow about who knows what? Emmanuel Bruno closed his eyes and the door to the past, as if it were an old Randolph Scott movie he had seen a dozen times on TV. With the same mental motion he slammed shut future doors, that being no way out either. For what it was worth, he settled for now, but as a last resort, the lesser of three evils, not as top choice. Many roads lead to Rome, the mood of the piece being Italianate.

Sidney eased the Lincoln alongside the low house, talking it slowly into the curb like a skittish horse, and got hell from her for scraping the tires. He was used to wearing blame and he put it on without complaint. Pretty soon everything fit whether it was his or not. He wondered what his mother-in-law had to do with Italians and gave the thought up quickly before she read his mind. She could do that, he was certain, and excoriate him when she chose. It was an Italian house, unmistakably. Vines all over trying to strangle the place like a tank of green octopi. And flowers. Whole sections of flowers that somehow only blossomed and gave off fragrance for them. Jews couldn't raise flowers like that, they hadn't the patience, the secret knowledge. Jews raised azaleas and rhododenron, shrubs without prejudices, that perform for anyone. But fat yellow roses and multicolored hollihocks and sunflowers that looked down and smiled like doting parents—that was Italian magic.

His collar was soaked, he perspired cold sweat like a man perpetually under the sentence of death. Somehow he just couldn't muster a drop of warm sweat. Again a chauffeur for her. The thought of it, compounded by summer's heat caused large cold pools to form on his neck, then unexpectedly plunge down his back, only to thin out again at his puffy waist and into his boxer shorts.

"It always gets hot around Rosh Hashana," he noted wisely. "Are we lucky (he thought he was superb at irony). We sit and stew in a hot temple. Then go out into 85, 90 degree heat for some cool breezes. Are we lucky. Hitler should be so lucky."

She left telling him to wait a few moments. But a few minutes could be God knows how long. Time to think while she was away and couldn't intercept what his mind told his soul in strictest confidence. It came to him, the way messages came to the prophets of old, alone, despised, degraded, that much of his life was dealt away in small bits, in chips placed on losing numbers. He was like a bettor at the crap tables in Vegas. That was the essence of his life. A thousand pieces of nonsense, a thousand losing numbers. Not a heavy bettor, his chips were tossed away one at a time. Standing in line to pay for groceries Carol was too lazy or too busy to buy. Baking in that Sinai desert of a parking lot, waiting for the bus to take the kids to summer camp. Idling the motor while the gas tank was being filled and waiting again for the change of ten. A few chips there. On a line to buy tickets to see a movie judged awful by the critics and rated X by the censors. More chips. He had given up attempting to be clever. It was too taxing and it led nowhere. The house winds up with all the chips, anyway.

When Pearl slammed him hard he knew how to spend his chips, to say "ouch" under his breath and suffer like the little boy with the fox under his coat who saved his country. "Caution," Carol said, "Momma can't go on forever. And, God forbid the day comes (it should be a hundred years from now) you'll see, Sidney, we'll be rewarded for our caution." Till then he must grin and swallow large bowls of crow soup, eat chopped crow liver, and, as a main course, large portions of boiled crow. Wasn't that better than saturated fats?

To say that she used her wealth as a weapon is like saying that Don Rickles is a bit rude, that the Hydrogen Bomb causes damage. She would just note its presence the way Gary Cooper noted the presence of his holster. Her wealth came from Mr. Fialakoff,

177

a passing stranger, who, as far as the world knew, never had a first name. The girls called him papa, and their mother simply referred to her husband as Fialakoff. Waste not, want not. When he left, she nicely expanded his real estate dabblings as if she had suddenly been given hotels on Boardwalk and Park Place. Sidney helped collect every time she passed Go, as the insurance broker for the Monopoly Board scattered throughout Crown Heights, Flatbush, and Boro Park. Actually he was only a well-paid foot soldier, someone to fire drunken supers, threaten a tenant, and make sure the inspectors were greased when they came to look for trouble. When Fialakoff died she lost her punching bag. It was a blessing that Sidney allowed himself, in the name of caution, to become her sparring partner. Too big to miss, too spineless to duck her punches, and too dazzled by present premiums and future ownership, Sidney swallowed garbage and called it caution. And poor Sidney never could get out from under. Heading toward philosophy, the place people go when they feel they've lost all their effectiveness, Sidney thought of his cold sweat again and came to the conclusion that it was really the tears of his soul crying because he was almost out of chips.

Pearl slammed the door of the car and grinned with her eyes. Grinned because the slam would give Sidney something to think about. Let him suffer a little instead of counting her money. No fool, she knew that her son-in-law and others unmentionable were figuring the logistics of slicing up a big pie.

She told no one about going to see the old Italian. What for? Sidney took her, but he didn't know why. Sidney was a yenta. It wouldn't take long for Carol to know, then Barbara, then everyone in New York State. Three sisters should be like three fingers on a hand, all equal. But it was no state secret that Joannie was her favorite. If she were a doter, Joannie would be the dotee. A source of friction with the other two who smiled and joked about it yet feared the subtle influence it had on mama's will. Certainly they would not close ranks on Joan's problem, that being an excellent source of inheritance leverage.

Face to face was the only way. Hand to hand, it really was, considering Pearl's method of problem solving. The face of the little Italian bubba with apron and noticeable moustache, was empty and open. Words slowly fell out of her mouth, telling her that Emmanuel was in the garden resting. Pearl nodded thanks and marched into the mass of flower beds and bean poles that the old lady called a garden preferring not to waste words on someone with side combs, a crucifix, and gold teeth.

*His* garden. They all tiptoed or walked like they were in a hospital. That was all he asked anymore of the world. But it would have been useless to tell that to Pearl. She tiptoed for no one. Not for her husband, not for her children, and not for Calvin who his wife thought was a combination of Albert Schweitzer and Clark Gable. Pearl never thought much of Schweitzer, anyway. A Jewish doctor who's crazy to work on colored people.

"Mr. Bruno," she said somewhere between a question and a command.

Manny rotated his head just enough to sight her with one eye and saw her looming over him, tall, wide, and deep. His first feeling was of pique. He willed her to vanish quickly, he was losing the warmth of the sun and the warmth of fond clarinet-days in Fiorenza.

"I'm retired lady. I don't work no more. It's my son's business, now." He then took her out of his line of fire and reset himself. Maybe the magic would return.

"I know that, Mr. Bruno," she said with the dignified patience of an executioner.

She looked around the garden, searching for a way in. Tomatoes and hollihocks, string beans and roses. A mishmash. These Italians . . . no sense of order, no planning. And this little old pink man with a cigar in his mouth like some dead·insect. She could buy and sell him, so why the high horse, mister? Like a warship's cannon she moved her nose, constructed on a grand scale into postion. Her target: a blue Madonna holding the child Jesus, also painted blue.

"Nice birdbath," she granted him over-generously.

The rocking stopped and his head clicked into place like a remotely operated toy to which she had the controls.

"That ain't a birdbath, lady," he said.

"What is it then?"

"It's a Madonna and child. Jesus and Mary. It's a religious statue."

179

"But the bottom, it gets filled with water when it rains, no?"

"Yeah, so what?" he said.

"And the birds. They drink from it, don't they?"

"I guess."

"Then to me it's a birdbath, whatever you call it."

"Whatever you say, lady," he surrendered with a voice that sounded like the crackling of dried newspapers. He thought she had assassin's eyes and a voice like a fire engine.

A magnanimous sweep of the head. She could afford to give back a little. The sun, the garden made her feel good inside. "You grow all these things here, yourself? Every year? From scratch?"

"No, lady, I just plant the seed. God does the rest."

She was annoyed. Irritated, too, at college games from an illiterate laborer.

"I know *that,* but God needs willing hands and a strong back to get the job done."

"God don't need nobody. You, me, the Pope, Joe DiMaggio. He does a good job by Himself. It's the people that louse things up."

"You don't want to give me a thing, do you, Mr. Bruno?" she said.

He stopped rocking for good. The little pleasures of the day, the only pleasures of the day, were over. Maybe tomorrow.

"First place, I don't give to strangers. Second place, you come here to see me so you want something you think I got. Why I gotta give you anything just because you want? You do the giving, Mrs., and don't make jokes about my religion. I don't practice, but that don't give you the right to walk all over it."

"I don't make fun of religion. I'm just not used to these things and I ask questions and I look for answers. Don't be so sensitive. Besides, we got more important things than religion to talk about." She had pride in the way she handled difficult people—tenants, inspectors, the City. She spoke plain, bone plain truth. Truth was one of her weapons, deadly when used with skill.

"We better be nice to each other," she said cryptically, teasingly, as an appetizer, or "or we got a lot to lose, Mr. Bruno. A hell of a lot to lose. And you can tell the world Pearl Fialakoff said so."

Manny folded his hands over his belly, leaned back as far as the laws of physics permitted and gave her a look he usually reserved for his grandchildren when they, too, said something foolish. "Lose, lady, lose? I gotta maybe five years left, if I'm lucky. Or five minutes. *That's* all I can lose. I got no money. I'm not in high society. Nobody is gonna put me in jail. What I got to lose?"

"Mr. Bruno," she said, ignoring all his claims to unassailability. "I'm here to talk to you about your son, Victor. Do you understand?"

"So what did he do? Spoil your petunias, or something?"

Rosa Bruno stood at the back screen door, her small hands like dogs' paws, nervously wiping and rewiping themselves on her red bordered cobbler. Still, after decades she hadn't the courage to confront him in his courtyard. Through the screen door she received some protection from his look of blue ice yet it allowed her to peek at the big Jewish lady who had some business with her husband. Instinctively she knew it was about Victor, about something Victor had done.

He saw her and he stared back. The King was displeased. Now, right now, he wanted her away from the door. If he wanted her outside, next to him, he would have called her. Since he didn't, she should have gone deep within the low, flat house. Simple logic.

Rosa's vague silhouette disappeared. There would be something to say to her later, Manny promised himself.

"I didn't come to talk about roses, Mr. Bruno, or statues. It's a very serious and a very delicate matter. It's about adult-try."

"What kind of tree is that? What are you talking about?"

"You and I are in the same boat, Mr. Bruno. We both got in-law trouble."

"What in-laws? I aint' got no in-laws."

"Bruno, your daughter-in-law and my son-in-law are doing some heavy fooling around. Do you understand me now? Is that plain enough, Mr. Bruno? Is that more serious than roses and birdbaths and Medinas?"

"Madonnas."

"Whatever."

A pause. The unmistakable sound of fish taking hook, knife hitting bone. No one flicks off insults to one's children. Jews,

Italians, Aborigines. A child's hurt is a parent's hurt. All parents were alike, she was sure. They all have babies the same way—painfully. And that was only the downpayment.

"Okay lady, you got the floor. Make your point." When he flicked an imaginary ash from a cigar that had not been lit in days, Pearl knew that she had pierced an artery.

She was still standing. "A minute," Bruno said, disappeared, then returned with a white kitchen chair from his shed and invited her to sit with a small flourish of his hand.

Finally hit him where it hurts, she thought, and the good manners pop out. The peasant. So much for getting his attention.

Coming out of the veronica, his eye caught the rustle of the window shade in the bedroom. *La stupida*, again.

Equals now, or at least eye to eye, she spoke. "Now that I've got your ear, I'll give you facts and figures. For a couple of months, I ain't exactly sure because my daughter, that's Doctor Bernstein's wife, ain't too willing to tell her own mother the details, your daughter-in-law and the doctor have been making you-know-what all over the Island. Picnics and motels and a week in the country. All the trimmings like they say. Men get that age they get a little crazy. This mishuggena son-in-law of mine is doing a terrible thing to my Joannie." Up close she looked more weary to him than dangerous. "She's a good woman, but a little crazy too, thanks to him. You know what I mean by a little crazy? Too much money, too much freedom." Whether he wanted a definition or not he got one. "She's worked it out so the four of them have this agreement to keep the whole thing going like a business."

"What kind of business?"

"A business business. A deal with her as chairman of the board. They actually agreed to keep the ball rolling. I wouldn't be surprised if they formed a corporation."

His jaws began working the cigar, rotating and chomping. A steady stream of tobacco juice oozed into Manny's stomach. At the first wave of pain he threw the cigar striking the Madonna on her cement thigh. A brown spot, like a bullet hole, marked the point of his anger.

She recited dates and places, streets and roads, almost as if Joan had written them down. Nothing was left to the imagination

182

except what they did for each other when the doors were closed. That did not require imagination, just the memory of an oasis in time's desert when he did those things, too.

Dirty whore, dirty filthy whore, he said to himself. She finally did it. Finally started cheating on that weakling. Opened up his shame for the whole world to laugh at. Not enough she shamed him in his own house, in his father's house, too. Now out in the street, all over, like manure. He wished for the cigar back. It was at Jesus' feet, covered with ants. Someone like *her* had to come and tell *him*. A Jew yet. Who else knows? How many people are sitting around their tables, eating and drinking and making jokes about his son and his son's wife? And Victor himself, one of the partners. In on the deal, that jackass. His leg had fallen asleep so he shifted his weight. The rushing blood tingled his foot back to life. Pearl thought he was squirming.

Why didn't the boy come to me? he wondered. His poppa? I'd give him advice, good advice. Show him how to handle a bad woman. And the acid came pouring into his stomach, adding to the cigar juice, subtracting from his ability to hide from her what she had no right knowing.

"Listen, Mrs.," he said through stained teeth showing like headstones in an old cemetery, "what do you expect me to do? I'm the boy's father, sure, but he's grown up. What should I do? Holler at him? Make shame, shame? Beat him with a strap because his wife is hot in the pants for the doctor?" Questions with no answers. She couldn't give any. Besides she came just to turn a lock, open a door, show him pictures.

"Whattaya think, I snap my fingers and they dance like windup toys?" He spat a wad of phlegm to her right, the overflow from his drowning stomach. "Pfooo." It landed between Jesus' mother and Joan's. "This ain't Italy. This is America. You say 'Come here' and they say 'Aw, what you want? I'm busy. I'm watching my programs. Is it important?' He spat again close to the same spot. "They gotta *be* ready, twenty-four hours a day ready. But it ain't so. I'm only kidding myself when I think like I'm back in Italy."

A robin plopped out of nowhere, like a glider and landed on the fig tree behind Pearl. The bird warbled a long clear note, sharp, crystal, and mournful. One robin note matched one Bruno

183

note that had suddenly come to life. A living thing fluttered within him, new energy crackled. It was like the lights in a large building suddenly being turned on at midnight. He would do it. Try one more time to breathe life into a corpse. One more time to stop them . . . her. Time to confront Tessa and walk away a winner. Purposely he had avoided Victor and his too-American wife. Maybe it was hopeless, maybe the two of them deserved to roll in the mud and make fools of themselves, but *he* was no clown, no after-dinner joke. Maybe his last fight, another Caporetto of the soul. And he would be just as brave as when the Austrians stormed down the mountain.

"Maybe you want me to smack Teresa around. I can't do that, lady. The two of them together, they're pretty tight. Like Abbott and Costello. So what do you want from me? Why can't *you* grab your daughter and shake her up a little? Maybe you can get something moving there. You don't look like a soft lady."

"Don't you think I would if I could?"

"I don't know, that's why I asked you."

"Don't you think if there was any other way I wouldn't come here and make a fool of myself like this? We don't like to walk around naked either. You think only Italians got pride?"

Manny grunted.

"After all," she continued, "I don't know you. You ain't family and it ain't easy. It ain't easy being her mother. My daughter is one of them liberated women. Like your Teresa."

"Not *my* Teresa." He spat her out like a fly caught in his mouth. He spat twice to make sure.

"Anything goes with this fancy crowd." She rolled on as if Manny was just another bean pole in the garden. 'I wanna fool around,' he says. 'We talk about it,' she says. 'Be discreet and have a good time,' she says. 'You want tuna or egg when you go on your fooling-around picnic, honey?' she says. Talk, my foot. If my late husband ever told me he wanted something on the side, I'd have picked up a pot and smashed his head in." She stuck her square heel in a small gathering of ants that had formed to investigate the matter of Manny's cigar. "Then I'd take the wise guy and throw him out of the house, the wise guy. When you're married you don't fool around. Ever. I don't care what the latest

184

thing is, or what the marriage counselors say. Let them keep their new ground rules. I go by the old ones."

"Hmm," Manny commented. A delicate yes.

Pearl slowly deflated like a puffed adder undergoing analysis. It was pointless for her to talk non-stop, she realized. This little pink man must have something to say, some indication of what she might expect in the way of action.

"All these new rules, Mr. Bruno, they're no good. I'm glad I won't be around much longer. The world is too crazy for people like me. I wanted strong, successful children to take care of themselves, to give me pleasure. Do you know what *naches* is, Mr. Bruno?" His look answered no. "It means the pleasure of parents, in my religion. Instead God gave me weaklings, three weaklings. Killers in their mind. They're counting my money already, they're fitting me for a coffin with their greedy eyes. And the best one of the lot lets that no good son of a bitch out on a long leash. I'll tell you what I would do," she said to Manny, "I'd throw that leash over the branch of a tree and hang him from his you-know-what.

"But I said to myself, Pearlie, you ain't gettin' nowhere, daughters being what they are in Jewish homes, today. You Italians, you got a strong fist. I figured you'd tell your Victor straight up and down, that he's got to shape up. Get that wife of his out of our lives, all our lives, and fartig, it's finished. But I see I'm wasting my time (she thought not, macho-making being a delicate art). I see you Italians are like us Jews, helpless." She pulled her wool skirt around her legs like a blanket at a football game. Enough pump-priming, she thought. You can't get seltzer from a dry onion. If it's there I'll get it. If it ain't, well, we cut another pattern.

His DiNobili on the ground, thrown in anger and pain, hitting an innocent bystander, caused him shame. A loss of self-control, emotion before a stranger, the accidental target, were all ingredients in the stew, but not the whole of it. He pitched forward, left the chair to rock on its own and squatted before the Madonna for the butt. Pearl noticed the age spots on his hands and the growth on the back of his neck like a tiny brown button. Did his doctor ever check it? Does he *have* a doctor? Manny placed the cigar in the outstretched right hand of the blue Madonna, as if she had asked for a drag. He felt better, his own sense of balance restored.

"Listen, lady," he said, "I see we both in the same boat. We're both old timers, we think like old timers, but we got kids that won't stand up straight." He looked at the Madonna, noting to himself that she was excused from the conversation. His complaints were limited to this fat Jewish lady's kids and his. Not hers. "You know what the whole story is, lady? I think we've been too good to them. Spoiled them rotten." Wisdom delivered as if he were disclosing a revolutionary breakthrough in parent-child reactional psychology. "Spoiled them rotten," he repeated. "Made weaklings out of them. The momma and the poppa mean nothing. What the friends say, what the TV says. It's like a poison." Nodding all the while, she was, at last, pleased with the familiar ground they were walking together. Disregarding what it really was, this could have been a meeting of Parents Anonymous or more accurately the start of a weekly Battered Parent session, if one existed. Actually the oldest of the maltreated groups since Cain turned out to be such a rotten kid.

Not one to overstay her welcome she grasped her knees for support and rose. Manny rose with her and took his cigar out of his unusual ashtray.

"Come, I walk with you to your car," he said like one dignity to another. Pearl had broken the ice. He may have fallen in. Both monarchs saw nothing unusual in their walk together down the acid-cleaned flagstone to the car, since protocol's rules vary on the subject of grand exits.

Sidney sat mopping his neck and chin, watching the slightly muscular, slightly bowed legs of a young mother as she pushed an occupied baby stroller down the street. She had a well-rounded rump and Sidney devilishly wondered why asses should not have handles to make grabbing easier. The picture of it tickled him. Pearl intercepted the leer and the lust behind it. Her Tartar eyes vowed vengeance on him which caused Sidney's sweat mills to go into overtime. Manny ignored him as if he were invisible.

"You do something, Manny. Anything. I get this feeling, talking to you, that you're a man who gets things done."

Manny turned his palms up to the sun as if to empty them of

186

any contractual obligation. She tapped the right one, nodding no, negating his confession of helplessness.

"I ain't promising nothing, Mrs." She was not about to leave his table full. This Jewish lady came and demanded. He saw and was touched by her mirroring his anguish. But still, so what? He didn't give to strangers. "It's not my headache. I'm retired Mrs. Pearl, from everything. But maybe I don't take a snooze on this one. Maybe." That was as far as he would go. Perhaps too far. The lady was persistent.

**13**

Something terrible was happening all around her and she felt shut out. It was like hearing a houseful of people cheer something on television while she was preparing dinner in the kitchen. The lady who came to see Manny, his quietness, his frightening extra quietness that followed her visit like the silence that came after an earthquake. Then his disgust with her when she looked into his face begging answers with her eyes. He was like that. Everything kept to himself. Answers locked in, she locked out. Something was simmering alright, with her baby Victor in the middle, in trouble. Manny in it, too. With that Jewish lady stirring up the pot. And she was so afraid.

Rosa was almost used to being left out of things. Were she more sophisticated, she might have built on that base of Manny's indifference toward her, a separate but equal life. But she was incurably *la stupida,* and accepted, like a trained house dog, a peripheral existence as her fate, her penance for this enormous, unspoken, pervasive sin she had committed. Why wasn't she told, though, what the sin was? If she only knew. If only she had the chance to confess and receive absolution, life would not be so hard, so fruitless.

Father Rossetti could not tell her though she plagued him every week after mass, her silent, patient face, her tiny clasped hands shouting in his ear. And Father Rossetti was an educated man. He knew both Bibles, the Jewish one, too. He knew the lives of the saints and spoke so beautifully. Yet, when it came to her case, only a smile like the martyrs in her religious books.

"You have the cleanest soul I've ever listened to, Mama Bruno," he told her.

"Then why am I being punished?" she asked, a look of torment worn innocently on her small round face.

"Who is punishing you, Rosa?" he asked with a monotonous patience that skirted the edge of boredom. He did counseling, too. This was his counselor's voice. To be said in his defense, he had heard Rosa's lament repeated weekly for years. They both agreed that she had four fine sons, good men and healthy, too. Also eight fine grandchildren, less a point or two for the ones that tended toward their mother's church. She lived comparatively well and enjoyed good health. So what more could she want?

"Who, who, you ask?" she said. "Emmanuel, that's who."

"Ah Emmanuel," he answered with the indifferent interest of the psychiatrist who claims it is objectivity. "Now, Rosa, that is something I will not insert the Church into." His square cherubic face, misplaced on a forty year old, gleamed with the look of one who sees light at the end of a tunnel. "What happens between a man and a wife, I feel, is very personal and very private, Rosa. I won't, I can't, mix in. If you and Manny came to me and jointly ask for counseling, okay. But I don't have to tell you about Manny Bruno. He's a universe unto himself. I'm afraid he's hopeless." Father Rossetti had the unmistakable look of a man just removing a pair of very tight shoes after a long hike.

Ann Landers did not know, either. Rosa sent America's spiritual adviser and confessor many letters hand printed on good stationery, in bent English. But the lady was too busy with women who smear themselves with jam before they go to bed with their husbands and ask her if it's alright.

Emmanuel would not tell her. He knew. Of course he knew, but he was angry. The two of them, uneasily yoked together for forty years shared a few things. Talking together was not one of them. That she was guilty of something was one of them. So why didn't he ever sit down with her and say, "Rosa, you did a bad thing. You did this or you did that." Tell her, for the love of God, so that she might know and earn forgiveness.

Yet, how could she not know? Didn't he call her *stupida* every day of their life sentence together? Everytime she slipped or fell, in his eyes, he trotted out the same comment. Sad, sad, for at the

189

bottom *stupida Rosa* was too stupid to realize that her great sin was stupidity and it was committed against her husband. For that, despite a lifetime of goodness that counted as nothing to her judge, despite her gift of four innocuous sons, Manny had sentenced her to a lifetime of emotional Siberia. This was one sentence served without the hope of parole because she repeated her crime whenever she opened her mouth.

Like now, when he asked her for his good clothes to be laid out on the bed.

"Why?" she asked, confirming the fairness of her sentence. "No one died. There's no wedding until Umberto LaPreziosa's son gets married on Thanksgiving."

"*Stupida*," he said reflexly without malice or hate. "Does it make a difference why? I got some business to attend to. Family business. It don't concern you."

A picture of the heavy Jewish lady came to mind. That visit caused the clothes to be laid out. It was best to walk around him. But she had to know. She had a mother's right to know.

The black suit with the pin stripes, cleaned and pressed after each wearing, lay flat on the bed. Next to it the white on white Arrow shirt with French cuffs and a set of pearl cuff links that Carmine Bilello forced Manny to accept for nursing his Irish setter back to life. On the floor, under the suit were a pair of tiny, pointed black shoes that shone like the hood of a new Cadillac. It was all displayed in a fashion befitting a ceremony of dress for a matador.

He had reluctantly taken to wearing a belt after a lifetime of buoyancy by suspenders. It was right to have one's pants held up instead of held against. Pressure should be on the shoulders, not against the gut. But a small matter of only symbolic value. He made the concession to America with the understanding that a concession is not a surrender. His gray Homburg, purchased a decade ago for fifty dollars, lay in its crypt on the shelf in the closet. It was never touched by anyone except Manny. In his mind he called it the John D. Rockefeller hat and endowed it with reverence far beyond its price tag.

And the dapper uniform changed the man on the outside as well as internally. He told himself he was the same Emmanuel Bruno whatever he wore, but he knew it was a small fiction. The

190

truth is we are all prisoners of what our eyes see and Manny saw white on white against his pink skin, shiny black shoes, and a soft felt Homburg. No longer a gardener, a broken-nailed laborer who cut grass and spread fertilizer. The mirror told him he was a statesman, a prince of finance, someone to be feared and respected. Somehow, on this Sunday in September, when the first frost had ended the lives of the tall sunflowers outside his bedroom window, Manny looked taller than a mere five feet. A matter of great delicacy, of some importance, he told himself, would be decided today. He would be ready.

Teresa was his main target for today, but she was not just a daughter-in-law badly in the need of a tongue lashing (really a horsewhipping were he permitted proper latitude). Truly she was, in his old fox eyes, the living embodiment of all that was wrong in the world. The world that really began going bad in the thirties. During the thirties total bankruptcy and decay set in. Teresa had a lot to answer for on both levels—her own conduct and the world's.

He tossed aside Rosa's suggestion that he wear a top coat. It was not even worth one *stupida*. A disgusted stare was all she deserved.

By ten o'clock he stood in front of Victor's split-level on Constance Avenue in the lower middle class section of Hewlett. Manny grunted his disgust grunt, the one especially reserved for his opinion of where his sons lived. The other boys had homes in similar surroundings. He spit clean spittle into the leaf-covered gutter. When so dressed he never smoked or even permitted himself a DiNobili to rest in his mouth. Too afraid a brown stain on his shirt would destroy the miracle of the clothes.

Manny never cared for their taste (Tessa's taste) in houses, in neighborhoods, in anything. A split-level was a nothing house, typical of Teresa, typical of America. No real downstairs, no real upstairs. Just steps. Plenty of steps all over the place. Down to the den where there was a room that everybody owns and nobody owns. The kids watch TV, the parents entertain friends who sometimes sleep over in that same room. It had no character. At his place there were rooms to sleep in, a room for company to sit, bedrooms for the boys when they were small. Different rooms. The way it should be. And here, steps up to the kitchen. Silly nonsense to have to walk upstairs to get to the kitchen. A kitchen should be a place you walk straight into. There was something dishonest about so many steps.

The neighborhood displeased him, too. All the same houses, just painted differently. As if that could hide the monotony. She choose to live on a block with some Irish (dirty kids), some Jews (dead lawns), and even a colored family (dead lawns and dirty kids). From the Bahamas, Victor told him, as if that made a difference. Her own kind wasn't good enough for her. He hated those neighbors who completely replaced their lawns with nugget-sized stones. What did they expect to grow? Boulders? A sacrilege to put stones where living things should be.

All the wrong things that girl did. Now he had the clincher, the wedge to really let her have it. To get ten years of stomach-eating silence out of his insides. Before noontime she would know that old Manny sees her and knows her for what she really is. Maybe something will come out of it. He thought not. Maybe Victor might be pushed to make a fist . . . and use it. He picked up a yellow ball, covered with a coat of dew from their lawn and opened the front door without knocking.

Sounds of Sunday breakfast came from up in the kitchen. Knives clattering, plates clinking, slippers shuffling, boys laughing, Tessa talking non-stop as she often did with the boys when atop an emotional high, and Victor spacing the babel with one word sentences. And Sunday smells, too. Bacon, sausages, eggs, and rich coffee aromas. Tessa percolated coffee never having surrendered to the slick sell of instant. The fragrances of food tormented Manny. Once they were pleasant smells, when he had all his stomach, when it didn't rain acid every day inside on the half the doctors left him.

"Poppa," his son announced when he saw Manny's Homburged head showing on the top kitchen step. It looked like a magician's illusion, a head floating in space.

"Look, kids," Victor continued staring into Tessa's face, "look who's here. Poppa Manny."

Tessa, startled, looked first at Victor and then at what Victor saw. Her lips parted and she mechanically sealed the neck of her

192

terry cloth bathrobe that had carelessly showed a disinterested audience more plunge than she was now willing to expose. Manny didn't need any more ammunition.

The boys were eating and giggling. To this full slate of activity they added a few whoops and a short wave at their grandfather who somehow looked different. Not a real wave, though, just a flick of the palm. Tessa noted in the vengeful part of her brain Manny's lack of grandfatherly enthusiasm. His others get hugs and kisses. Mine get a nod from the neck up. Like it costs money to give away a kiss.

"The kids left the ball outside," he said instead of hello. "Don't they know people steal things?" He dumped the ball in Victor's lap and made a show of wiping his hands.

"They always do that and I always tell them not to," Victor said in what seemed to Tessa a whining apology. "But no one steals around here," he added.

"Sure, sure, this is the Garden of Eden and everyone here is a saint," the old man said acidly. Tessa thought he looked at her on the word "everyone."

"You want some coffee, pa?" she asked unenthusiastically. "Some eggs?" He took the coffee and declined the eggs. She could count on one hand the number of times he had had coffee in her house.

"How are you, Poppa Manny? Stephen asked sweetly. She thought that the kid was a saint, unquestioning, forgiving. The constant bickering over Manny went unregistered with both children. To them Poppa Manny was just the little old man they saw once in a while at parties and weddings. And daddy's father. He also smoked little cigars that smelled very bad.

"Just fine, sonny," Manny force-smiled and took off his hat. Victor pulled up the extra kitchen chair next to the refrigerator and his father sat down. Manny then placed the hat inverted on his lap for safekeeping.

Bastard, she thought. He doesn't even know what to call the boy. She was constructing a state of mind and knew it. Like she knew a storm was brewing and was tying things down. She also knew that Victor saw nothing having no barometer to measure such things. Just like his mother.

"Let me take your hat, pop," Victor offered.

193

Manny smiled again. Just like his mother to say something like that, he thought. "No, I'll keep it here."

Victor grinned at his father, considering that safe, and sipped coffee from a Budweiser glass. A family joke. He thought it was nice of the old man to stop in on his way to someplace. Or maybe he just came over to be friendly. And it was about time the old buzzard made a gesture. After all, Manny sees the other boys. He certainly was no bum. He makes a living, takes care of his family. Maybe the old boy was mellowing. It didn't make sense, just because of Tessa. Tessa was his problem, his business. Why hold grudges just because she isn't a quiet girl who says yes when Manny asks for a yes?

"The sun is a little too strong for my eyes," Manny said and moved to Victor's seat. His son surrendered his chair, at the head of the table, and switched places. Now Manny had the same place at the table he enjoyed at home and he was more comfortable. The hat found its way back into Manny's lap.

The old man laughed out loud, a short strangled laugh to act as overture to a Sunday matinee. "Some fat Jewish lady came to see me on Thursday. She came with some crazy story that made me laugh and laugh. I tell you I ain't had a laugh like that in years." But his eyes weren't laughing, nor was his mouth. It had snapped shut and remained that way. Tessa inspected his every word like luggage at the airport during a bomb scare.

"Yeah, what did she say, pop?" his son asked, bracing himself for an overhearty laugh to please his father. Tessa and the old man simultaneously felt a twinge of revulsion. He, because his son was so willing to spend a laugh to pay for peace, she, because Victor could not see the punch line coming.

"Now get this, you won't believe it. She said these four married people, two couples, sat down and worked out a sweet little deal to keep a very dirty thing going. She said that one of the men and one of the women were having this good time. With each other. And the two left out of the fun and games, they okayed the deal. They were going to play ball and shut up about it. Like they formed a company to keep it going. To keep it to themselves and to keep it going. Now ain't that the funniest story you ever heard in your life, Victor? Tell me, you ever heard anything funnier?"

Victor's eyes, at first eager to cooperate, suddenly went dead. He put down his coffee and stared at his hands as if they had just been added to his body. Having no use for them he gave the new members the job of holding his knees. Which they did poorly, sliding and slipping off.

"Boys," she said softly, "take your bacon and eggs and finish in the rec room. It's okay," she said to quizzical eyes that seemed to question her sanity. "I said it's alright. Go watch your cartoons there and I'll call you when it's time to get dressed. Go, go, go."

Like good soldiers they did as they were told. I love them, so, she thought as they filed past her. She hated Manny even more for giving of himself not a smile, a tap on the head, a pat on the rump as the boys marched by.

"Tell us more about this funny story, pa. C'mon, pa. I could use a good laugh."

Victor sat glum and speechless as he did when the Jets blew a big one.

"Enough, enough of this game," Manny shot out at her. "You know damn well what I'm talking about, wiseguy." The way it was said sounded like the hiss of an arrow just before it strikes its target: mean, angry, vengeful. "You and that doctor friend of yours."

"So?"

"So? What kind of an answer is that? 'So' ain't no answer. You're just rubbin' my face in it."

"In what, pa? Whatever it is, it doesn't concern you."

Manny bristled. "Doesn't concern me? That hunk of horsemeat sitting between us is my son. You put the horns on him and he's dumb enough to wear them along with a big fat shit-eating grin. So what do you mean it doesn't concern me? You take me for a fool?" His face was turning florid.

"Pa, listen," Victor began, his voice hoarse with a great weariness.

Which triggered Manny who came to talk and to be heard. Listening was not on his agenda. "You shut up," he snarled. "You're as dumb as your mother. You I don't want to talk to." By now his neck had reddened to match his face. "You let them Jews talk you into a set of horns. And this one, too (fox eyes at Tessa). She's just like a Jew. Her mouth, her mind."

195

He did not want it like this. She was sitting like a princess and he was smoking and spitting fire. He brought himself back from the edge. With a palm grown soft he patted the crease in his pants that had ruffled as he ruffled. "Victor," he crooned, "I don't know what the hell's wrong with you. You were brought up good, from a good Catholic home. Why are you making your life a three-ringed circus? Your kids, they don't have to see this, this . . . cesspool."

Victor's eyes blinked more than once, probably to start his brain, she thought, as she sat watching father and son with an inordinate degree of objectivity.

"Ain't it bad enough she's no good? You gotta be part of it, too? What gives, Victor, you foolin' around, too? With the guy's wife?"

"Oh, no, poppa, she's a fancy lady. She doesn't do that number," Victor replied with horror obvious. "She and I have the same interest. We want to save our marriages and families."

"Hey, what the hell's going on here? Black is white? Good is bad? You fool around to stay together? You violate the family to save the family?" Manny's words came in small explosions.

Tessa pushed her seat back increasing the distance between them. She lit a cigarette and watched the match die above the glass ashtray she won in Coney Island. "You know, of course, pa, that you're not entitled to know a damned thing from us. What I do, what Victor does is nobody's business. Private property. And don't hand me that crap about the grandchildren. Mix them in a crowd of small dark-haired kids and you'd never be able to pick them out, devoted grandfather. So don't hand me a number. I read you very well. It's the same book I read when you tried to blackjack me before the wedding."

They glowered at one another like dogs itching for a fight. Tessa continued while she had momentum. "The whole world is Manny's world, and Manny's world is the whole world. Right? You're interested in things only in relation to yourself. When one of your boys hit a home run it was Manny's kid at the plate and Manny did the scoring. Your glory. And when they did something you thought was wrong it was a reflection on you. Never mind what they felt or how they bled. You never had children, you had extensions. A damned octopus is what you are. They rise

196

and fall according to how well they perform for you or bring glory to your name. You make me sick."

Manny showed indifference by toying with his hat, spinning it slowly in his lap first clockwise, then in reverse. He refused to look at her during her silliness.

"Pa, I want to say something," whispered Victor, edging in carefully not to get caught in the cross fire. "Tessa and I are working it out. Really, we're working at it. And we *will* find a way out. So just hold on for a while. We ain't a hopeless case." He glanced at Tessa for her reaction and had he been made of wood her glance would have changed him into a fine white ash. He read her and could not understand her anger. Nor could he understand his father's. Manny stared at the kitchen table until Victor had returned to his more natural silent state.

"You know, my son, my thick, thick son, you are worse than hopeless. An idiot. At least a guy that's in the shit house says it stinks. You say it smells like lavender and you want your poppa to agree with you. No, I ain't goin' to do that. Shit is shit and lavender is lavender. You're a real loser if you can't tell the difference."

She rubbed her oversized red slippers together, taking sensual pleasure in the soft friction. She kept contained. To snap the bonds and liberate the hate that was flooding every pore was to forever cut the ties that kept Victor alive. Then the cripple would be marooned forever, having no source of psychic energy to get himself back into orbit and home. Victor was still so weak, too weak. He would never make it without her, possibly not even with her, and surely not without this dandified tyrant with the pearl cuff links. Certainly she would not eat dirt. Victor or no Victor she would defend herself when not to do so meant spiritual obliteration. So it was in Manny's hands, as it always was. If he knows when to pull out of the dive, fine. If not, then expect a damn big explosion with lots of casualties.

Talking time again. She would not crawl, that was already decided. And raising her temper and her voice was out. But she could be firm and honest, not that those two popguns rang Manny's bell. It just made her footing more secure. Tessa retightened her robe.

"I really don't think I owe you a damned thing, Mr. Bruno. I already indicated that. Not a thank you, not a forgive me, not

197

even a period at the end of a sentence. But since you crashed this party and because some gossip came to your house with stories. . . ."

"Not *some* gossip. It was the lady's mother."

"Doesn't matter. Since you were made a junior executive with our firm I'll tell you what the company's policy is."

"Very funny, just like a heart attack."

"I will never leave Victor. In my own way I love your son and I'll take care of him. But alone he's not . . . enough (she hated herself, but she just could not find the right word at once) for me as a person, as a woman. You had a lot to do with that. You gave me a bird with a broken wing. And *you* broke the wing."

His collar felt more and more like a noose. Manny loosened his black silk tie and opened his collar button. "Teresa, I gave you a good boy. He was a good boy when he married you."

She nodded, agreeing easily with his characterization. "Kind, thoughtful, industrious, and all that jazz. And I'd trade the whole box of candy for a man. A whole, a complete man. A man who . . . why do you know, when we first got married he would stand up whenever you came into the room, like you were a general and he was a private. Now I ask you, is that any way for a grown man to act?" She felt a little sick, like she was getting her period. A prolonged battle was not her cup of tea. But, by unwritten agreement they were on Manny's timetable, using his set of rules. So she would just have to sit on her small waves of nausea and ride it out.

"Hey," Victor suddenly called out, "what's going on here? I don't have to sit and listen to you guys talk about me like I was dead or something." He released his knees and made motions to leave.

Tessa welded him to his seat with her finger. "You stay right here, Victor. You just sit. Don't go running away. This is important. I don't want you to get the story second hand." Victor sat. His hands, reassigned, were folded over his chest. It made him more masculine looking than holding his knees.

"This other man, Dr. B., we'll call him," she continued, "finishes the picture. I'm a complete person, now. I'm happy and I *don't* intend to change that for anything."

If Manny had an unlimited assortment of words to select from, he would have told her that she was blatantly vulgar for exposing her lack of modesty and morality as well as her overabundance of libido. Lacking the words he settled for the crude stone age tools that carried him until now. "No, no, lady, you're teasing an old man. You don't mean that. It's a joke. You want double what everyone else got. Some ladies got one car. You want two. Some ladies got one husband, so sure, you gotta have two." He smiled at her and shook his head tauntingly. "You sure got one big set of balls, Mrs. crazy lady."

She almost enjoyed the performance. The cuckold husband's father. No one, in her memory, in literature or music, ever constructed such a part. Manny had the whole territory to himself. He could write his own part, act out the role, even play it on his clarinet.

"You just heard what you wanted to, pa. I told you very simply that I'll take care of Victor even though, thanks to you (said with a sweet smile), he can't return the favor."

"I ain't buying."

"And I ain't selling. Take it or leave it, but I'll say it again. I'm no Florence Nightingale. I'm a good person, but not that good. I expect to be dead a long time. I want something out of life. It's all very simple and it's not all sex. And that's not hard to understand if you think about it. But you'll never understand and I don't expect you to. Just remember that I'm not asking for your blessing. Just putting it on record so you'll know. If anything changes you'll know about it. But you'll have to ask first. I won't tell you."

"Can we come up yet, mommy?" asked Victor junior as he handed her their plates.

"Sure Victor, sure," she said her eyes caressing his. "Listen, soldiers go outside and shoot it up a while." She patted his black silky hair. "I'll call you when it's time to get dressed for Cecilia's party, okay? Just don't get too dirty or I'll shove you both in the washing machine. Clothes and all."

Grins in triplicate as they deployed outdoors. Oh, God, she thought, I've been keeping them prisoner for *him*, that misery. The thought of it primed her nausea again.

It was not going well with Manny. Although Victor was flustered, on the verge of a rout, Teresa was not in tears. Nor was she going to be. He expected a caught-in-the-act tearjerker. Instead he got defiance and a spray of buckshot. So it was true that his son was part of the plot. God, that he had to live long enough to see such a monstrosity. And a woman talking about sex as if it were a recipe for tomato sauce. But the kid wasn't really a full partner. That bitch pushed him in. He was only a cover for her activities. He saw through that at once.

Again he played with the hat, turning it over and reading the label and hat size as if it were a newspaper. She was meaner now than when they first got married. Tougher and more brazen, too. That comes of letting things go too far.

Victor. That's all that remained. What you cannot break through you go around. Maybe there was something left in Victor to touch, some small, almost dried up well. Something under all that American garbage. Maybe a small stream of good Italian blood that can be made to boil. One last shot at it before he went home to change clothes and play the game behind the school where the Parks Department set up a boccie court because Modugno's son was assistant commissioner. Not for the old Jewish elephant—she doesn't need his help. She's got plenty of tricks up her sleeve. Maybe for Victor Abruzzi and for Teresa's father who found him green with seasickness and fear a thousand years ago on the decks of *The City of Ashland*. He was glad her father was dead. He would never have survived the shame.

"Victor, you wear your horns like it was a nice new hat. You must like wearing horns."

"I don't think I'm wearin' horns, pa," he replied innocent as a third grade play. "I knew about it, I went along with it to hold on to what I've got."

"Well they ain't earmuffs, sonny boy."

"It's nothin' pop. I'm wearin' nothin'."

"Agh, you're eatin' garbage so long you enjoy it." Manny held his chin imitating the act of contemplation. "I think, Victor in the hospital they made a switch. I think they gave momma some Polack or Jewish kid instead of my son. *My* sons got Italian blood, proud blood. When someone sleeps with an Italian's wife he gets mad. My son, my real son, would get *agita*. A Polack would say, well it ain't so bad. You're a Polack, Victor, if you don't get mad."

Enough. It was time to end the bearbaiting. Even gentle Victor had a boiling point. When she boiled she quickly recovered. Victor was quiet, and when finally his safety blew it took a lot to patch up the damage. She wasn't looking for a major catastrophe, today, thank you. But the old bastard, who should know about boiling points, was desperate and dangerous. She stepped between.

"Listen folks, my niece is having a birthday party, lots of relatives, lots of noise . . . it's going to be a long day. It's been a long day already. We have to get started. Like now. I don't like being late."

Invisible smoke issued from Manny's ears. He was making progress; the patient was coming along and now this bitch whore steps in. Without his knowledge his fist slammed down hard on the table sending the cups and plates into frenzied shock.

"Not yet," he shouted. "When I'm finished you can go to your damned party." So intense was his anger he failed to see his own half-filled cup of coffee teetering on the edge of the table.

"Victor, until you get control of yourself and yours I'm going to make believe you're dead. Don't call on the telephone, don't come to the house because the dead can't walk or talk. I mean it. And I won't even mourn for you. Become a man, Victor, and you'll come to life again. Otherwise, I'm down to three sons. For God's sake use force if you got to." For emphasis his fist slammed the table again and this time the cup took the plunge and dove into Manny's Homburg nestled invertedly in his lap. The lukewarm coffee first formed a lake in the felt bowl then its level dropped as the felt absorbed the fluid like a blotter. Manny sat horrified, his power ebbing as the coffee spread through the soft gray material darkening wherever it touched, like a cloud covering the sun.

With great dignity composed in no small part of shock, the broken man rose and sleepwalked down the steps and out of the house. He held his hat in front of him as if he was serving it for dinner. He seemed smaller than sixty inches, considerably less than the Manny Bruno who entered. Victor's head was bowed in his best church manner. Tessa held back both tears and laughter until the impulse to exhibit either had passed. She thought while dressing, about that second, that rare second in time, when Manny

201

realized that he had drowned his Homburg. She took a picture of it for all time to rerun when things got rough and she needed a laugh. Pink face going to white to beet red. Homburg from felt gray to coffee brown to slate gray. Blue suit turning black in the crotch from what leaked through as if he were incontinent.

"We'll be late, Victor," she said, hushed as if she, too, found herself in church. Silently she brushed his shoulder and he rose and went to dress. He also seemed shorter than his customary height.

Late at night, after the party, after the eating and the drinking and the dancing, which Tessa did with all her might, they lay together quietly and talked.

"Tessa, he wants me to wack you around, like my Uncle Vito sticks it to my Aunt Anna. Tessa, I can't do that. I ain't made that way. I smacked you once when I was very mad. I can't plan to do that."

"I know, Victor, I know."

When she realized that he was crying she took his big teddy bear head in her hands and laid in on her breast.

"You meant it, Tessa, didn't you when you said you'd never leave me. You did mean it?"

"I mean it, Victor. I'll always be here. Shh, poor baby, it's all right. It's all right. Go to sleep."

His sobbing ceased after a while and Victor fell asleep on her breast between her hands. She patiently extricated herself from under his weight and left the bed when he began to breathe rhythmically.

It was warm out on the sun deck. The wood planking returned the heat it absorbed during the day. Tessa sat on a redwood chair in her nightgown and chain smoked until the sky looked as if someone had struck a match behind the ocean. Nothing in particular entered or left her mind. Just a pervasive sense of peace with all the parts of her that she managed in some thirty odd years to contact. The kids, upset at not finding her in bed, found her on deck and brought the morning with them.

Long ago, in the Dark Ages, there lived a mighty king. This king had the power to command large armies. He ruled over vast areas of land. Or was it the Middle Ages? Victor was unsure, history was not his best subject in high school. Anyway, this king defied the Pope and, though an arrogant and absolute ruler, he was obligated to crawl on his knees to Rome as punishment for the sin of disobedience. Perhaps the story was not even true. No matter. Victor knew how the king must have felt, fact or fiction. He too was in defiance of a mighty pope of sorts. However even if he paid the price, even if he kneed the two miles to Magnolia Street where Manny wore the miter it was highly unlikely that forgiveness would await him there. Crawling on his knees the distance between homes in order to walk like a man might satisfy the Pope, but not his father. Tessa's head on a platter would. That's what it really boiled down to, he had to humble Tessa as well.

For the first time in his life Victor weighed equally unacceptable alternatives. To save himself he had to blow up one terminus of his bridge. To keep the world of his origin, his childhood, he had to destroy his adult years. On the other hand, to keep his self-image as a married man intact, or reasonably so, required the amputation of a filial relationship whose power over him was as real as it was massive. So real and so massive that he never questioned its right to exist.

Tess contrite? Impossible and unthinkable. Without knowing the term Victor was strung out over a dilemma. And as infection

203

produces pus, so dilemma spins off tension and anguish. Life since Sunday was unlivable. Victor was miserable and by transference so was wife and family. Unshaven, unwashed, with eyes like a cow entering the slaughterhouse, his constant companion was a half-emptied can of beer which he swished around then drank in single gulps. She found the aluminum empties where he finished and left them. Television gazing became the vital part of his life. The lawns and hedges of the Five Towns would just have to await the resolution of his gory impalement on the horns of the two bulls charging in opposite directions.

"Stephen, get me a beer, huh," said with feet propped on her prized coffee table, with a slack jaw that had sprouted a new lawn of reddish black needles.

"Oh daddy, do I have to?"

Victor bloodied the boy's nose with two swift slaps across the face, leaving both father and son stunned. A thin red line trickled down Stephen's face which showed more surprise than pain.

She heard the rapid staccato and before she stuck her head in the living room she knew where it came from. On the edge of a volcano, she knew it was only a matter of time.

"What did the kid do?" she asked and condemned in one. Missing the shame and anger on Victor's face she watched, instead, the small stream swell on Stephen's. A scene, in front of the boy, would only magnify things. She sent him to wash his face.

"I asked him for something and he gave me back talk. I don't have to take that crap from my kids."

"And for that you have to make him bleed?"

"Big deal."

"Big deal? Is that all you have to say?"

"Yeah."

"That's a real horse's ass answer."

"That's because I'm a real horse's ass. Didn't you know that? Sure you know that." Then he cut bait. Paul Lynde had just said something hysterical, something off the top of his head and Victor had just missed another Hollywood Squares nugget.

She found Stephen in the bathroom looking in amazement at his own blood, as if he doubted he owned any and finding the proof of it pleasantly surprising. "Daddy's not feeling well," she

204

said dabbing at his face with her own saliva. She was annoyed at herself for not using the faucet.

Victor ended up going to the refrigerator himself. He got two Buds, one for himself and since he had company, one for his anguish. Soon frustration and self-pity came to call and he took out two more cans.

Tessa ignored him the rest of the day, but not out of fear or anger. She knew he was roasting on a spit and that slowly cancelled the animus over the bloody nose. A child forgets, Victor needed her more. Her job was to soften the edges, try, if possible, to stay out of his way while the gaping hole inside begins to heal. She was sorry about the horse's ass bit. But she wasn't that sorry, in retrospect. Let him take it out on her, not the innocent.

The man felt all the symptoms of an existence in Purgatory. Life floated by. Time had no meaning. He measured it by beer cans. His work, when he worked, was performed with a sullen vapidity despite a sudden chilling frost and a string of nippy days when the sun lost its magic. Manny had cut Victor's emotional mooring, surgically, without the comfort of anesthesia. And still with all the time in the world to let his mind roam free, that crippled child never wandered into forbidden rooms. The real question of the origin of his current misery remained behind locked doors that had no keyholes. And he just moped, sent his fingers through his hair and watched TV from the early ladies' programs until Errol Flynn ran Basil Rathbone through with one hand and held Olivia DeHavilland three inches below the breast with the other. Flynn at four AM and David Hartman at eight the next morning. And beer. And potato chips.

With Flynn swinging from the chandelier he wondered when it would end. When will the old man take back his curse so that he can go on living again? He had bad pains in his stomach. Did he inherit his father's ulcer? Maybe that would make Manny proud, that his son finally showed a Bruno trait. Last Sunday, it was all a bad dream. Manny had never come to the house, never wiped him out, and never dumped coffee into his own hat. If only it never happened. If only the coffee didn't spill there might have been a chance, a crack in the door, a goddamn place he could crawl through. The next morning he would have called up pop and said "Heh, heh, heh, you sure were mad yesterday. You really made a big stink about nuthin', nuthin' at all. Suppose we forget the whole mess, okay?" It had worked before, like when Tessa got her way with Stephen's name. He was mad for a while, sure, but it blew over. After a while they were friends again. But before wasn't now. Now was now and it pinched. He became political out of desperation, but like most of his history he botched that up, too.

"Mama," he said in front of Rizzo's meat market where he knew she would be on Friday morning. "Mama, speak to him. Tell him not to be so stubborn, so hard on me. Tell him I'm trying. I'm not a bad son. I'm good, you know I'm good. You're not ashamed of me, are you, mama?"

He would have bled his whole life in front of Rizzo's, if she had not taken him by the hand like a little boy and stuffed him into the alleyway between the meat market and the paint store.

He lowered his voice, finally, when he didn't have to. "I'm not a bad person, mama. You tell him that. And Teresa's not bad either. She's got different ways, but she's one of us. So what? She's good with the kids, with the house . . . with me. So what?"

Rosa, at the first sign of a problem, began wiping her hands. She wore a thin black topcoat but began to treat it as if it were her kitchen apron.

"Mama listen to me," he shouted into her face. Desperately he reached down and smothered her dainty hands in his bear paws.

"She's *not* a bad person, mama. We got a relationship that we live with. We ain't hurtin' nobody. I love her, mama. I don't want no one else." He was shouting now and this disturbed her. Noise brought people and if it ever got back to Manny her life would become double hell.

She looked deeply into his twisted face, her expressions mimicking his. Haltingly she had followed every word he said, even lipped some of them a split second after he did, but she hadn't the smallest notion what was bothering her baby. No one told her. He could have been a Roumanian reciting in his native tongue for all she knew. Manny had come home, last Sunday, red in the face and without his hat. In clipped terse American she was told under no circumstances was Victor or his wife ever to come to the house or call on the telephone. The red face, the missing

206

Homburg, and now this thing with Victor. What did it all mean?

"Dead ducks, Rosa, that's what they are. We forget now we have Victor until I tell you different."

"Why?" she asked almost inaudibly, as one whispers to the dying.

"That's between my son and me," he spit back at her.

"And Teresa, too?" she asked, inflaming him.

"Especially Teresa, that . . ." Manny often left the sentence unfinished but not its meaning.

She wondered how anyone could say anything bad about Teresa. The girl called her mama and kissed her every time they met. She remembered her on her birthday and always brought a little something when she came. Just like a daughter. The others . . . like statues. They avoided kissing her like she had something catching and they always came emptyhanded.

When she asked for a second hearing he put his hand on his hip and glared at her. She knew better than to press him when the hand went to the hip. It was easier to put a sweater on a chicken than to open a door that her husband shut. Her hands went into spasms in her apron that Sunday afternoon.

Now in the alley where cats shopped Patsy Rizzo's garbage cans she stood with her son, her hands held limply as if the bones had been removed and ached with him. If she could only help. If she only knew what caused the breech.

"Victor," she said, with innocence and anguish inseparably intertwined, "your poppa. He's not a easy man. He gets crazy, you know. I still can't figure him out. Forty years and I can't figure him out." She was building a case for inadequacy. It required little preparation, she had been in rehearsal almost forever.

"Mama, mama, please go to bat for me." His words were running together now. "I'm drowning, I'm drowning. I don't know why. He ain't no God. He ain't worth all the sufferin' I'm goin' through. You gotta do it for me. You gotta do it."

"Whaddaya mean he ain't worth it? He's your father. He ain't a bad man. A little, you know, hard, but he's treated you good. Okay so he's crazy. We all got something wrong."

"But he's makin' like I'm dead, like I'm an orphan. No mother, no father. He don't want to have nothin' to do with us no more. Me, Tessa, the kids."

"No, not the kids," she said. "Just you and Tessa. I don't think he meant the kids, too."

"Will you tell him I'll try? Tell him I'll do my best to be what he wants me to be. Tell him I feel lousy about the whole thing. Tell him parents shouldn't fight with kids. Tell him he's only got a few years left. Oh, Jesus tell him any goddamn thing you want to, only patch it up."

People stopped between the stores and began looking at them, at him, a shaking hulk, screaming and crying at the little black beetle. Some might have wondered if there was any danger in the alleyway. The ones who thought that violence was imminent hurried on to avoid involvement. The others stopped, looked disinterestedly and slowly went about their business.

"Listen to me, mama, I'm in terrible pain. I'm suffering. He's just killin' me to death."

Slowly she extended her hands as if presenting him with his baby. She touched him lightly with her fingertips. "Victor, Victor," she crooned, "whaddaya want from me? You know poppa. If he says no, it's no. My hands, they're tied," she said, raising them joined together by imaginary ropes.

Victor inhaled deeply then exploded. "What the hell good are you?" He gave her five seconds to answer and left before a trembling Rosa could assemble a reply. She composed herself and finally turned the matter over to God, who, like a waiter, would clean up the mess people had left.

A bar on a sunny day is one of the darkest places in the world. And if the place is air-conditioned it adds to the blackness because cold and dark is blacker than warm and dark. Victor interrupted the bartender's love affair with a new color TV, fine tuning and knob turning. He took his beer to the farthest corner of the long rectangular bar so that he might sulk in grand isolation. The drink lived but seconds. He returned in deadly silence and rapped for a refill. Tommy, the bartender, pulled the tap and cut the foam off the top of his glass with a professional sweep. He made a project of handing Victor the drink.

"The suds of the day for the man of the hour," Tommy chirped.

Through hating eyes Victor growled like a dog having a nightmare. "Stick to pouring drinks, pal. Let Longfellow make with the poetry."

Tommy pushed on unaware of the ticking, ticking.

"What's the matter, Victor me boy, your blades dull? Your weed killer ain't knocking 'em dead? Your hoses dripping?"

He had heard it all before. Many times before. Standard gardeners' jokes. He turned his back on Tommy and shuffled off to exile. Sitting there he felt as if he were slowly dying. He would welcome the end and the release it would bring. All hope faded when his mother showed him her wrists, bound together with cowardice. His sweet, loving mother. She knew better than anyone what that man was like and yet she left him dancing in the air like the little pigs in Rizzo's window.

Strokes of genius explode at odd times. Victor's winning number had come up in Tommy's saloon after another three trips to the bar. Floating by four o'clock he stumbled out of the dark like a prisoner released from solitary confinement. The fading light had blinded as his pupils contracted protectively. The plan was so simple, so beautiful that he couldn't help but throw a few pieces of it Tommy's way. The bartender listened and smiled. It seemed almost funny.

The truck coughed its way along Central Avenue like a consumptive, mirroring Victor's state of tipsy. Other drivers passed by, hurling invectives in pantomime at him. To which he responded by inserting his middle finger straight up into the air. The silent man's scatology. He smiled a blowsy smile and his plan grew more brilliant. Soon he would be master of his house again, the horns he said he did not wear would fall off and his father would welcome him with open arms. The maples on both sides of the wide avenue had turned colors, the product of infinitely complicated chemistry. Such reds and golds and oranges would have flooded his normally receptive sense of nature had it been open to suggestion. But the plan, more its aftermath, had completely consumed him. He had become a totally dedicated man.

Cal sat in the backyard determined by willpower alone to suck up the lovely day. He was most alive in autumn. The combination of temperature, position of the sun, composition of the air

209

opened psychic doors. Even his painting was going well. His mood, his libido, gave him hints that he might live forever. He wondered if it were possible to follow fall around the world as if it were a sweetheart who had scorned him and who he must have, nevertheless.

Tessa had begged off the day. Too many problems at home, she explained; he understood. The summer had passed reasonably well between himself and Joan. No serious friction, a few shore dinners with the kids who were surprisingly civil to them. Perhaps they knew. A little touchy around bedtime, but they managed a few guarded laughs, some serious talk, even moments of passion. A new beginning? He thought not. More like a period of re-adjustment. He had become becalmed and was quite happy about it.

He caught up on his *Journals*. A new treatment for ulcers. There was always a new treatment for some ailment that turned out to be less than a miracle. They sold medical miracles the way they sold soap suds. The change in the audience dictated a change in technique, but the mechanics were the same. Usually he read his *Journals* in the screened room between the garage and the house. Sibelius' music provided the background. There in the natural darkness provided by huge oaks outside the door he would lose himself in the quiet Finnish forests, learning of new chemo-therapeutic approaches to leukemia, osteoporosis in the elderly, or the incidence of depression in the post-partum mother. There was a time he could spend weeks here in salutary confinement. But the day was perfect and he wanted some of it so he camped out under the apple trees and began to read.

Hours passed. The report on the dangers of mammography was depressing. The treatment had become as bad as the disease. Who said medicine was without humor? Glasses off he rubbed his eyes and smiled at his own sophomoric cynicism. Nothing new. He had been there before, asking questions about his profession. No, cynicism was a dead end. Tessa was one of those things that proved it. The last time he had dug deeply was in Greenport with her. She put a frame around things that gave them form and substance. His mind began to sail like a glider and he dropped the journal. One full week to wait for her. He would have to busy himself until then.

Shadows on the grass grew longer. He looked at the flowering cherry, a whirl of white blossoms late in May, a day or two of life and then it was over. Very short and very sweet.

One shadow was moving rapidly, like a black arrow aimed downward at his shadow. He turned and myoptically saw Victor, puffing and sweaty, his right hand raised high above his head, tightly grasping a small pair of green garden shears. Victor was not looking at him. He looked as if he had a quarrel with Cal's back and was about to rectify it.

With death in Victor's right hand Cal did the natural thing. He panicked. And in his panic tipped over in the slatted lawn chair that had held him so comfortably all afternoon. Victor, his senses reduced to slow motion, was unable to adjust to the situation and proceeded to plunge the shears into the space where Cal's back had been seconds earlier. He lost his balance when he struck the September air and fell over the lawn chair and its frightened occupant, neatly slicing a bloody path along his left arm as he went down.

"Victor, what the hell are you doing?" was all Cal could muster on such short notice as the gardener lay on him bathing him in his blood.

"Oh Jesus, I'm sorry, I'm sorry, I'm sorry. Oh Doc, what did I do, what did I do? I did a terrible thing."

Cal ignored the attempted murder and concentrated on the accident. "My God, Victor you're bleeding like a pig."

Strangely Victor never realized that he had slit his arm. He rapidly sobered, realized his crime and was engulfed by the horror of it. Finally he saw the gash, almost ruler-straight from elbow to wrist and vomited silently into the base of the flowering cherry. Cal applied pressure just under the gardener's arm pit and the flow of blood stopped. Victor more closely viewed the damage done, and vomited again over the latest edition of the *Journal of the American Medical Association.*

Suddenly, Victor burst into tears. "Oh my God, what did I do? Oh Jesus, Doc, don't be mad at me." If Cal hadn't been holding Victor's arm above his curly head to stem the gush of blood, Victor would have been down on his knees begging forgiveness.

"I'm not mad at you right now, Victor. I swear I'm not. I just want to patch you up. Then I'll decide if I'm mad at you." With his hand in the dike he shouted for Joan. She, her makeup set, dressed, and she thought, looking especially well in her blue and white sailor suit was about to leave for a United Fund meeting. She was just poking her head out of the kitchen door to say good-bye.

Both men were covered with blood. At their feet lay a bloody pair of shears. She rushed outside her heels clicking wildly on the patio steps. Up close she smelled the beer vomit and saw the blood-stained grass.

"Oh, Lord, are you hurt Cal?" she asked touching him all over.

"No . . . no Joan. It's Victor. It was an accident. He had a couple of beers too many and tried to trim the hedges. He ended up trimming his arm." He knew she would never accept that story but it would have to do until something better was available.

"It was an accident, Mrs. Bernstein. I didn't try to kill him. I swear I didn't," Victor cried with large warm tears.

"Joan," her husband said still holding Victor's arm aloft, "take the bag out of the car then go into the office and clear the books off the examining table."

Her heels played a more rhythmic tune as she headed for the garage. At the office door she met Cal with his bag and Tessa. Victor looked at his wife as if the sun were in his eyes. She looked first at the red highway down his arm then touched his face.

"Are you alright, Victor? You're so pale. Did he lose a lot of blood, Cal?"

"Enough."

"Tommy called me up. He said you were talking foolishly about killing three birds with one stone. Joan told me the rest. Are you sure you're alright Victor? Is he, Cal?" When she was finally sure she turned back to her husband. "Victor, what the hell's wrong with you? You almost let that old man destroy you with his voodoo crap. Oh Victor." There was disgust in her voice and tenderness, too.

"I'm sorry, Tessa," Victor said, still unable to meet her eyes. Cal and Joan closed the door of his almost defunct examination room. It was seldom used now. Emergencies only.

Joan found an old surgical gown and covered her sailor suit. Cal cut off Victor's yellow sport shirt, the one the kids gave him for Father's Day. He was very white and full of I'm sorries. She worked with Cal as she had in the distant past remembering again how quickly, how professionally he practiced his art. A twinge of pride rode up and down her spinal column at his calm and skillful procedure.

But it was Tessa who surprised her most. She was not surprised at Mrs. Bruno's strength, spunk, or integrity. During the summer she had pulled her own weight, showed no fancy notions about becoming the next Mrs. Bernstein. Two or three times she telephoned the girl to talk about what foods to please steer Cal to and from. Tessa, at first laughingly, then when she realized that Joan was not being stiff-upper-lipped bitchy, seriously promised to walk away from French fries and desserts and toward salads and poultry when they dined together. Aside from the fact that the young lady seemed firmly entrenched in her life, Tessa was to be admired most for not knuckling under to people like herself. It appeared to be a circular, involuted reason to like someone, but there she was, the object of Joan's admiration.

What amazed Joan most, and it said as much about her as it did about Tessa, was the tenderness, the almost motherly concern, that the younger woman had just displayed. Anger, viciousness, and a sharp tongue should have come first, just now, given a weak schlemiel and a clever, feisty woman. She herself being steel and plastic, she found it difficult to absorb the fact that it was all held together in Tessa with tenderness. That girl was full of hidden corners.

Victor babbled on while they worked on him. Cal shot him full of antibiotics, anesthetics, and anti-tetanus. "She's right, she's always right. I should never have let the old bastard push me into it." The needle was almost misdirected as he grabbed Cal's arm to beg forgiveness for the hundredth time. "Oh Jesus, Doc, I'm sorry," he cried as if he said it for the first time. "He buried me alive and I had a few beers and I began to feel sorry for myself. I don't know why I did it. I musta been crazy."

Caught up in the surgical process Joan mopped Cal's brow (which was dry) and ignored Victor's (soaking wet). She dabbed when told to and fetched when ordered. She felt wonderful. "Hold on Victor, it's almost over," she said without any timetable to refer to. Squeemishly she peeked at Cal's embroidery and quickly turned away. Victor seemed oblivious to his wound and worse, ignorant of his true offense. Joan reminded him at once. "I'm really surprised at you, Victor," she began. "I thought we had a deal. I thought you believed in what we worked out."

"Oh, Mrs. Bernstein, I did, I did, but I don't know. I just fell apart. Give me another chance. I'm getting stronger. Look, he's sewing me up and I didn't even blink an eyelash. You see, I can be strong."

Cal concentrated on the surgery. The damn fool had come dangerously close to a large artery. Luckily nothing major had been severed. Like most horizontal wounds it looked worse than it actually was. A few capillaries bisected, but little else.

Victor droned on, his litany beginning to annoy doctor and nurse. It ended on a new note. "Doc, I'm ready to take my medicine," he solemnly announced. "You can call the cops now. Only don't let Tessa see them take me away."

Suspended between a laugh and a large portion of pathos, Cal tried to show neither side of the coin. "I have no intention of calling anybody. This is between us. We'll settle out of court, Victor."

His face shone as if newly polished. A little bloodletting and it was all youth and innocence again. He was once more a sweet little boy, almost but not quite a murderer.

Joan washed her hands in the small sink, pleased with Cal, pleased with herself. He looked at her, bent at the sink the way she had looked in the apartment on Empire Boulevard after he had come home after a long stretch at Kings County. His throat tightened as the past invaded.

Poor Joannie, he thought, she thinks she's fighting for her life. But listen, ice lady, I'm not going anyplace . . . far. I just love this girl, this strange lovely girl and I'm afraid of loving her and I'm afraid of losing her. Can't you see that, Joannie? You read everyone but me and her so well. She's what I should have had to begin with, but I didn't know it until it was almost too late. And if I had had her I might not have had the wisdom to appreciate what a jewel she was. But here I am because you just can't cut out twenty years of yourself and expect the patient to survive. If only you were more like her. If . . . if . . . if.

"Thanks, hon," he called out to her back as she prepared to salvage at least part of the afternoon. "You were a first-rate nurse. Damn good job."

He had not called her "hon" in years. It was nice to hear and nicer to know that it still had the power to warm. Like usable matches found at the bottom of an old mineshaft. Damn fool, she told herself, satisfied with so little.

In the den she found Tessa on her third cigarette, which she snuffed out when Joan cleared the air for her. Victor was fine and whole again. She was genuinely relieved. Another few minutes would not matter so she stopped to chat.

"You know, it's a shame," Joan said.

"What is?" Tessa asked.

"That we had to know each other, this way."

"Well don't let that wipe you out, if you're serious."

"As a matter of fact, I won't," Joan replied in her perky manner.

Tessa still did not know Joan well enough to determine if she was being lined up in the lady's sights or if she was serious.

Cal was not ready to release Victor yet. "Before we wind things up, Victor, I have to tell you that I'm going to continue to see Tessa and be with her when I can. I hope we don't have to go through this blood bath every now and then. You might get the hang of it next time. Just remember I'm really doing you no harm. I thought that was understood. In fact I'm preserving your marriage. Someone else might have forced Tessa to go away with him. Permanently. This way, God, I don't want this to sound like a lecture, you have her because I have her, too. Doesn't that make sense to you?"

"Most of the time it does, but sometimes it don't. Like when the old man starts working on me. That's what this whole thing is due to. I'm just six years old when he's around. But you know, for some strange reason I don't care anymore whether I'm in or whether I'm out of his picture. Fuck him." He held his mouth as if attempting to lock in precisely what fell out. "Jeez, I'm sorry I said that in this house."

"This house has heard it before, Victor. Say whatever you like."

215

"I don't need him anymore. I probably never did. He just wanted me to think so." During the patching another great idea hit him. He had his teeth in it and would not let go. "I don't care what the hell he thinks," he said.

He swung off the table and tried out his legs. They worked. "Listen, Doc," he said, confidence swinging skyward, "you sewed me up real good. Great. Thanks very much. How much do I owe you?"

"Nothing, Victor," he said with a wave of the hand. "You were here on a social visit."

"Thanks, thanks a lot, Doc. You're a helluva guy. If I ever lose Tessa to anyone I wouldn't feel so bad if it was to you. Oh, one thing I better tell you," he said, his hand swallowing up the doorknob, "I hope you don't get offended. I uh . . . intend to fight you for Tessa. I want her back, all of her. You had it easy up to now 'cause I gave her away. Please forgive me, but I'm going to try like a bastard to push you out. No rough stuff, nothing like this," he said and pointed to his arm. "Maybe it's too late." He shrugged. "She's a pretty solid woman and once she sets her mind, that's it. But I'm going to try." He squared his jaw as if that was the start of trying.

"Don't bully her. That won't work, Victor."

"No, no, I'm going to do it by being different, by trying to change."

Cal, because he could really do no otherwise said, "Okay, Victor, that's fair warning," and opened the door.

Victor told her everything, about the length of the wound, the number of stitches, how well the team sewed him up and his own feelings during the ordeal. What he did not tell her she would find out sooner or later. Probably sooner.

"Where are the boys?" Victor asked.

"I left them at Margie's, next door," she answered.

"Let's pick them up and go to the Pancake House. I'm starving. Besides this is an occasion. It ain't every day I get thirty-eight stitches."

"I'm game, Victor," she said and led him to the door as if he were blind instead of stitched.

Cal winked at her before she closed the hall door between them. She responded with a long soft kiss and nudged it his way.

216

Tied to the kiss that wafted across the room she tagged on a whispered, "Next Friday, love," and closed the door between them for at least seven days.

He stood in the hallway still engulfed by her presence and thanked God, or providence, or his stars for Tessa.

## 15

Joan was incensed for good reason. Gambling in high school by the students had gotten so out of hand that two of Peter's friends wore broken arms to class as a warning to welchers. Peter told her in clipped, non-committal words. She sweated the rest out of him by withholding the car until he completed the scenario.

Hundreds, even thousands of dollars changed hands in the halls of learning every Monday morning over the results of weekend football. The teachers knew it; the principal knew it. Where were the police when debts were cancelled by the breaking of limbs? Infuriated, Joan wanted answers and called together an ad hoc committee on a day's notice. She needed less than that but Marsha had just returned from Estoril and needed the day.

The meeting at the high school went well. Joan's opening remarks dwelled heavily on the innocence of children and the taxes paid to prolong that delicate condition. It can't happen here, she said, setting herself up on purpose, but it had. And it must stop. The large turnout was deep into swapping charges and distributing guilt when Joan, enlivened by the verbal electricity around her suddenly came to a dead halt. What was Tessa doing there, in the back rows, arguing with that noisy group of negatively charged parents? Why was she so pregnant? Why was she pregnant at all? Joan shuddered and turned away. The girl, continued her upstaging act, pointing out that schools cannot do everything, parents must set the standard, causing a commotion with her big mouth and bigger belly. But, of course it wasn't Tessa. Her brain had given her a private showing of Tessa carrying Cal's child (who else's?) and the shuddering became very noticeable.

"Joan, what's the matter? You catching cold or something?" Marsha said as regret after regret beat at her crumbling defenses. Shuddering first, then the tears that fell like a soft, unannounced summer rain. Why had she let it go so far? she wondered. Did she have to be so clever, so modern, so hard and sparkling like a diamond while that girl whisked him away right under her nose? She couldn't see the other parents, she couldn't even see Marsha, offering the refuge of her skinny arms. She did see herself and into herself, the silly need to be top dog here on the hustings and there at home. She regretted not having the simple intelligence of any fool to see that she had just given him away, being too clever to be direct and simple, that marriage just wasn't out-foxing him and her.

When the shuddering and the tears became noticeable even to the back rows, Marsha, with greater dignity than she knew she had, led Joan offstage and into the small room used for scenery, sat her, docile and meek, in a wooden folding chair stained with the paint from *Damned Yankees* and called Cal at the office.

"Bring your little black bag. I don't know what it means medically, Cal, but she's shivering like a wet dog and the tears, it's like you turned on a faucet."

The meeting was abruptly ended, cancelled by Joan's strange behavior. They filed out in small clusters aware only that their leader had had a sudden attack of intestinal virus. All the lights were turned off except a small bulb over the emergency exit and in the room where Marsha sat and held Joan's cold hands.

Cal rushed into the darkened auditorium still wearing his white examination coat and almost fell over the custodian who had just swept away the cigarettes from the night's activity.

"Where . . . ?"

"Behind the stage, doctor. You go up the steps on the left, through the opening, and straight down to the last door."

The door was closed and Cal opened it without knocking. Marsha sat opposite Joan, baby-talking her, trying to act maternal and doing a very decent job of it all to a very non-responsive subject. Cal looked at his wife and saw how close she was to hysteria.

219

"What happened, Marsha? Did anyone say anything to her? Was there a battle? This is not like her. I don't have to tell you."

"Nothing, nothing, Cal. She was sitting there, running the show, having her usual damn good time, working them up into a frenzy and all of a sudden she begins shivering and crying to beat the band. I never saw anything like it in my life. Joan, of all people. She's Mother Courage herself." Marsha held her heart. "I tell you, it's rattled me something awful to see her like this. I'm devastated."

He wasn't listening. He just waited for Marsha to get it all out and then leave. Politely, because she proved to be a friend, he said, "Marsha, thank you very much. I'll take over from here." He kissed her cheek and sent her home.

"Joan," he said, as if trying to gentle her from sleep. "Come, dear. We're going home now." Gentler than any time since that second birthday party when Peter had stopped breathing and Joan fell apart while he cut a hole in the baby's windpipe. He led her by the hand to the car, his exhaust still chugging smoke into the early winter night. Her crying had stopped but the shaking was just as strong. He took a blanket from the trunk, the one that he had shared all summer with Tessa and covered Joan with it. It began to drizzle so he turned the wipers on. Like accusing fingers they wagged under his nose and droned to him, "You did it, you did it."

She was easy to undress and after he tucked her in and gave her a shot of Valium he almost fell over Peter outside their door.

"What's wrong?" the boy asked, his head hung low, his eyes puzzled and sad. Cal had never seen that particular combination in him. It hurt and pleased him to see it now.

"Nothing . . . nothing, Pete. She's a little tired. Working too hard. A couple of days' rest and she'll be bitching about the beer cans in your room." They smiled in unison, as if agreeing on it would insure its coming to be.

"Cal, don't leave me," she called catching him in the doorway.

"Don't worry, honey," he said as he hovered over her, "I'm not leaving you." She smiled like a woman who has just given birth and fell asleep with his words providing the direction she was groping for in her Valium fog.

He didn't have to sit up all night. The shot would do fine as guardian of her mind, but sleep would have been an unearned luxury. Besides, he wanted to be there next to her for a reason he hoped might become clearer as he sat.

Tessa. Oh my God, Tessa. What would become of them? Strange and terrible that with Joan, helpless, perhaps hopeless, his hand stroking hers, he should ask himself that kind of a question. And not feel shame. But shame was never a part of it. He was never, even unto this minute, ashamed of any part of his life with Tessa. And he wouldn't fake it in a false act of contrition to fool his soul. Guilt was there, but only because Joan had injured some metaphysical limb. He had acted according to the fixed rules of his conscience which is often called honor. Nothing hidden from Tessa or Joan. Tessa knew the game. Yet Joan, a pro in all departments, fell apart. Where were the warning signs? Pneumonia begins with a fever. Some doctor, some husband, he decided derogatorily, he had seen nothing coming.

So he accepted the guilt of omission which is the mildest of crimes and vowed to serve only a light sentence for it. Beginning here, at her side. But she said don't leave me, and it stunned him. Never had she come close to that kind of dependency before. It touched him deeply and he tried not to measure it. He would take care of Joan and do whatever was necessary to get her going again and somehow he would keep his balance. As long as whatever was necessary stopped at Tessa's door. To even contemplate a world without Tessa was like picturing his own death. He loved her. Even now he saw Tessa's face and lovely back and wanted her.

"My throat is so dry," Joan said sensing his presence.

"Here, drink some water," he said, glad finally to be of some use.

"Why don't you go to sleep?" she asked from deep within her nebulous world.

"Soon, soon. . . . I'm not tired."

It'll be fine, he promised himself and fell asleep in the chair.

Quite early in the morning he called their friend, Dr. Daniel Glazer, who served on committees with Joan and to whom Cal sent patients who needed the services of a competent psychiatrist. He appreciated the man's non-doctrinaire approach to fiddling

221

around inside a person's head. Beside, he was one of the few shrinks he knew who didn't convert to wearing medallions or chains around his neck or long hair when that was in vogue.

Dr. Glazer sat next to her bed on the tufted chair meant to hold bedspreads and not people. He tugged at his red-brown moustache as if to straighten out the wrinkles and joshed easily with Joan. She had properly attired herself in a quilted robe and dabbed on a little lipstick when Cal told her he was coming over.

"Listen, kiddies, I ain't going to make a big deal out of this. Number one, you get professional courtesy so there are no fortunes to be made here, and number two, it's not that serious." He looked back and forth at them as if he were carrying messages. "We got a hairline fracture and nothing more if, *if* steps are taken. You listening to me? This would never have happened, Joan, if only you were weak. That's the big problem. Or very wise. The weak ones bend and lean on others. That's how they survive. And the wise ones (he threw his hands up in the air as if he had just given up looking for them), where the hell are they? Frankly I never met one. They're wise enough not to try and be so strong. Strong people break, you know. They don't bend. They're my best customers, the strong ones. It usually takes forever to put them back together again." He grinned puckishly. "They're the ones that keep my twins in Med school.

"So, now I'll get personal. In this particular case you are and have been children. Both of you. I don't like to rub it in, but I must if we're to heal this fracture. This has been coming for years. The only question in my mind was which of the two of you would slip first. We got here two strong nitwits, moving fast in opposite directions. And you thought, both of you, by not talking about it it would go away. Bad. Bad in theory, bad in practice. You, Cal, licking your wounds in dark corners, and you, Joan, acting like a bitch, sometimes. Forgive me, but it's so, dear lady. This is just the right setting for such a minor tragedy."

Cal looked out the bedroom window at the glistening blanket of new snow that had fallen unexpectedly during the night. It had begun as a drizzle. Was it only just last night? His neighbor's snowblower cut a path down his driveway tossing white foam to the left and to the right. No one removes the stuff anymore, Cal thought, they just rearrange it.

Dr. Glazer pursued them, both strangely silent at his analysis.

"Well, we just shot the past. Let's talk present tense. What you got, honey, you didn't acquire in a day and it won't wash off in a day. The way you come out of it, if you both think you want to get together on this, is with time and patience. Your time and patience, Doctor Bernstein, your time and patience, Lady Bernstein. You think you got some laying around the house, kiddies? Now," he said in summary, "I'm confining you to house arrest for the next two weeks, Joan. Just rest and relax. Talk a lot face to face. Say something that means something."

Downstairs Cal began to look for Dr. Glazer's hat and coat. He had forgotten where he stowed them. Together they finally found the clothes and Cal said, "Some things were pretty much on target, Danny, things I just realized myself. Other things you are probably speculating about and there's no point in laying it out in front of you. Maybe it's not too late to make a fresh start. I have a lot of thinking to do. However it comes out, I'm going to bleed a lot."

He walked the green carpeted steps back up to the bedroom not knowing what to say, where to begin, how to begin. She smiled and that opened the door.

"Joan, I didn't know you were that vulnerable."

"Don't blame yourself, I didn't know either."

The call to Randall cancelling all appointments for two weeks was easy. The call to Tessa was harder and it felt like suicide to cancel this Friday and the next. He explained why and asked for patience. She was very understanding, told him to take his time and call her please, please, when things were stabilized. She'd be okay, he wasn't to concern himself with her. (Impossible request.) After he hung up he felt the pain of a fresh wound. He had surrendered the one day of the week that gave meaning to the other six.

The house was holding its breath. Joan was sound asleep. Cal had all the time in the world to face himself, which is another way of saying he had no place to run and hide. He made some tea and thought soon he would have to face unpleasant facts. He was good at it if it were other people's facts, telling patients what they had a right to know. Just a few days ago he had told himself, behind his own back, that she was becoming intertwined with his very thought down to the cellular level. Addicted, someone might say if he were cruel; emotionally engulfed, were that someone kinder. The day before Joan slipped he finally began admitting to himself, this time face to face, the possibility that oscillating between two poles was not working anymore. Things were getting out of hand inside himself and the scales were tipping.

Now the world had stopped and spun again in a different trajectory. He sat in the kitchen, reading teabags, trying to slow its centrifugal force, to hold it still while he added the Sweet 'n Low and found some truth. He burned the roof of his mouth and continued the search. No matter how he assembled the pieces it came out impossible. As he washed out the cup and put it in the dishwasher he thought of Joan. And pity dredged up a mixture of old memories to stand beside his newer ones of Tessa. Greenport and visiting the park on Sunday, the four Bernsteins, with day old loaves of wholewheat bread to feed the ducks. Tessa's way of looking over her shoulder at him and laughing and Joan announcing that yup the rabbit died and you're going to be a daddy. How much she got under his soul on Ellis Island and how very proud he was of his wife when she punctured some stuffed shirt's inflated ego and he floated on the released hot air.

He kept in touch with the office, just barely. Randall, with expected efficiency, banked the furnaces and closed shop. Though he ached just thinking her name, he didn't speak to Tessa. He made Joan's convalescence the center and circumference of his life. He even learned to scramble her eggs in the morning. By the second day bed bored her and she left her cradle to sit wrapped in Laura's old bathrobe by the garden window in her blue room where she carefully watched the world of clouds and the shapes that filled it. Curiously she seemed content to study trees, wind, and snow.

Life at first was unbearable for Cal. He would have much preferred to be the watched instead of the watcher. So many things assaulted his mind and they mostly concerned Tessa. He thought that any minute he would drop what he was doing, break her door down and beg forgiveness. When he did call, she said it was still alright. She understood. Her voice was so reassuring, soothing him, stressing that she was still Tessa and she was there to pick up the strands whenever. He felt so rotten.

To fill the days, which had become enormous in size, to nudge her back to health, he began to read to Joan. The children were who knows where. Peter came and went and was a very muted giraffe. Laura, instead of going to the Bahamas with her friends over recess, stayed home and baked cookies and burned most of them. Every afternoon Cal made a large pot of Chinese tea and read to her. How did he remember, he wondered, that she loved Willa Cather's novels? Something jarred it loose from a tenacious yesterday. He read *My Antonia* to her and somehow it gave him deep satisfaction to do so. He even began looking forward to their literary afternoons, alone together, doing for her.

Finally she began to pour the tea herself. He had prepared it in an exotic pot bought in Portsmouth during the first vacation they were rich enough to afford.

"Is the tea too hot?" he asked.

"No, dear, it's fine, just fine," she answered uttering her first complete sentence in days. "And please don't fuss."

"That's okay . . . I want to fuss."

"You do?" She was surprised. "Then by all means, fuss."

By the time they started *Death Comes for the Archbishop,* she began to talk freely with him.

"I haven't seen much of the children. Are they alright?"

"Fine, Joan, they're fine. They're children, you know, involved in their own lives. But they ask about you all the time and I catch them peeking while you're asleep. They love you. We all do."

Why did he say that, he wondered. Danny Glazer wasn't there to read for the part of his conscience. He didn't *have* to tell her that, but he wanted to. It was a sentence looking for a place to be said, he told himself later.

It was time. Tessa had to be told and he had to hear himself say it, too. He would try not to think about it because to do so would start all kinds of revolutions inside. He still loved Tessa. That was fact. It might lessen later on, but it would never disappear. He looked at the phone until it grew almost larger than he. Her voice entered every pore and showed him how much he missed her. She said that the office was fine for a meeting that night though she sounded to him like dry twigs.

The buzzer sang announcing her presence in the lobby. He picked up the intercom, made sure it was Tessa and pressed the button near Randall's desk. Her silhouette appeared and he opened the opaque glass door before she knocked.

"Hullo, Cal," she said and smiled, but only at the corners of her mouth.

"Hi," he said and kissed her. Her lips were day old toast. "How have you been?" he asked cheerlessly.

"Oh, not too bad. The usual assortment of coughs and colds. How's Joan coming along?"

"Slowly, but surely," he said quickly.

She brushed by him and took off an ankle length coat with a luxurious fur collar and threw it across the waiting room couch. All in blue, looking better than he ever knew her to, she stunned him and he blamed it on his perverse mind making what he must lose so very desirable. On purpose? he wondered. Did she know and was she punishing him, taunting him with her loveliness? He felt a sharp stab in his heart like angina when she smiled. He had arrived early, telling Joan he had some unfinished business to settle and spent the past hour in the dark constructing courage as if that nebulous quality lent itself to carpentry. But his house collapsed around his ears when he saw her. She had put on some weight and it was quite flattering.

He picked up the coat and caressed the collar. It was a pointless act but it gave his hand something to do. Finally he put his arm around her shoulder. "Come . . . come into the office. There's a pot of coffee and I even have an ashtray that I hide from Randall." It didn't get the smile it deserved.

She stared at him and wondered why he had such difficulty in speaking. It was either sex or pain that gnawed at him and she could handle both. In the office his symptoms seemed to grow so intense that she was prepared to step out of her skirt and begin unravelling immediately. He dropped her coat on the floor and kissed her desperately and she knew things would never be the same after that. Her fears began taking on flesh and she grew dizzy.

"What is it Cal? Tell me. Please tell me. Something is very wrong with us. I knew it over the phone."

He looked at the way her eyes widened and her hand stopped in midair near his cheek. "It's Joan. Her breakdown. It's shown me something about her, about me, I never knew. Probably I never wanted to know. She's very soft inside and I always looked the other way about it. I've failed her. I realize that now and that upsets the whole applecart." He heard himself saying these impossible things to her, watching her face as his words twisted the ends of a very desirable mouth. He swore, in the dark of his office the hour he tried to find the right words, that he would not take his eyes off hers. Part of the penalty for hurting her was to watch them. Now he did and it was like someone had pulled down the shades in a very lively house. With little effort he could easily hate himself.

"This is hell, Tessa. Worse. I love you, I want you, and I just can't say what I have to." He took his eyes from hers and looked out the window at the shivering trees, their branches clutching the night sky. "Tessa, I've got to back out of our relationship. End it, call it off. Everything. And I'm just destroyed over it." He paused to catch his breath as exhausted as a cross-country runner after the race. His voice, at first emotional and tremulous had become drawn to a fine point and if she were five feet away she wouldn't have heard him at all.

"I'm such a damn fool for everything. For letting you go, for thinking I could have gotten away with it from the beginning." She sat on his studio couch looking at him as he fell in a heap in the patient's chair. "I thought I could have it both ways, Tessa, but I can't and it's eating me up alive. I still want you and her, but now the difference is I know I can't have it both ways. She needs me. She's just not that strong Cossack I thought she was and that makes it a kind of choice. I started getting to the point where I was going to try and push you into leaving Victor. That day I lost you on the ferry and nearly went berserk I started to think in terms of either/or. I figured Joan was tough enough to handle a divorce and the kids. Well, the kids wouldn't care too much. Peter would get a Corvette out of it and Laura would have another place to run to. I didn't even consider how you would handle Victor. Then this thing with Joan and the nice way we

227

all closed in to help her. I learned some hard facts, Tessa. The age of specialization just doesn't cover marriage. I can't have one wife for sex and play and another for the rest. I'm not a Frenchman. I'm just a damn fool."

Tessa sat very still, occasionally touching, scratching her acne scar. She searched the floor once in a while, rubbing the carpet pile when nervous energy had to be discharged.

"Are you sure you know what you're doing, Cal?" she asked with a deliberate slowness designed to make him reconsider. "You've got three lives in your hands not counting Victor, and I've nothing to contribute to the decision. Be very sure, Cal . . . please. I'm willing to be very patient and very understanding. . . ."

"Yes, yes, goddamn it. I know what I'm doing and it hurts. She needs me and has for a long time. I never realized it, never even thought about it until . . . until just recently. I can't walk around that fact and if I tried I'd end up losing both of you. There was a complete, a beautiful innocence when we went off and made love. Adam and Eve in the garden of Long Island," he laughed painfully. "But the way things would be now I'd only be using you for sex and a warm glass of milk and at the same time feeling guilty as hell leaving her at home. I'd always have it in the back of my mind when I was undressing you that she might be slitting her wrists in the bathroom because of it. And Tessa, you're not just a piece of Kleenex to use and throw away even if I were bastard enough to shut her out of my life."

Tessa nodded slowly, accepting, rejecting, then accepting again. Her tongue followed the line of her lower lip which had become intolerably dry. "That's funny," she said finally, without a speck of humor, "I thought when it ended . . . if it ended . . . I'd be the one to cut it off. That you'd become a bore to me, or the pressures from those clowns on my side would become too much. But I guess it doesn't really matter who cuts the string. It still leaves two separate pieces. I feel so empty, though, babe, so damn sick, too. I'm almost tempted to say I'll forget what you told me, you go home and think about it again or let's have each other whenever you can slip away, but that wouldn't work. I even thought of really turning it on so you'd make love to me and can-

228

cel the whole good-bye scene. Maybe that's why I tried so hard to look well. The new coat, the skirt and blouse. But I really couldn't handle a shape-up situation. One day yes, one day no, though so much of me says, yes, give the guy the option."

"I wouldn't do that to you. You're not a ping-pong ball."

She lit a cigarette and sat back against the couch. He watched the blue curls of smoke vanish on the ceiling. "Right now I don't know what I am, Cal. I do know we had a beautiful, beautiful six months, which is more than many married couples do. No matter how cynical I become I'll remember that." Remembering that she promised Stephen to limit her smoking she smothered the cigarette. "You'd never know it, looking at you, champ, but you can really hurt a girl."

Curiously the cigarette looked like an airplane shot down, its nose buried in the ashtray. "It . . . it would be pointless to hang around waiting for something to happen. Victor's been bugging me for weeks about California. His Uncle Angelo has a landscaping business he's dying to give away to a deserving relative. Victor says a fresh start would do wonders for our marriage. I think the poor guy deserves a shot at it. After the hell we put him through. Who knows what that California climate might do?" She never took her eyes from that broken Marlboro.

"I almost forgot about Victor."

"I won't be coming back, or sending postcards from Disneyland. I'm not made that way. I don't like loose ends." The mascara she wore to showcase her eyes was retreating slowly down her cheeks, but it was dark and Cal held her so close that it didn't matter. "Oh, I wish I could be a ping-pong ball for you and use all those tricks to keep you from feeling guilty, but you're a real cuckoo, you know, and I'm one, too. You just won't become a lying, cheating son of a bitch and I'd probably grow to despise you if you did. Funny, but I'll bet that you and Joan grow very close. I've a lot of respect for her, especially since she took a fall. It shows she's very human and loves you a great deal."

"She's a good person," he said and let it go at that. His arms were still very tight around her.

"Well," she said, "what now?"

"Would you mind, Tessa, if we just sat together in the dark for five minutes? I'm in no mood for sex or saying nice things. I just want to hold you and remember a little."

"Oh, Cal," she said, and he turned off the desk lamp.

Five minutes became half an hour then longer. In that half hour they relived their half year together. More than once he inhaled the perfume of her hair and kissed her neck and more than once she kissed back.

Tessa broke the spell partly because of what Ecclesiastes said about a time for everything. "Listen, babe," she whispered, "I'm going now," and finally he offered no serious resistance. Their last kiss was less desperate.

His angina-type pain began again, but he knew it was the only thing to do. He held her coat and she slid in. Turning slowly after tightening the belt she held his face, and kissed it without expecting one in return. At the door, she stopped, looked at him and said, "We had a time, didn't we, love?" and hurried down the steps rather than wait an eternity for the elevator. The one thing she was not looking for, she told herself as her heels clicked down the steps, was the time to feel hurt.

He didn't phone her immediately from the darkened office. So many things to sort out. Besides, the ache would be quite apparent even to a Joan operating at less than one hundred percent.

She picked up on the third ring.

"Hello." Her voice was getting stronger.

"Hi, how are you feeling?"

"Oh, it's you. I'm fine. I slept a few hours."

"Good, good. That's very good. Say listen, I . . . took care (and he gritted his teeth at the choice of words) of that unfinished business and I'm just about ready to come home."

"I'm glad, dear," she said. "Is everything okay?"

The stabbing pain again. "Not exactly, Joannie, but . . . I guess it will be." He barely said it and it flared up.

"Suppose I bring home a quart of Lobster Soong and a couple of egg rolls? You think you might help a guy eat his way out of it?"

"It sounds wonderful, Cal," she said, "but go to Wong's on

West Broadway. That cheapskate on Central Avenue practically threw one of my ladies out when we were collecting for Little League."

And that sounded wonderful, too, to Cal.

For days now he was anxious to tell her what had been alive and growing in him. It started as a seed two weeks ago over Lobster Soong. At first he called it pity, maybe it was back then (he doubted it now) but tadpoles become frogs and butterflies grow out of something entirely different. He was child-like in his desire to blurt it out. And adult in wanting the right time and place.

Sunday night was usually theirs by default. On this one Peter had the car and a willowy blond who always left pistachio shells in the ashtray and Laura had gone to look at wedding pictures that belonged to a friend whose marriage was annulled before the album was ready. He put a Sterno log in the fireplace and waited until it caught well enough to give off crackling sounds and yellow and blue flames.

"Joan," he said as they sat and watched the dancing colors, "I think I'm far enough past what happened to really see what it was. Do you want to hear about it?"

"I do, very much."

"First off, I'm not going to ask your forgiveness. At least not yet. I don't think that's the main issue."

She felt compelled to reply, but didn't.

"Those two weeks you stared out the window, when I read to you, were busy times for my head. And after that. I learned a lot in spite of a strong desire to wrap myself up in self-pity. I didn't want to learn anything because I loved that girl. So help me God I loved her."

"I know you loved her," she said quietly.

"Then, and I don't know when it happened, it hit me, Joan. It was as clear as day and right in front of me all the time." His face glowed in the fire light. "You see, Joan, Tessa was really you. You as I first knew you. Gutsy and crazy and tender and so easy to be with. Before we began to do things that put distance between us."

231

Caught in an outpouring of knowledge he couldn't control and didn't want to, he turned his chair to face her. She was beaming with a child-like joy he thought she surrendered back in the fifties. He slowly extended his hand, and, as it grew easier, he touched her.

"Joan, Joan, don't you see what I'm saying? I love you. It's still there. Above the prettiness and the fresh excitement of other faces, love is still there, where it's been all the time, ever since I picked you up in the hospital cafeteria when you were waiting for Arnie."

"And the bastard never showed."

"Joan, I love you. I always have. Even when your name was Tessa."

She was crying now, her tears like drops of honey in the fire's glow, openly, freely, without glancing around to see who might be watching. She didn't care if the whole world were witness. And laughing, too, in easy balance with her tears, nodding at his every word.

"I thought . . . with Tessa . . . I found it again. Found you again. (Oh, God, did I give that poor kid a hard time at the end.) But I never lost it. Listen to me, Mrs. Doctor Bernstein, I'm asking for a second chance, a chance for both of us to rebuild something good with what we have left. And we have a lot left. So we're not the same two terribly eager, terribly energetic kids we once were. So what? We got experience and you can't beat experience." Unaware that she was surely sold before he began, he sped on. "Are you willing to try? Say you're willing to give it a shot, to donate yourself to a real worthy cause."

"Oh shut up already, Cal. Yes, yes, oh God, yes, I'm willing to try. I haven't heard you run on since . . . since . . . I don't know since when." She blinked to chase the tears that blinded. Once, twice, and by the time she could see him clearly he was holding her very tightly. For the first time, not counting those rare moments in bed they had which really do not figure in the totals, anyway, he kissed her with a passion absent since Laura was born. He thought he might have forgotten how with her, but it all came back, that marvelous sensation, first in a trickle, then in a downpour. It was wonderful to feel that way about her again.

She found herself touching him, squeezing his fingers, buzzing his lips, things she had turned over to the dead past as she had with the idea of eternal youth and round-the-clock energy.

"No promises, Joan, now. Only children make promises."

"Then let's be children and make promises. At least about some things. Children can keep promises. Let's promise to come to each other when we have something to say. Small, medium, large things. Instead of running for cover. You know, once the kids finish school they won't be coming back. It'll just be the two of us, so let's promise to live for each other. Cal, we can do it. Oh, I'd like that so. But it won't be easy." Her eyes looked large and deep as the log slowly changed into flame and smoke. "It won't be easy. I'll slip a little, I know. I'll still want to keep active while you're out there destroying germs."

"Keep your groups. Just make me group one."

"Of course, of course. I'll back off the campaigns when you're home and I'll keep all the new assistants. We'll go away for a day, a week, a month. Anywhere you like."

"We'll decide that together, like we used to pour over the maps together before the kids came."

"Yes, yes, it sounds very exciting."

"It won't be easy for me, either. I'll still slap your mother down."

"I'll try not to take sides."

He grew somber. "And I'll still think of her, once in a while." His hand dropped limply from her and he looked distant for a moment. "Not a conscious thing. It'll just sneak up on me. It was a beautiful time in my life."

"I know, dear, and what happened then is just as much my history as it is yours. But maybe, if I'm very lucky, she'll fade away and merge completely into me. If I'm very lucky. But we *are* two very lucky people. We have so much goodness and love left to give one another. You're right, so very right. It didn't die, though there were times . . . oh, there were moments . . . well, we passed that turn. Hopefully."

They rose together, as if on cue, and he kissed her lightly again. Just like leaving for the office back in Canarsie. Memories of long passionate nights in small basement apartments returned like

233

friends at a class reunion. Love among the textbooks. Sex on a studio couch and *Diseases of the Eye*. Calvin Bernstein grew warm in that special place where the body ends and the soul begins and thought that even if love doesn't cure all it certainly provides one hell of an environment for the patient.